FIVE NIGHTS OUT

HUGH WARWICK

Five Nights Out
Published in Great Britain in 2024
by Graffeg Limited.

Written by Hugh Warwick copyright © 2024.
Designed and produced by Graffeg Limited copyright
© 2024.

Graffeg Limited, 24 Stradey Park Business Centre,
Mwrwg Road, Llangennech, Llanelli,
Carmarthenshire, SA14 8YP, Wales, UK.
Tel: 01554 824000. www.graffeg.com.

Hugh Warwick is hereby identified as the author
of this work in accordance with section 77 of the
Copyright, Designs and Patents Act 1988.

A CIP Catalogue record for this book is available from
the British Library.

The publisher acknowledges the financial support of
the Books Council of Wales. www.gwales.com.

Printed and bound in Great Britain by Clays Ltd,
Elcograf S.p.A.

ISBN 9781802587487

1 2 3 4 5 6 7 8 9

FIVE NIGHTS OUT

HUGH WARWICK

GRAFFEG

Five Nights Out

We are an animal of the day. We rely on our eyes to bring in the most important information about the world around us. Yes, we use our other senses: sound, smell, taste and touch, to help paint a fuller picture, but it is sight that is key.

It can be easy to think that we live in a daylight world – we see the flowers, hear the birds, watch butterflies – then we go to bed and it all stops. Or rather, we stop paying attention.

However, what goes on at night is every bit as, and I would argue often more exciting, than what is around in the day. If we shut our doors, windows and curtains, we could be missing out on half of the life with which we share the world around us.

Stories dating back generations tell of the night being the time of fear. We suffer from nightmares, we are warned about monsters under our beds, we tremble as a branch taps on the window during a storm or creates the shadows of monsters on our walls.

There are good reasons why the night has been a time of fear. When we were living more like animals, many thousands of years ago, when we did not have buildings and relied on caves or other rough shelter, the night was a time when predators would prowl and we had good reason to be scared.

Now, we have far more safety and the only threats we have are from other people, so it is important that we take care but not fill ourselves with so much fear that we never get out into nocturnal nature. I have been scared at night, but every time it was down to something harmless, combined with me being tired. If I had listened to that fear, I would have missed out on so much amazing life.

Five Nights Out is here to introduce you to some of the magic that might be missing from your life and will hopefully encourage you to open up all your senses. You will be surprised by just how much you are missing. Let's dive deep into the night, my nocturnal world.

Hedgehogs

I did not intend to become a nocturnal naturalist, but when I got an opportunity to study hedgehogs, well, I was thrust into this very different world. Of course, I knew what a hedgehog was – I had read *The Tale of Mrs Tiggy-Winkle* by Beatrix Potter, or, more likely, the book had been read to me. While there are other animals around the world that have evolved the same form of defence – most famously porcupines, but also tenrecs from Madagascar and echidnas from Australia and New Guinea – hedgehogs are the UK's only spiny mammal.

Hedgehog spines are made from the same stuff as our own hair and fingernails, a protein called keratin. If you look at one of your hairs under a microscope, you will find it very similar to a hedgehog spine. There is a bulb in the skin, then a narrow neck before the spine gently curves. This curve is important as it helps the spine act as a shock absorber.

Famously, hedgehogs also roll up into a ball

to protect themselves. It is a brilliant technique against many predators, though not so good with cars and badgers. Interestingly, the first thing a hedgehog does when bothered is actually to frown. Go on, try frowning. The muscle you feel tightening on your forehead goes all the way down to the tail on a hedgehog (yes, they do have a small tail, but it is usually hidden). When they frown, the spines, which are normally lying flat, get pulled up into a jagged pattern.

It is quite possible to stroke a happy hedgehog, but I would not recommend doing that with one that is frowning. The spines are really very sharp. In fact, on the whole, I would not recommend touching hedgehogs unless they need your help.

They also have another special muscle that acts a bit like the drawstring at the top of a sports bag. This is the muscle that allows them to remain rolled into a tight ball for hours. Their nose is tucked into the tail and there is no way in for a predator (well, nearly no way – we shall learn more later). Oh, and if you have heard stories or seen cartoons (I am looking at you, Sonic) suggesting that the hedgehog can roll when it is in a ball, that is simply not true. That is all the sort of thing you can learn from bumping into a hog in the garden. To find out more of what a hedgehog gets up to, you need to adopt their lifestyle.

The first work I did was looking at whether they were causing a problem for ground-nesting birds on the small island of North Ronaldsay, the most northerly of the Orkneys, off the coast of Scotland. I was staying at the bird observatory, and one of the hardest parts came in the evening, after dinner, when the bird watchers would settle down for a night of music and merriment and I instead got kitted out for a night of wandering around on my own, looking for hedgehogs. The birdwatchers were all asleep by the time I got in at four in the morning.

Sleep is always a problem with this sort of work, as I had information to collect during the day as well. A very stressful part of this was watching Arctic terns. Now, you might wonder what would be so stressful about watching birds. Well, these birds live in a colony and nest on the ground. My job was to count the amount of food – mainly sand eels – that was being brought to the chicks to see if they were being fed enough to thrive.

The stress came because these birds are known as 'peckie terno' on the island, and they will, if they can, jab the top of your head with their very sharp beak! I had to sit with my back against a wall to stop this happening. They would hover above me and then dive and shriek as close to me as they could. Walking around at night counting hedgehogs was far more relaxing! This work, while important and very interesting, only allowed me to bump into hedgehogs when I met them. To get to know what they really get up to, you need to follow them, quietly.

I was lucky enough to be invited to radio track hedgehogs as part of an RSPCA project. We were trying to see whether hedgehogs that had been taken in by a wildlife hospital as youngsters would be able to cope with life in the wild after a winter away from those conditions.

To do this we attached a small radio-transmitter to their back. We clipped a patch of spines between their shoulder blades and then glued it in place, with a thin aerial running towards the tail. Each transmitter is set to a specific frequency, and to find the hedgehogs out in the wild I needed to tune into each hedgehog using a receiver. The signal I get is a beep – nothing more exciting than that. When the aerial I am carrying is pointing towards the hedgehog, the signal is loudest, and when at 90 degrees, quietest.

Complications arise from the fact that the

beeps are almost as loud when I point the aerial in the exact opposite direction. When there are ditches, buildings or walls, the signal can get bounced around, so I spend ages walking in circles, trying to find the hedgehog. Oh, and it rains. A lot. Or at least that is my memory – lots of rain in April as I trudged up and down hills. Though, to counter that, you do look like you are operating your own remote-controlled hedgehog when you eventually track them down! I can't complain, I had some of the most amazing times, because when I was doing this in Devon it was the first time I had really got to know individual hedgehogs. These bundles of prickles are full of personality.

Let me introduce you to some time in the company of hedgehogs. During the day, the hedgehogs are tucked up in a nest. They don't climb trees to build their nests but make them on the ground. These day nests can be quite flimsy, sometimes little more than a pile of dried leaves they have collected together and into which they crawl.

As a nocturnal naturalist it is best to spend as much of the day asleep as possible – just like the hedgehogs – but this can be tricky, as there is always something to do. During the day I would do a walk around the site checking where all the hedgehogs were sleeping so that I knew where to start my evening's activities. I would then write up the data I had collected from the night before, making sure the batteries were all charged for the radio receiver and the torch and planning the next night, not forgetting that the shops aren't open in the middle of the night either.

Cooking during this project was quite limited. I had a small gas cooker in my caravan, a caravan which was remarkably close to falling to pieces. There was no bathroom, of course, so I had a small spade for dealing with the necessary. And as for washing, the wife of the farmer on whose land I was working would insist, every week or so, that I come in and have a bath. Other than that, there was a tap in the field which allowed a bracing wash. On a good day I would not only get a bath but also bake some bread to take back up to the caravan with me. Work tended to start at around 8pm, when I would collect my electronic tracking gear from a shed and see who was up and about.

The job was simple, in theory. Every night I had to find all twelve hedgehogs that we had released at least once, plot their position on a map, record those positions as a grid reference and weigh the hog. How does one go about weighing a hedgehog? My supervisor and mentor on all things hedgehog, Dr Pat Morris, designed a cunning device with his wife, Mary: a modified pillowcase into which the hog can be gently placed and then suspended beneath a spring balance. It only took a moment and the results were some of the most crucial information to be collected, the reason being that if the hedgehogs were settling into their new home they would not dramatically lose weight. If they did, that would be a cause for concern and require a return to the hospital. The idea was to do this for a couple of months.

Maybe I could have let the twelve go and then come back to see what was left in two months, but the reality is hedgehogs can move 2km a night and therefore, if I wanted to have any hope of keeping up with them, I needed to be out every night!

That might sound like really hard work, and it was physically demanding, but the opportunities were amazing. I have always loved wildlife, and I love wandering around the countryside looking at – and for – wildlife, so this was perfect! While it was hedgehogs that were my main concern, there was all the other night life to see as well.

Wandering up one slope in search of 298,

who became known as Freya (now, I know I was not supposed to give the hedgehogs names, but I was out all night with them and it just made the work easier if I had someone to talk to!), I was given a jumpscare by a sudden noise.

I had a torch, of course, but tried not to use it too much, as when you get used to the dark it is amazing how much you can see. (Try it – if you can get somewhere fairly dark and let your eyes settle. It can take 15 minutes or so, but you will be amazed at how much you can see.) In this case my shock was caused by two badgers, tumbling and play fighting out of the hedge to my left and rolling just a few metres from where I stood.

They were so involved with their game – and this was play – that they carried on for a few minutes, running back into the thick hedge then tumbling out again. I must have been downwind of them, or I am sure my scent would have sent them scurrying. It was magical. I had been standing absolutely still and my toes were going numb with cold, so I shifted, ever so slightly, and that was enough. They realised I was there and vanished back into the undergrowth.

Badgers are beautiful (more on them soon), but they present a problem. They can, and do, eat hedgehogs. Their claws are longer than hedgehog spines and very strong. They leave a distinctive hollowed-out shell of a hedgehog – just the skin and spines. Three of my study animals ended up being eaten by a badger, but I don't think it was the ones I saw at play. I think it was an animal on the move who had learned the technique.

This made me very nervous, and every time I could not find one of my hedgehogs I would start to worry. Most of the time, though, there were not such stresses, and I gradually got to know my hedgehogs. Strange as it may seem, the hedgehogs also got to know me! For example, after weeks of being followed around by me, some of the hedgehogs decided I was not a threat and would just dart for the undergrowth when I got close, rather than frowning and rolling into a ball. This meant I was then forced to chase after them.

I was aided in this by small lights that glowed on the back of the hogs, which in turn gave great amusement to the farmer's wife, who had trouble sleeping and would enjoy the small hours watching the lights dance around her garden.

The distance they can travel is remarkable. Towards the end of the night I was looking for

Hettie, more formally known as 248, for the final check (I tried to see each hedgehog twice during the night). The earlier I got to see them, the closer they were likely to be from where I saw them last, theoretically making my life a little bit easier. This female had always hung around the same part of the farm, so when I could not find her I did start to worry. There was a hint of a signal coming from the south, so I followed that and realised it was leading me towards the busy road that skirted the study area. Now I was getting more concerned.

Roads are a problem – it used to be that many hedgehogs were seen squashed on them. As the number being killed this way decreased, there were stories in the press about the possibility that hedgehogs were learning how to cross the roads safely. Unfortunately, that is not the case. In fact, we run a 'citizen science' survey called Mammals on Roads which shows very clearly that hedgehogs tend to get run over in proportion to the population, meaning that we can learn how the population is doing by counting corpses.

This does not tell us how many hedgehogs there are in total, but does tell us whether numbers are going up or down. I headed towards the road deep in worry, though the signal did still seem to be moving, which was some relief. On and on I went, until I got to a farm I had not been to before. The yard was full of old equipment and her signal seemed to be coming from underneath a bit of rusting tractor. I poked around, hoping not to wake a ferocious guard dog, and eventually found her. She had walked 2km (as a straight line on the map) from where I had last seen her.

My walk home (well, to my caravan) was much later than usual, and the sun was not far from rising as I came to a hill. Across the field I could see a small herd of deer who caught sight or scent of me and quickly vanished. One minute they were there in the predawn light, and then they were gone. I was fascinated, so trudged a detour to where I had last seen them and found that the hedge they had been near had a gap in it – a gap which opened into a new world.

They had darted into a well-hidden green lane. These are the remains of the earliest roads. This one ran between two hedges and was clearly part of the old route over the hill. It had been worn down into the ground by thousands of feet, hooves and wheels. It really felt like a magical world had opened up to me, though it would have felt a little more amazing if the farmer had not used it as a dumping ground for tyres and fertiliser sacks. Other nights ended earlier, thank goodness.

One of my highlights happened when I had finished my rounds, packed up the kit and stepped back out of my caravan to clean my teeth (like I said, rudimentary bathroom). Toothbrush in hand, I spotted a figure. It was Nigel.

Nigel was distinctive. Not that he looked different – no, he just reacted differently to all the other hedgehogs. While some rolled into a ball and some ran, Nigel just carried on without a care in the world. I had checked whether he was deaf or blind, both of which might have left him more carefree, but nope, his senses all functioned. He would flinch at torchlight or if I made a sharp noise.

It seemed to me that he was just comfortable with me around. However, if I had a visitor joining me on the nightly rambles, he went back to being far more cautious. It is not unlikely that I had developed a very distinctive, and probably quite hedgehoggy, scent! On this early morning he was just snuffling and feeding. I could hear the distinctive sniffing noise, and then he would stop and chomp.

I popped my toothbrush into my pocket and

decided to head after him as he went out of the gate to my field. It was the peace before dawn, a hint of the change in the light that would come with sunrise, so no need for a torch. I crouched down to watch Nigel at work as he snuffled along the tarmac of the narrow lane, darting his snout into the grassy verge when there was something to eat.

I realised that this was a risky strategy for both of us, as by now I was lying in the road to get a better view. The reason I did this was that the road was dry and relatively warm, while the verge was thick with dew. I am sure that is why Nigel chose to walk on the road too.

The road was quiet and I would hear any cars coming, so I felt safe. However, two of my hedgehogs did get killed on this stretch. None got killed on the busier road though. This made me wonder whether the nastiness of the busier road just kept them away, whereas the quiet one lulled them into a false sense of security, the only car they met possibly being the one that killed them.

The problem hedgehogs face is a lack of fight or flight response. Most animals, when they feel threatened, either run away or turn and bite. Hedgehogs don't, they stay still, knowing they are protected. This works for many things, but not cars. Luckily for us, the road remained empty and I found myself in the unusual situation of being nose-to-nose with a hedgehog. There was a moment where it became clear that he had noticed me – seen me and paid attention – before snuffling back to the slugs.

This carried on for a bit longer until he dragged a bigger, black slug out onto the road from the grassy verge. Before eating it, he scraped it across the tarmac, repeatedly. I think he was trying to get the slime off the slug before he noisily started to eat. It really seemed like this was only being eaten because he felt he ought to. It was the hedgehog equivalent of giving a toddler a Brussel sprout!

After eating this slug he moved on to a dandelion leaf. I was confused. They are carnivores, they eat meat. He was not, though, eating the leaf, but just chewing it and building up a mouth full of frothy saliva. Then he started to squirm around, spreading this froth all over his spines. This was the first time I had seen a hedgehog doing what is known as 'self anointing'. There are lots of theories as to why they do it, but know one really knows!

If you ever are lucky enough to find a hedgehog out at night, just keep quiet. It will probably roll up. If you are able to, get down to the hedgehog's level and wait for it to relax. This might take a while, so use that time to look closely at this amazing animal and have this thought in mind – it is an amazing predator (if you were a worm, you would be nervous) and is bigger than 99% of all animals that have ever lived, in the top 1% with the blue whale, Tyrannosaurus rex and us!

If they are out in the day, they are probably poorly and need to get to a rescue. You can find your nearest one by calling the British Hedgehog Preservation Society at 01584 890 801. You can visit their website at www.britishhedgehogs. org.uk for more information.

Badgers

Badgers are amazing animals. Beautiful, playful, fascinating, so powerful and strong. As we have seen, they also include hedgehogs in their diet. This might be enough to put off some hedgehog lovers, though the only people who ever really complain are those who want to persecute badgers. People who understand nature realise that predation is part of life.

I love badgers – I occasionally see them when taking my dog for a late-night walk down my street. There is even a blond one which might be an albino, but I have not seen whether it has a red eye. Coming home from a party late one night, I heard heavy scratching paws on the pavement and turned in time to see this ghost of a badger disappear into a neighbour's garden.

There are really blondies, known as leucistic. In fact there are also erythristic ones too, which have red fur.

Nights out with badgers have been an accidental part of my work with hedgehogs.

While I have never studied these black and white beauties to the same depth as I have hedgehogs, I've picked up a lot along the way and I also know some people who love badgers with just as much passion as I have for hedgehogs.

Badgers are mustelids, the same group of mammals that includes the weasel, stoat, polecat, pine marten and otter. Most of them have a similar design – they are long, thin and possess very sharp teeth – but the badger is a bit different; less long, more stocky, and while the others are almost entirely meat eaters, badgers have a wider diet and therefore have less specialised teeth. I would not want to be bitten by any of the mustelids, mind you.

Largely nocturnal, they all rely heavily on scent, so deliberate badger watching takes a bit of planning, like making sure you are not wearing any perfume, and that you are, if possible, sitting downwind of the inquisitive noses as they emerge from their sett.

A sett is where badgers live. They dig into the ground, usually into a slope, so that the holes don't just fill up with water when it rains. The main tunnel leads to small rooms, which these amazing animals build beneath our feet. It is here that they hide out during the day, raise their young and spend a lot of the winter tucked up, relying on fat reserves.

Tonight I am off to see if I can spot some very special badgers, and one very famous badger in particular – Luna.

Luna is an albino, meaning that she also has pink eyes, as well as no black fur, and she is famous because she lives in a field that some people want to turn into a housing estate. There is a campaign in the little village of Iffley (which is more just a bit of Oxford than a stand-alone village) against this development. We all know that there is an affordable housing shortage in Oxford, but digging up some of the precious green spaces to meet those needs has to be resisted, especially when 'our' new homes will come at the expense of those of Luna and her family.

It had been raining a lot, so I'm dressed for the weather, in waterproof trousers, boots and a heavy coat, and go to lock my bike up at my friend Dominic's house. His day job is as an ecological consultant, but he has also been at the forefront of campaigns to stop the destruction of special patches of our countryside by those who see an easy way to make money. He gives me the map to show me the site of the sett, along with advice on where best to position myself.

I have not been out alone at night to sit in

a field for a long time and I am really rather excited as I wait for the path to be clear and climb over the fence into a brilliantly rough field. Neat and tidy fields and gardens are the enemy of nature. Now, this was far from perfect, some idiots had used the corner by the path as a dumping ground for loads of litter, but beyond that, things improved.

Or rather, were not improved. There is a tendency to 'improve' fields to make them more productive, but this one had been used for ponies and was patterned with droppings among tussocks of grass. A perfect habitat for small mammals, the mice and voles that owls and foxes like to eat. I was over the fence at 6pm, and there was still plenty of light. I had a short walk across the first field to a great mound of brambles that looked like it had once been part of a hedge. That was my spot, and ahead of me, about 30 metres away, were more brambles and evidence of disturbed earth. The timing was right to let me be settled in place before the expected arrival of the badgers at 7pm. Dominic had told me that this was when the trail cameras had been seeing them emerge from their sett.

Everything was perfect. The wind blew gently into my face as I looked at the badgers' home. This meant that my scent was not being blown into their faces! I had also not gone to take a closer look at the sett, as again that would have disturbed them. The mess of brambles and trees behind me meant that I was leaving no silhouette – if it was just me and an empty field I would be much easier to see.

Next time you are out in a rough field, just take a moment to look, and you will see the paths that animals leave. I had positioned myself at the end of one of the very clear paths that ran out from the sett. Settling down to wait I began to concentrate on what the twilight was bringing me. Second week of March, mild weather, a bit of moisture in the air – and birds. Not many species, but quite a few blackbirds and wrens declaring their presence, though the poor birds were having to compete with one of our often overlooked acts of pollution: sound.

The ring road around Oxford is not too far from this beautiful scene. The same breeze that is keeping my scent from the sett is also washing us all with the noise of cars and trucks – a deadly drone that has been shown to impact the ability of wildlife to communicate, leaving aside the millions of animals killed each year.

The peace of the evening is being disturbed, as it will be every evening, by this noise. I have been one of the drivers, I am responsible too, and I never think about the noise I am making when in my car.

While I am trying to ignore the noise, I spot a movement. The light is already beginning to fade, but there is still plenty enough to see a female roe deer emerge from the hedge on the far side of the field. Despite everything I have done, she is suspicious. She keeps looking in my direction; she can tell something is different but not what. I sit still, then, after a minute or two, she lowers her head, seeming to relax, and is joined by two more deer, including a male with antlers rich in velvet.

Let me explain the velvet: deer grow antlers each year, then shed them following the breeding season. Roe deer start earlier than most, in December. Now, the bone that the antlers are made from is covered in a layer of skin and fur. The antlers need a blood supply, which is in the skin, and the fur insulates this.

Soon, the antlers will be fully grown and the deer will scrape the fur off on trees, revealing the hard bone that will be used to fight other males. For now, this fuzzy-antlered roe just posed for a while before following the other two across the field. I felt pleased that I had not been too obvious. As a prey animal, deer are more sensitive to potential threats than a badger, though there are no wolves or lynx around these days to catch them.

By 6.30pm, the clouds remind me that they are wet – nothing too serious, just a light smattering of raindrops. Two crows fly in, announcing their arrival with rich caws. They settled into a bare tree and I realised that the other birds had stopped singing too. Bedtime for the birds, it seems, though every now and then there is the high-pitched note of a redwing, a beautiful thrush that overwinters in Britain.

Light is now really drained from the view. Details are reduced to textures. I can see more than if I had just arrived, the time letting my eyes get used to the dark helps enormously. There is one problem, though. My right foot has gone to sleep. Sitting on the ground with my legs crossed was a silly idea. I have to move, and as I struggle up to kneeling, I put my hand onto something soft.

It's a molehill. My fingers explore the soil that these busy miners have brought to the surface. It is such fine soil, and also a reminder that this field has plenty of life out of sight. Moles make the most out of places with lots of worms. Worms are also important food for badgers.

From kneeling I moved to standing. I realised that my red-light torch was only good for reading or writing and the beam wasn't full enough to allow me to see further towards the sett. Red light not only allows you to retain your night vision but also is less likely to upset wildlife.

I could still see enough, though. Or could I? I found that I was noticing movement, which I took to be the shapes of badgers, but when I checked with brief illumination they turned out to be tussocks of grass. I remembered what it was like following hedgehogs around at night, especially up in Orkney, where I was not using radio tracking, and I would see a shape in a field that was definitely a hedgehog. I'd climb over the fence and run into the field, only to find it was a cowpat! My ears were becoming increasingly important as I waited to hear movement, straining to filter out the noise of the road. It is such a disturbance.

Movement – 7.10pm. There was definitely someone out there, and given everything about the evening, probably a badger. I waited, but there was something not quite right about the movement, so I risked another splash of light from my torch, only to find that it was a rabbit. That was good news. It meant that I was able to spot movement and that badgers would be easier than rabbits because they are larger and much less stealthy.

So I waited. I concentrated on the sounds, filtering as much traffic out as possible. I looked indirectly in the direction of the sett, which might sound odd. I should explain. As the level of light is reduced, the bits of our eyes that work best change. The central bit, where we concentrate our vision when we stare at something, specialises in colour. But if you look slightly off centre at something, you will find, out of the corner of your eye, that you will see more when the light is fading. In particular you will be able to pick up movement better.

By 8pm, though, I had to admit defeat. It was now as dark as it was going to get and the badgers would already be out doing their thing. I stiffly gathered my things and headed back across the field, expecting that at any moment a badger would jump out and tell me it was a wind up.

No such luck. I got back to Dominic's house and thought I ought to report on what had not happened. Sitting at the kitchen table with a cup of tea, I explained how the evening had gone.

'Oh, they probably used the backdoor,' he said. It turned out that while they usually use the entrance I was observing, they have another way out they sometimes use – he knows this from the camera footage he has seen. There was nothing I could have done. I could not have been at both at the same time. It is a good reminder though that badger setts can be really quite large! The biggest ever is in the Guinness Book of Records as having 879m of tunnels, 50 underground chambers and 178 entrances!

'You know what, you've seen a badger before, so just relax,' he said. I protested that I had never seen Luna. 'Well,' he continued, 'we can sort that out for you right now.'

With that he went to get his laptop.

The collection of videos of the badgers from that sett are far better than anything I could have seen in person. If I had been as close as the cameras, they would have never come out at all. The first video is actually an edited short film narrated by local superstar Peggy Seeger. She is a world famous folk musician who has been writing, singing, performing and campaigning since the 1950s.

The film is just a five-minute introduction to the presence of Luna on this land – and the importance these fields have as her, and her family's home. The fascinating realisation is that the badgers have probably been there for hundreds of years. While developers can state that they will move – relocate – badgers, which they have to do as badgers are protected, this ignores the attachment to the home in which these badgers have lived for generations.

One of the things you learn when watching these videos of badgers is that they really do play. There is no other word to describe it. Remember when I talked about being spooked by the playful badgers when out hedgehogging – it is the same here. Some people complain when I use words like, 'happy' or 'playful' when talking about animals. They say that I am putting human emotions onto them.

If you have a pet cat or dog – or know anyone who does – try and spend a little time with them and watch how they play. Centuries ago, animals were dismissed as just being soulless machines. This led to some people thinking it was okay to treat animals in horrible ways. Now we, well, most of us, know better.

There is one video where Luna has climbed up a tree stump, grabbed onto a bit of branch and is hanging upside down, playing with the others. Okay, it might be a step too far to say she is smiling, but it certainly looks like it. What is clear is that this is fun.

Play is an important part of life – play is how animals learn. The badgers are open-mouthed play-biting. No one is getting hurt, but they are preparing for more serious times, when they work out who is the strongest. Actually, the badgers seem to love hanging from the tree stump. The next video has Luna playing by herself, holding onto the branch with her front paws, while beside her two others are enjoying a game of tail biting. Luna then tries to scratch while hanging and promptly falls to the ground. There is no sound on the video, but if there was, I am sure the other two would be giggling.

I am beginning to wonder how coordinated this blond beauty is. The following video has her stretching up a tree-trunk before slipping down and collapsing into a hole. It does not look like that was part of the plan. Maybe that is why she has a nibble at a rear leg to teach it a lesson.

The video of her and a sett mate mutually grooming each other shows that there is a more tender side to life in this family. By this stage my second cup of tea had gone cold. Watching these amazing animals I can really understand why people become so very attached to badgers. The amazing thing is all this wonderful wildlife is just out there – these fields back onto the gardens of people living in the village. The badgers I see when walking the dog are right in a housing estate.

A couple of days later I bumped into Dominic. I was really pleased to discover that he also failed to see the badgers at the sett to which he had directed me. He went out the night after me, with his night-vision equipment. This reassured me that I was not just being a clumsy wildlife watcher, and that the badgers were really just being very crafty!

For more information on badger welfare, protection and conservation, visit www. badgertrust.org.uk

Bats

I have spent a lot of time in the company of bats, but not purposefully. They are some of the most deliberately nocturnal animals we have. They are around us, but to our ears they are silent. With the right tech, however, we can drop into their world and find out who is flitting around our heads.

There are a few things to straighten out first: for one, there are no vampire bats in Britain (and even if there were, they tend not to nibble people, preferring a tiny drop of blood from cattle). Also, bats are NOT going to get stuck in your hair or bang into you.

Bats have got such an amazing navigation system. As they are able to weave through woodland and snatch a moth in flight, they are not going to bump into us! The fastest bat in the UK is called a noctule, and they can fly at 50kmh, but that is nothing compared to one of the fruit bats found in South America, the Brazilian free-tailed bat. This has been recorded flying at 160kmh, faster than any bird!

So, how do they do it? How can an animal navigate at such speed and with such accuracy in the dark? The amazing thing is that they do this with sound. In the same way we use light in the dark, shining a torch out into the world for our eyes to see the light reflected back to us, bats use sound and can 'see' the world through the echoes as they bounce back.

That sounds far fetched, I know, but humans can also do it on a small scale. If you make a noise when you are in an enclosed space filled with soft things – a wardrobe, maybe – and then compare that to what it feels like to make the same noise in a railway station, you would probably not have any trouble in working out which you were in from the way the sounds bounces back to you. Well, bats do that, but MUCH better!

I already mentioned that they are silent to our ears – that is because the noise they make to enable them to find their way around is at a frequency too high for us to hear. Actually, young people can often make out some of the lower sounds bats make, but as we get older we lose that ability.

However, we should be thankful that we can't hear them, as they can be loud! The loudest bats shout at 140 decibels. Rock concerts tend to peak at 120dB, and the pain threshold for people is around 125dB. Night-time rambles after hedgehogs would not be quite as peaceful if my ears were being bombarded by this volume.

To really hear what is going on, we need to use a machine that converts the high-frequency noise down to something in our range. These are called bat detectors. Each species of bat has its very own call sign, so the detectors not only translate the sounds into something we can hear, but also tell us who is there.

I live near the Boundary Brook Nature Reserve, run by the Oxford Urban Wildlife Group, surrounded by schools, allotments and houses. These urban reserves are so important for wildlife. Our gardens can provide many things that help nature, but not everything. And it is not just the wildlife that benefits, it is us too – these reserves are a great place to share and learn.

I arranged to meet my bat-loving friend Steph Holt at the reserve on a May evening. She spends much of her time working at the greatest building in the country, the Natural History Museum in London, but lives on the same estate as me. She also has a bat detector.

The path that runs from my street to the

reserve is a feeding ground for bats. There are some gentle street lights, but nothing too intrusive. The bats can be spotted if you take care and look for them, flitting against the sky, their small silhouettes darting.

The flight of bats used to be dismissed as chaotic because people did not understand what they were doing. Now we know more about it, and are, or should be, amazed. They are not seen around lights so they can see better, but because insects are attracted to the lights.

When I meet Steph this is one of the things I ask: are our street lights a good thing for bats? It turns out that this is not a simple question. 'Some bats can cope with the light,' Steph says, 'the pipistrelles that were flitting around over your head will enjoy the insects, but other bats steer clear of the light. What makes this worse is that some of the insects that they might have fed on in the darker corners of the reserve will have been drawn to the light.' That also answers another question, as to who was flying overhead.

Fascinatingly, light has been shown to have a dramatic impact on a bat's ability to behave normally. Researchers have looked at how bats respond to different levels of light and found that even a full moon is enough to keep some bats skulking in the undergrowth. This means that they are not feeding, and for such a busy animal, food is so important.

'They have to eat so much to keep themselves going. Did you know that these little bats need to eat around 3,000 midges and other small insects a night? That is four or five a minute, all night long!' Steph tells me.

People think of bats as flying mice, but in reality they are more like us than they are mice. They live for a long time, some up to 35 years, and usually only have one pup a year, investing lots of time nurturing and teaching their young.

Pipistrelles are our smallest bat, and while it is great to see their dark shapes it is even more exciting to hear them on Steph's detector. It really is an extraordinary experience to be let into this other world of which we are so ignorant. There is a background white noise and then, as they dart over us, a series of, well, if you make a clicking noise using your tongue against the roof of your mouth, that is not far off it. (I am now just taking a moment to imagine you all doing this as you read!)

Over the next half an hour or so we get nothing but pips and an owl, but that is not the right animal for this chapter. 'This reserve is great for pips,' Steph says, 'but we can get to see some other bats if we head towards the water.'

That is easy, meaning a short walk to a brook. This one is not very idyllic, as it is a concrete channel now, but the insects don't mind and therefore the bats don't mind either. It is still only pips we hear, though, as we wander towards the Thames.

I have seen a few bats up close, when they are being looked after by people with the correct training and licences. Bats are very well protected by law and it is illegal to interfere with them or their habitat. I start to tell Steph about the most beautiful bat I had met. 'Was it a brown long-eared bat?' she asks. Well, yes, it was, and we both get a little excited describing our experiences.

I had gone to a rescuer who had one of these bats. She reached into its enclosure and gently took hold of a bundle of brown. As she opened her hand, the long ears of the bat (their name is quite accurate, if not very creative – they are brown and have long ears), which were folded forward over its eyes, lifted slowly, revealing a nose that twitched and was covered in the cutest freckles!

'They are also known as the whispering bat,' Steph explains. 'There is an amazing arms race between moths and bats. The favourite moth of the brown long-eared bat is the large yellow underwing. This moth has found a way to escape a hunting bat. When it hears the echolocation it simply folds its wings and falls towards the ground, so the bats have started to shout more quietly. This bat also listens very intently with its amazing ears.' The bats then swoop on the moths, scooping them up in their tail basket, a flap of skin that connects the wings at their rear end, and takes them to a quiet spot to feed. 'They are terribly messy eaters,' Steph says. 'They will eat the body of the moth and then drop the wings, which, given how many moths they can eat, leads to quite a pile.'

After crossing a road we come to a recreation ground – a flat, grassy space used for football and frisbee. Steph gets her detector back out and fiddles with the settings. I ask what she is doing. 'Here we might get a soprano pipistrelle,' she explains. 'We used to think that there was just one species of pip, but now we know there are three, one of which shouts a little higher than the common pip, so we called it the soprano! Then there is Nathusius's pipistrelle, which shouts somewhere between the two.'

We stop and listen to the background hiss, but there is nothing. Looking up, there are no signs of bats either. Steph is not downhearted. 'Lots more ahead of us, I am sure,' she says, stowing the box and striding on.

I ask how many bat species we have in the UK. 'Well, we have 17 that breed here, and then there is the greater mouse-eared bat that we think does not breed here, but visits. If it does breed here, it will be our largest bat. Around the world there are over 1,400 different sorts of bat. They are quite amazing animals, I don't understand why more people are not as fascinated as I am!'

As we walk over a cycle path, the air is beginning to feel damper. If it were colder I would expect to walk into a mist, but the warmth of the evening keeps the air clear. Perfect for moths!

The meadow we enter has been radically changed over the years. It was massively overgrown with brambles and scrub, but now a lot has been removed and new trees have been planted, though plenty of rough ground is still to be found on the margins. On the whole, rough, scruffy ground is good for nature – sports pitches are less so.

'Right, let's see who we have here,' Steph says, reaching for the detector again. 'If we are lucky we will spot a serotine bat. These are much louder and deeper than the pips. They will eat anything they can fit in their faces!'

The white noise of the detector is undisturbed

by serotines. As we walk on towards the river, I do worry about the lack of insects. This is something that bothers Steph and pretty much every other ecologist too. We might be happier not to have insects in our faces or on our sandwiches, but without them we will have no bats and far fewer birds and hedgehogs too.

'Okay, let's try to see if we can pick up a Daubenton's bat,' Steph says, twiddling the dials on the detector to set it to the correct frequency. The Daubenton's bat is also known as the water bat, which is why Steph thinks we have a good chance. 'It likes to feed on insects just as they emerge from the water,' she says. 'And they then swoop on them with these great big hairy hobbit feet...' I had to stop her there. Hobbit feet? On a bat?

'Okay, maybe not as big as a hobbit's feet, but still big for a bat, and definitely hairy,' she explains. 'They use them to drag along the surface of the water and scoop up insects. There is another thing that makes them special – they have a white tummy which you can see in torch light. In fact, you don't need a detector for a Daubenton's bat.'

Steph has really increased the anticipation – I hope the bats live up to her hype! There is a spot by the river where the dogs love to jump in, with a bit of a beach that means we can get closer to the water. Detector in hand, she turns it on and we are greeted with the usual static hiss.

'They will often roost during the day in cracks under bridges,' Steph is saying, when suddenly the hiss is interrupted by a sequence of quite urgent clicks, very different from the pipistrelle. 'That's one,' she says, grinning. I am delighted, even if I did not see one swoop onto the water or catch a glimpse of a white tummy. It is just so lovely to meet another one of those animals of the night with which I share this corner of the country. Without the kit, or Steph's skill, I would never have found one of these amazing bats.

There are people like Steph all over the country who have this knowledge and the desire to share it. It is one of the things I love about the naturalist world – mostly people are kind, welcoming and generous. No one was born knowing everything, everyone was at some time helped by someone more experienced.

There are bat groups in many towns, as well as a national Bat Conservation Trust who might be able to link you up with an expert. You can visit their website, www.bats.org.uk, for more information. If not a bat group, there may be a county mammal group local to you. Getting out into the wild (or even not so wild) and meeting amazing animals is such a delight.

Owls

Nocturnal life is perfect for learning more about owls. These amazing birds have not always been a part of my hedgehog work. Up in Orkney, the bird that used to keep me company at night was the corncrake, a now rather rare bird with the most remarkable call. Their Latin name, the name that scientists give all animals and plants so that they can be understood all over the world, is *Crex crex*, which is very appropriate, as that is the noise they make. It is a strange, rasping noise that used to drive locals mad, as the birds would often use their stone cottages as a sounding board.

Now when it comes to owls, we know what noise they make! Twit-twoo... Well, only some owls make that noise, and if I am to be very accurate, no one owl makes that noise. This is the call of the tawny owl, our most common owl in the UK and the one you are most likely to hear near where you live. In fact, the call is a call and response, with the female going 'twit' and the male going 'twoo'!

To learn more about owls, I was lucky enough to be able to visit my dear friend Miriam Darlington. She is a poet and author who has written a book all about owls called *Owl Sense*, and she is the perfect guide into what makes owls quite so special.

It is a short drive from her Devon home to a perfect owl habitat. We park down a small lane surrounded by what looks like rough pasture. Like most wildlife, owls prefer things to be a little rough – they are less keen on the neat and tidy. The reason is that the animals owls prey on like a scrappy landscape. Miriam is taking me to find the owl that looks most like the owl we imagine – the barn owl.

Barn owls love voles. How do we know they love voles? There is an easy way to find out what an owl has been eating, and that is to find an owl pellet. Owls swallow their food whole, with none of this ripping into little pieces that other birds of prey do. When the vole, mouse or shrew reaches the stomach, the digestive juices get to work. After all the goodness is stripped away, the remains are cleverly wrapped up in the fur and coughed up. They don't particularly smell and they contain an amazing amount of evidence.

When they have dried out, these pellets

can be teased apart, revealing the bones of the animals that have been eaten. From this, ecologists have calculated that each owl can eat up to 2,000 rodents a year! Now, I am not an expert, but when you are in the company of someone who is, you will quickly learn to spot the lower jaw of a shrew and how different it is to a mouse. For some this might be a step too far into the gruesome; for others, it is like opening a curtain and seeing a completely different view of what is going on around you.

Barn owls hunt in silent flight, with feathers so soft that they just tickle the air. I have only seen barn owls a few times, but they are very memorable. They hunt by 'quartering' a field of rough grass, flying across it, listening. Their hearing is so acute that Miriam calls it 'earsight'. Amazingly, inside their brain, the bits which process sound are linked with those that process sight.

Miriam describes it as we walk. 'This super-powered owl aids its earsight by bobbing, dipping and turning its head so that its sound scanner – the facial disc – can capture sound waves and transport the faintest of whispers to the ears.' If you have already found an image of a barn owl, you will see the facial disk straight away. The face features a white heart shape in which the eyes and beak are obviously set. The way that this disc is shaped is like a radar dish, or even the radio-telescopes that 'look' deep into space. The barn owl does not need a vole to squeak – just the slightest movement, even chewing, is enough to guide its attack.

Their ears are of slightly different sizes and one is higher on the head than the other, with the ear holes hidden by feathers. This means that sound reaches the ears at fractionally different times, allowing the owl to refine its focus. Experiments that blocked one ear proved that the owl became 'blind' and was unable to hunt in the dark. Their ability to hunt so effectively in darkness is one of the reasons that barn owls were treated with fear by some, it being thought that they must have some power to do with the devil or witches.

Another potential superpower possessed by these owls is the ability to see where voles and mice urinate. It has not been fully proven yet, but we know that kestrels, those amazing hovering birds of prey, can see the trails left by rodents, and there is every reason to think that the barn owl can too.

Now this is a bird that does not twit and twoo; in fact, this beauty has a harsh call, almost a scream. This is not a relaxing noise at all and does absolutely nothing to rid the owl of spooky origin stories.

We wait beside a field that Miriam thinks might generate results, leaning on the gate. It is early spring, and the air smells like the world is waking up. I have been lucky to do a lot of my field work at this time of year. Yes, it can rain (a lot!), but there is a feeling of life blooming all around you.

We are talking quietly, even though the owls, if they are around, will know we are here. They will have heard our breathing! Less is better when it comes to noise and the nocturnal naturalist. It feels quite dark, though actually, I don't think my eyes have quite acclimated to the lack of sunshine – remember, it takes a good 15 minutes to get your night vision up and running.

Miriam was telling me about the amazing experience with long-eared owls she had seen in Serbia, and how the reason they were doing so well was the lack of use of poison to kill mice and rats, which also kills them. This is not a commonly seen owl in the UK, but when she was in Serbia it was possible to see over 20 roosting in a tree, but only if you know how to look, as they are beautifully camouflaged to blend into the woodland.

'There,' she says, dropping out of her memories into the present. 'You see that movement?' I had missed it and did not quite look in the right direction, though now I was alert. I may not have earsight, but I can concentrate a bit more than I was, remembering to look more out of the corner of my eyes than full on.

There it is, sort of like a tea towel flapping, despite the lack of wind. You can see why owls get a spooky reputation. Never mind the screech of the barn owl – this movement, when seen unexpectedly at night, could easily be a ghost.

Then it is gone. I did not see it drop, and the vole on which it fell probably had no idea what was coming. We wait to see it lift off, but must have missed it flying away. 'Come on, no point just waiting here, there are more owls to find,' Miriam says, and off we go into the damp Devon night.

How many more owls are there? We had talked about the long-eared owls, which don't actually have long ears but rather tufty feathers sticking up where ears might be expected, and the tawnys as well, with their twit and twoo. Who else is out there?

'We must not forget the short-eared owl,' Miriam says. 'There are more of these around during the winter as they migrate from colder places. Again, no obvious ears, just short ear tufts. Oh, and it is a bit odd, as it is often seen out in the day.'

Miriam continues, 'There are no prizes for guessing that the little owl is smaller than the others. These have a shrill yelp of an alarm call.' I remember I had seen a little owl on a walk once – it was sitting in a hole in a tree and it was so well disguised that I was fortunate to spot it.

'Little owls love to feed on beetles, so they love a field that has lots of horse poo in it, as this attracts the insects,' Miriam tells me. 'At the other end of the scale, there is the eagle owl.'

When it comes to these majestic beasts, I know a little more about them. There is a wildlife hospital I visit which has one which was previously a pet and cannot be released into the wild. She is magnificent, with golden eyes, and huge. They can have a wingspan of up to two metres. When looking at the bird on the perch, it was the talons that really made me stare. They can be up to 6cm long.

It is no surprise that where they are mostly found, on the continent, they are one of the few predators of the hedgehog. In fact, I was sent a photograph of one of these amazing birds flying to its nest clutching a poor hog.

Only seen occasionally in the UK, these birds

are probably visitors from Scandinavia, though some might stay and there may be others that have escaped from captivity. We are not going to bump into one of these owls tonight.

Miriam is leading me towards the dark. Out where we have been, in the fields, there has been enough light (once our eyes are accustomed) to be able to walk by moonlight. The moon is not full, but gives enough to guide us.

'We are heading to find a tawny,' she says. 'They are around here, I am sure.' I had not heard the distinctive calls and ask how she knows. 'Well, they are often here, but did you hear those blackbirds all kicking off and making a fuss? That was very likely to have been caused by a tawny being too close for their comfort.' And with that, we walk on, enjoying the peace and dusk.

I love the word for this time of day – crepuscular! I also love a good bright moon while out working at night – not just because it makes it easier to walk around without a torch, and not just because I love to see my moon shadow. Have you ever seen your moon shadow? Please, have this as a target for the next time you are out at night. Find somewhere dark enough on a clear night with a bright moon and you will see it.

A thing about that shadow. The moon, as I am

sure you know, does not produce its own light. All the light we see from the moon is reflected from the sun. So countless tiny packets of light, known as photons, are flung from the sun, and some of these hit the moon. While most of them will finish there, some are reflected on in their journey. When you see a moon shadow, you are seeing the result of these long-travelled bits of light hitting the back of your head!

Another thing I love about the moon, and this may sound a little soft, but when I was doing long nights of radio tracking hedgehogs in Devon the moon was there, most nights it was not raining. In Scotland, yes, there was lots of rain, but also the moon was just not in the same sequence as me. I missed the moon, she was set by the time I was out. I missed seeing the moon. I felt definitely more alone without her presence. It is also possible, however, that I was just getting very tired and over emotional!

I find that the night tends to generate tangents in my brain, so I will get back to the walk with Miriam. The moment of change is dramatic. We are suddenly in among the trees. The atmosphere changed, not just the amount of light. If I was to analyse it, I would probably find that the air was damper, cooler and filled with the scent of rot. A good old woodland with old trees and rotting wood is a gorgeous place to be, day or night.

Unnecessarily, Miriam tells me to take care. Each step is now quite tentative, but I could follow the shape of my guide, now slightly lighter than the surroundings. Our conversation drops to a whisper before I walk into her back. She had stopped without me noticing.

Further whispers help me get to the log on which she has stopped to sit. She leans closer and says, 'I know there are tawny owls here, I just want to get them to come a little closer.' With that, she cupped her hands to her mouth and hooted. I have on many occasions tried to do this, but have always failed. It is a delightful skill to have, and also something that children can use to really annoy their parents, like when they learn to wolf-whistle really loudly (I can't do that either!).

I ask, quietly, what she is expecting to happen, and she whispers, 'Well, a female might respond, or a male. More likely a male, as "we" are now a new bird in his patch. Maybe with a hoot of ownership, maybe more assertive. Let's see.'

Miriam also tells me more about the way males react. 'Tawny owls have territories, patches that they defend. They have spots where they like to sit and wait and pounce, not like the continually hunting barn owls. This means that they don't like to share!' This is one of the reasons they are so responsive to an invading owl, as they try and keep the patch clear for them.

Miriam told me a story of how someone had moved to a new home, and as soon as he got there started to do what they had done in their previous home. That was, check out the local owls, so he started to hoot. The first night there was no response, but the next night, there was and he was delighted. It became a nightly activity, going out to have a chat with the neighbouring owls, each of them asserting their ownership of the land.

A month later, this person was at a street party and mentioned to one of his neighbours about the lovely owls in the area. The person who responded said how lovely it was – there had been none until a month ago when he started calling to it, and they realised they had just been hooting to each other!

Back in the woods, the first few hoots were met with silence and I was beginning to wonder whether either Miriam was not sounding very owlish or that there were no owls! Then, after her next hoot, there was an answer. 'He is interested,' she whispers. She tries again, and then something strange happens. I do not hear anything, but sort of feel the slightest breath of a breeze on my cheek. Miriam feels it too. 'That was a flyby,' she says. We had felt the wind from the wing of an owl coming to see who we were. We had been discovered as hoaxers and dismissed. 'If we had been another owl, we would have known about it – they can be quite vicious,' Miriam says. Before emerging from the wood, we sit for a while longer, just enjoying the deep peace of this space, but there are no more owls.

Moths

I am very lucky to live in a house that is down a quiet cul-de-sac and backs onto a popular park. The sunrises over the park on spring mornings are filled with song thrushes, blackbirds, robins and jackdaws. As the day warms up, the red kites, relative newcomers, call and circle. Then there are the flurries of chaotic urgency from the even newer parakeets, all very obvious, bright, noisy and gorgeous.

It is at night when you need to work a little harder to spot the magic in the air, though some of my neighbours do make themselves known – the foxes in late winter make such a racket, the females encouraging the males for some attention with unearthly shrieks – and sometimes there will be the spooky bark of the muntjac. Both of these animals can cause quite a shock. We have already heard about the owls, but I have only ever heard tawny owls from my garden, sending their twit and twoo messages back and forth.

Oh, and the badgers. My rescue dog, Ogli, prefers his last walk to be down the street, to a small patch of grass at the end of the road where he likes to wee! Often, we will see one of these gorgeous beasts trundling across the path and into our friend Tracey's garden. As wonderful as badgers are, however, they have become something of a nocturnal menace on a Tuesday night.

Now that might seem strange, like they are keeping a diary or something, but Tuesday night is when our street puts out the bins, including the food waste bin. Badgers *love* food. They rummage through our bins if we have failed to sit them up high, scattering teabags, onion skins and potato peelings across the path.

Sorry, I do get caught up in the life that is around me – if you are going to be distracted, let it be by a badger or an owl. Back to the subject of this chapter. As I said, I am talking about 'magic in the air': moths.

Now, I can imagine a bit of a humph from some of you – what is so special about moths? Who cares about these dull things that flit around the lightbulb or nibble my favourite woollen jumpers? However, this is probably the most exciting chapter, because I imagine you had at least some interest in hedgehogs, badgers, owls or bats. A lack of interest in moths is purely down to a lack of experience with them. When you get the chance to really look at a moth, you will, I am sure, be blown away by their diversity and beauty, a beauty that is usually kept in the dark.

So, just what is a moth? Well, you might have an idea that the difference between a moth and a butterfly is that moths fly at night and butterflies fly in the day. In reality, that is not a good enough identifier – there are night-flying butterflies and day-flying moths. Basically, moths and butterflies are the same thing.

Another thing to remember is that there are so many different sorts of moth, over 2,500 of them, in fact. In the UK there are just 59 species (and of those, two are migrants). If you have a collector's mind – or if *Pokémon* is/was your thing – there can be little better to get excited about than moths. Can you catch them all? Probably not! Partly because of these 2,500, 1,600 are micro moths – moths so tiny that some need to be identified under a microscope. The bigger moths, known as macro moths, make up the rest.

There is another reason that it will be hard to 'catch them all', and that is because their numbers are declining at a terrifying rate.

Nearly all the insects are suffering. There used to be a regular summer problem that you would be driving along on a warm night and encounter what has been called a 'moth snowstorm', a great cloud of insects that would get squashed to the car windscreen and headlights, requiring scraping off to allow for safe travels. This cleaning job has all but vanished, and this is not because the moths have become smarter! It is because there are fewer of them out and about.

I had a moment a few summers ago. Cycling along the river on my way home on a warm night, I had a head torch on. It was only when I turned off the main towpath to join the brookside path that led home that I, literally, bumped into a moth. At that moment I realised I had not seen a single one on the ride, whereas I should have had my face filled with fluttering wings as they were drawn to the light and I barged into their nocturnal adventures. My heart sank – it was a measure of the decline in numbers, and I cried.

Moths and other insects are disappearing because of the way we grow food, the way we build and travel. Basically, we are the cause. It might seem like a small thing, the loss of moths and other bugs, but these animals are what the wonderful bats feed on. And their larvae – the caterpillars – are what keeps the blue tits and the hedgehogs, the toads and the blackbirds happy.

Let's leave the sad story for now and look at how we can get to enjoy some of the beauty that is hiding in the dark. Something that you probably know about moths is that they fly into the light. If one gets into the house on a summer evening and there is a light on, they will fly around and around it, making it very difficult to get them back outside. I will always try and get them out, not because I don't like them, but because there is nothing for them to feed on in my conservatory, and if I left them in there overnight they could end up dying.

Why do they fly around lights? This is a long-standing question and has resulted in many theories. One is that any light, whether that is a candle or a torch, represents the moon to a moth. Moths try to orient themselves, so they fly alongside it. If the moon is always on their left, for example, then they know they are going straight. With our light, though, it is so much closer and smaller, so the moth will fly in such a way as to keep the light on their left, meaning they just keep circling.

It could be that bright light simply confuses the moths. Another theory suggests that some light frequencies appear to the moth as the special scent released by the females, called pheromones. The truth is, we don't know. However, we do know that it works, and they are attracted. This is how we can get a closer look at them, by encouraging them to visit moth traps. Now, moth traps are harmless – they use a bright light to lure in moths, who then hide among empty egg boxes, scattered in the large container which has the light at the top.

Breaking out of the nocturnal theme for a moment and also reminding us that moths are not just found at night, let me introduce you to three of the most amazing moths (I would go so far as to say most amazing animal of any sort you might meet in the UK), amazing enough to make anyone fall in love.

The first is the elephant hawk-moth, which I have seen idling on my neighbour's window frame. You will know if you have ever seen one of these. No, they don't have a trunk, but they are extraordinary. That is partly down to their size – they are huge, up to 6cm, but that is eclipsed by the colours, browny green with pink stripes. Please – take a break from reading and go and find a picture. I need you to understand quite how amazing they are!

The great thing about the elephant hawk-moth is that it is so easy to identify, and I soon had a gaggle of passersby marvelling at the insect. Oh, I hear you ask, where is the elephant coming from? Well, their caterpillars are supposed to look a little like an elephant's trunk. Though I am not convinced.

You might see a connection now as I introduce the next species – the popular hawk-moth. Now, while I said the elephant was huge, this is in another league. With a wingspan of up to 9cm, it looks like rough-edged leaves, reddish brown in colour with occasional hints of purple. This one turned up at my local farmers' market. A child had found it and brought it to the chattering adults. Everyone was transfixed. This moth is so unusual in shape and size and a great reminder of the amazing life that is out there waiting to be found.

The final hawk-moth is the hummingbird hawk-moth. I have seen these while on holiday in Portugal, but they are becoming a more regular sight in the UK. What is special about these is that they are day fliers, and therefore much easier to spot, though many people who do are confused by this large insect behaving remarkably like, well, the clue is in the name – a hummingbird! They beat their wings very fast, and I mean *very* fast for an insect this size – 80 beats per second. This amazing flapping enables them to hover in front of the flowers on which they feed. They then extend their enormously long proboscis, the tubular mouth parts, into flowers to drink the sugar-rich nectar. And as they hover, there is often a humming sound.

Our cul-de-sac has a very busy WhatsApp group – and someone posted a short video of one of these amazing beasts humming and hovering in her hedge, but had no idea what it was. Again, there was soon a small gaggle of us watching this amazing animal as it fed on the sweet honeysuckle flowers.

The Oxford Urban Wildlife Group – where I started my bat walk with Steph – has also been running a year-long survey of moths. I realise that much of the moth magic is a bit out of place in this book as it takes place during the day. In mid-March, we set the trap in the nature reserve near my house on a damp but mild night. The trap we are using is different to ones I have met before. Rather than blast the night sky with bright light, it uses an ultraviolet bulb that is barely visible to the human eye. A slightly underwhelming amount of, well, violet light floats around the large plastic bucket in which we have put lots of cardboard egg cartons. The lid is a cone, or funnel, that while not completely preventing moths attracted inside from leaving, does not make it easy.

I left my house the next morning at around 7.30am to get to the unveiling, the moment we would find out who we had caught. The short walk is gorgeous. When I first woke at 5.30am I got my first clear blast of dawn chorus of the year – a delightful mix of blackbirds and robins, mainly. It lulled me back to sleep.

The walk was, as they often are, interrupted by interesting things. This time there was a movement of a bird that looked, from the brief blur of flight, to be an odd sort of sparrow. However, something was not quite right, so I paused and waited and then this delicately downward-curved beak appeared. It was a treecreeper – such a beautiful bird, with a bright white chest and great climbing skills, mostly when going upwards.

As I was watching the treecreeper, I heard other birds sing, but I could not put my finger on who they were. Fortunately, I have a free app on my phone called Merlin that will 'listen' to the singing and tell you! These were siskins, which are about sparrow size but with a definite yellow colour. It took me a while to see them, but there they were, flitting around above the treecreeper.

Mornings like this, before the rush hour (not of cars, but of primary school children on bikes and scooters, as this is the main path to the school from our estate) are full of potential. I wanted to share my sightings with someone, anyone. Even a dog walker would do, but no one was around.

The nature reserve's code lock had changed, so I had to rummage through my phone to find the email I had been sent. I could hear a few voices inside, so I was not too early. Helen and Richard were there, but were not expecting too many more people. Richard has been helping Helen at the reserve. I talked about the birds I had seen and was hoping for excitement, but, no. They see lots of them! I should get out more in the mornings it seems.

Small person voices arrive and along comes Freya. She is six, loves cats and lives a few doors down from me. Her mum, Sally, is a superb artist and they are full of delight at being here on the way to school. As we chat a bit, Jules and her eight year old, Isla, appear, with a very large trombone for her music lesson today.

We all walk over to the trap. The very wet weather has made the soil waterlogged in parts, so it is not in its usual place. We bring it back to a picnic table, around which we gather. The two kids have got the guide books in hand as the lid is lifted.

There is no great eruption of fluttering – the moths have largely gone to sleep, hidden among the jumble of egg boxes. Very carefully, Helen turns the first tray in the trap, revealing a single moth, and quickly reaches in with her phone to take a photograph. As she lifts the cardboard up she explained, 'It looked quite active, not sleeping at all, and I wanted to make sure we could identify which species in case it flies away.' As she handed the egg box to Freya, the moth took flight.

While some of the micro moths need close examination under a microscope, most big moth species can be easily identified by an expert from a photo. (Later, Helen sent me a message to let me know that her tame expert said the moth was a March tubic. I have tried to find out where the name comes from and what it means, but have failed! What I did find out was that they spend the day resting on the bark of trees and that the pale, patterned wings would make for a superb disguise.)

Next came two Hebrew characters – the names are as brilliant and odd as the insects. This furry brown moth has distinctive black marks on the wings, and I almost suggested that name when the first emerged, but did not feel confident until someone found it in a guidebook.

Then, what turned out to be a moth which should make a formal complaint to the naming people. Who called this beautiful animal the clouded drab? Okay, it is not in any way a showoff among moths. But drab? No!

The final moth was identified by my phone! I searched using the photograph I had taken and it really amazed me by giving the answer that it was a small quaker, which was later confirmed by the expert. Each of these moths are early fliers, none of them causing great excitement in the mothing world, but for our little crew, this was a brilliant way to start the day. The two children really enjoyed the experience and then used the final 10 minutes before school to head off to one of the ponds on the site, where they found frogspawn and the start of tadpoles.

Helen caught up with them, pointing out the small moving bundles of bits of plant in the still water. There was no current, no wind, so why were they moving, she asked the two girls? These were caddisfly larvae, which disguise themselves in bits of plant they find in the pond – and then move around.

Watching the children, and the adults for that matter, absorbed by the life in the pond, I did wonder why more teaching is not done outside in places like this amazing reserve.

So, that is a quick introduction to some moths, but we have so much more to do! Three hawk-moths, and the four from the trap – that just leaves us another 893 to go!

Final Thoughts

How do you feel about a nocturnal safari now? An adventure on the dark side? Can you be tempted?

The great news is that a lot of what goes on at night can be deciphered in the calm light of day – droppings, for example. Maybe this is a way to encourage you out for a walk if all that is left is looking at poo! Droppings are actually really useful. If you don't have a trail camera (one of those motion-sensitive cameras that you can leave out at night) then the best way to know whether a hedgehog has been around while you were asleep are a few deposits!

I hope that you are feeling warmer to the night. I know that there are challenges to being a nighttime explorer. Hopefully the excitement at the potential will overcome any fears. Being serious for a bit, whenever I was out doing nocturnal fieldwork, someone always knew where I was. Make sure you do the same. It is harder going, and the chances of tripping on brambles or falling into a pond are definitely higher at night. If you are somewhere unfamiliar it is also easier to get lost!

That being said, I would not want you to be put off a ramble in the dark. Just remember to tune your senses. When you have got beyond the street lights, or have turned off your torch, you still have around 15 minutes to get your eyes ready for the darkness, so start slowly and use your other senses.

What can you smell? I love the rising scent of damp earth. Maybe there is some blossom if it is spring. Some flowers smell strongest in the evening and you might get a great wave of honeysuckle if you are lucky. I find that the smells of the world are richer as we focus less with our eyes.

Listen – what can you hear? Have you lost the traffic noise? Or are you somewhere like I was with the badgers? You will start to tune out the drone of traffic as you pay attention to what else is going on. Some birds sing loudly at dusk – and then, well, there are the owls if you are lucky.

You may start to feel damp in the air. During the day water evaporates from streams and ponds, and is also pulled up through plants from the soil into the air. As the sun goes down and the temperature drops some of the water in the air condenses. Not only can it feel damp on your skin, but also it turns into dew – droplets on grass for example. This is because at ground level, where the air is even more still, more water is released. This means that it is worth preparing for a slightly damper and colder experience than you might think. Especially if you are planning on sitting down!

Why should we care so much about the wildlife of the night? I would argue that it is just a simple extension of the care we feel about the wildlife we more easily see. We know – research shows that having contact with nature makes us better. People recover more quickly from illness if they have even just a view of the natural world. Mental health benefits from time spent in nature are now so well recognised that the NHS is prescribing access to the green stuff! This is what they say on their website: 'There is strong and growing evidence that nature-based social prescribing plays an important role in improving mental and physical health and reducing loneliness.'

If we ignore nature at night, we are missing out on half of the nature that could help our lives be just that bit richer, fitter and happier.

Quick Reads

Quick Reads offer a series of short, engaging books which appeal to all tastes and reading abilities for the price of £1 each, encouraging less confident readers to pick up a book. These titles are aimed at adults who find reading a struggle or who've lost the habit of reading, and are also perfect for readers who are short of time. The initiative is coordinated in Wales by the Books Council of Wales and supported by the Welsh Government.

Lizzie Meets Her Match

An Allingham Regency Classic

Merryn Allingham

LIZZIE MEETS HER MATCH

This novel is entirely a work of fiction. The names, characters and incidents portrayed in it are the work of the author's imagination. Any resemblance to actual persons, living or dead, events or localities is entirely coincidental.

First published in Great Britain 2020 by The Verrall Press

Cover art: Berni Stevens Book Cover Design
Copyright © Merryn Allingham

Merryn Allingham asserts the moral right to be identified as the author of this work.

Chapter One

Sussex, Autumn 1813

I *am the resurrection and the life. He who believes in me will
live, even though he dies.*

Lizzie tried to arrange herself more comfortably on
the hard pew. She had never attended a funeral before
and it was proving a sombre affair. She'd hoped for a large
congregation and her wish had certainly been granted—the
church was packed to overflowing. It seemed the whole of
Rye had turned out to mourn the sudden passing of Sir
Lucien Delacourt. But the gathering of the fashionable that
she'd envisaged had not materialised. Her eyes travelled
over the crowded rows as the vicar continued to intone the
burial service. Not one bonnet worth a second glance, she
thought, then chided herself for her flippancy.

She sighed inwardly. It was a measure of her dawdling
existence that she'd looked forward to this event. Mrs Croft
was kind enough, but in the three weeks Lizzie had been at
Brede House there had been few visitors under the age of

sixty, and her days had been filled with a wearisome round of fetching and carrying.

A flutter of white handkerchiefs amid the unrelieved black of the congregation reinforced the sadness of the occasion. Adding to the gloom was the church itself, since it was vast, built at a time when the area had grown rich on the proceeds of wool, and beneath its dark and lofty beams, even such a large gathering as this appeared puny. Stained glass paraded along two entire walls of the building, their colours flat and opaque on a day of gathering cloud.

Only the flowers, vase after vase of them filling the altar steps, breathed light. But they were lilies, cold and white, with a perfume so intense that Lizzie began to feel nauseous. And though she tried hard to stop herself fidgeting, the bonnet ribbons tickling her chin were becoming more unbearable by the minute. She was as anxious now to be gone from the church as she'd been earlier to cross its threshold. Her restlessness drew a sharp glance from Mrs Croft: the dead man had been a great friend, Lizzie knew, and the old lady was finding the day difficult.

'My father, Lucien Delacourt, was once a soldier—brave, honest and true—and those were the qualities he made his own throughout his life.'

She was startled. A new voice had succeeded the vicar's and it was electrifying. Tender but strong, as though honey had coated steel with a sweet warmth. It cut through Lizzie's irritation and forced her bolt upright. Her eyes were drawn to the lectern and remained fixed there. A man she'd never seen before had begun to read the eulogy. Her heart gave a strange little jump as she drank him in.

He stood, tall and straight, his dark clothing fitting him with military precision, his face lean and tanned, as though he'd spent most of his life out of doors. He was surely a soldier. She watched his hands as he read—strong and steady even at a moment of great emotion. Only his hair flew in the face of such determined restraint, abundant and gleaming, challenging the dreariness of the place and the day. Even the dimness of the church could not suppress its bright glory, catching at highlights and dancing them in the air, until it seemed the man's head was circled by a veritable halo.

Lizzie sat mesmerised, as he spoke lovingly of the father he had known. The words themselves hardly registered. It was the music of his voice that caught at her, his presence that kept her still and breathless.

The service was over and she forced herself to muster all the patience at her command, while Mrs Croft slowly checked the contents of her reticule and began a search for a mislaid umbrella. *Hurry up, hurry up,* Lizzie pleaded inwardly, *he may be gone by the time we get to the door.* But he had not. A straggle of parishioners had lingered behind to offer their condolences and Sir Lucien Delacourt's son had a word for every one of them.

While she and Mrs Croft waited patiently in line, the clouds overhead began to mass, and it seemed doubtful they would make it out of the churchyard, yet alone reach Brede House, before the coming cloudburst. Lizzie, though, was sure it would be worth the drenching, and felt a small bounce of excitement as the last parishioner walked from the porch.

The young man stepped forward to clasp her employer by the hand. 'Dear Mrs Croft, my grateful thanks for venturing out on such a day.'

His voice was as beautiful as when he'd spoken from the church lectern, and it wasn't just his voice that was beautiful. He seemed even taller now, more upright, more hardened. Lizzie liked what she saw and, withdrawing into the shadow of the laurel hedge, she unashamedly looked her fill.

'How could I not come, Justin?' Henrietta Croft murmured. 'Your father was a dear friend, a very dear friend. And to lose him so swiftly. I can't believe he is no longer with us.' Mrs Croft dabbed her eyes with an already wet handkerchief.

'Nor I.' He squeezed her hands warmly, but his lips were compressed into a thin, uncompromising line. 'I had no idea how frail he'd become.'

'Lucien has not been well for some time,' Mrs Croft conceded, 'but a heart attack! None of us expected that.'

'I should have been here. I should have seen what was happening ...'

The man's eyes held a bleakness in their depths. They were green—or were they grey—or like the sea, ever changing? And like the sea, Lizzie thought, they spoke of restlessness, of constant motion. 'I should have realised how vulnerable he was,' Justin added.

Mrs Croft laid a gentle hand on his arm. 'You mustn't

blame yourself. You have been fighting for King and country, and very bravely by all accounts. It's what your father would have wanted. And he has left you problems enough, I don't doubt. The estate must be in a sorry mess.'

'You excuse me too easily, but you're right. Chelwood has been badly neglected of late. I can't make up for my prolonged absence, but I can set the estate on a smooth path before I leave.

'You're planning to leave Rye?' Mrs Croft's voice rose in surprise.

'I must return to my regiment as soon as I'm able.'

'But I thought...' her voice tailed off uncertainly '... I thought that having inherited the title and estate, you would be certain to sell out.'

'I shall never take that course, Mrs Croft. The army is my life. There can be no other for me.'

Lizzie's heart did another of those curious little bounces. She knew exactly what he meant, since didn't she also have the military in her very bones? He was a kindred spirit, she was sure, and she wanted to rush forward and clasp those strong hands in hers. Taking a deep breath, she walked boldly from her shelter and into their conversation. Mrs Croft seemed surprised to see her, as though she'd recently mislaid her companion as well as her umbrella, but was happy enough to perform introductions.

'Justin, this is my young friend, Miss Elizabeth Ingram. My cousin was kind enough to recommend her. Elizabeth has recently been a pupil teacher at Clementine's establishment.'

'Miss Ingram.'

He bent his head in the smallest of bows, but when he looked up, his eyes refused to meet hers. Or so it seemed to Lizzie. She was certain he had deliberately looked away, and was angry at her foolishness. Why was she always attracted to such unsatisfactory men? Justin Delacourt was cold and indifferent, she decided, and far too like another soldier of her acquaintance. Quite possibly he was short-sighted, too, since she knew herself to be a pretty girl and was unused to such treatment. Surely there could be nothing in her appearance to give him disgust? The dove-grey gown had been carefully refurbished in deference to the occasion, and a straw villager bonnet hid a dazzle of auburn curls. Did he perhaps not like women? Or was it simply snobbishness: she was a mere companion and not worthy of attention?

'I found the eulogy you gave most moving,' she said, determined he would take notice of her. He needn't know it was his voice rather than his words that had moved her so powerfully.

'Thank you, Miss Ingram. You are very kind.' Another dismissive bow and he was turning back to his father's old friend.

'Such a splendid congregation, don't you think?' she pursued. 'They were most appreciative.'

'I'm glad you feel so. It's difficult to distil into a few words all that one man has meant.'

'You must have succeeded. I didn't know your father, yet I was touched by your words.'

Lizzie knew herself guilty of flummery, but she'd spoken

the truth. And forced him to look at her. She saw his gaze travel over her figure and linger unwillingly on her face and, though he might wish otherwise, his eyes betrayed a flicker, a flash, of interest. He gave a brief nod in acknowledgement and then abruptly looked away to speak to Mrs Croft once more.

But whatever he was about to say was lost. A well-dressed, middle-aged couple had emerged from the dimness of the church and was hurrying towards them. There was a subdued murmur of greetings mixed with farewells and, in a minute, Mrs Croft was leading the way from the churchyard, an unwilling Lizzie in her train.

Chapter Two

'How wonderful to see you back in Rye, Justin, where you belong.' Caroline Martin held out impulsive hands to the young man towering over her, but for a moment received no response.

Justin was struggling to regain his composure. He'd caught sight of a light grey skirt half-hidden behind the greenery, but he'd had no idea of its owner. Then, without warning, Miss Ingram had arrived. He'd glimpsed a pair of the deepest brown eyes and a profusion of errant curls, the colour of fresh chestnuts, tucked beneath her bonnet. He'd been taken aback at how young and pretty she was, far too young and far too pretty to be anyone's companion, particularly a semi-invalid like Henrietta Croft. And far too interesting for his peace of mind.

Experience had taught him that women were either manipulative or missish, and neither held attraction for him, but he'd sensed immediately that Miss Ingram was different. She was no simpering miss, that was certain, but a bold and lively spirit. She was also quite lovely. In truth, he'd been unnerved by her and that made him feel ridiculous.

'Justin? How are you, my dear?'

He gave himself a mental shake and embraced Mrs Martin with affection, extending a warm handshake to her husband.

'My very humble apologies for not having visited you both. It's what I most wanted to do, but there has been so much to arrange at Chelwood and I've been home but a week.'

'We understand,' Caroline soothed. 'It has been the saddest homecoming for you.'

'Sad indeed, but I have the best of neighbours to support me. I intend to pay Five Oaks a visit next week—once the formalities are over—and will hope to find you both at home.'

'Whenever you come, you know you'll be very welcome,' James Martin said heartily. His eyes, Justin noticed, had slid uneasily towards his wife, and he'd placed what seemed a warning hand on her arm.

The Martins were life-long friends and their son, Gil, had been his closest companion for as many years as he could remember. But a note of discomfort had crept into the conversation and it felt strange. Perhaps they, too, thought he should have been at Chelwood caring for his father rather than fighting battles in Spain. In an effort to cover the awkward moment, he said, 'I collect that Gil is away on some adventure right now? As soon as he's back, he must ride over to Chelwood and confess all. We have much catching up to do. It must be over three years since

I was last home.'

To Justin's horror, tears began to fill Caroline's eyes and two large drops trickled down each of her cheeks.

'Mrs Martin, what have I said?' He was genuinely alarmed. In all the years he'd known Caroline Martin, he'd never seen her cry.

'I'm sorry, it's not your fault,' she managed at last. Then the tears became too much and she retreated into the folds of her cambric handkerchief. Her husband signalled urgently to the waiting groom to escort her back to their carriage.

'I must apologise for my wife's tears,' he said, once Caroline was out of earshot.

There was an uneasy pause until Justin asked, 'Can you tell me what ails Mrs Martin?' He felt upset as well as mystified. Caroline had been more of a mother to him than his own and he loved both the Martins.

'It was your mention of Gilbert, you see,' James said haltingly. 'The boy is missing.'

'Missing?' Justin's face was blank. 'But how, when?'

'He's been missing for three months and, as to how, we've no notion. That's the problem. One day he was here, and the next he'd gone. He simply vanished from sight, taking nothing with him except...' James hesitated a moment '...except a little money and a family ring. But they'd not be sufficient to sustain him for so long.'

Justin felt bewildered. 'Surely someone must know where he is. His friends? Your family in Hampshire?'

'We've sent messages everywhere, but no one in the

family has seen him. As for friends, Gilbert has very few. It was always you, Justin—he needed no other—and since you've been away... I think at times he's felt very lonely.'

Another reproach to add to the already long list, Justin thought. 'I've been away far too long, it's true, and I'm sorry for it. But is there no-one in the neighbourhood who might have an inkling of Gil's whereabouts?' It seemed impossible that a healthy, fit young man could disappear so completely.

'He talked a lot to the new excise officer. He was the only person Gilbert spent any time with. A good deal of time, walking with him in the marshes and on the cliffs. As he used to with you. But then the poor chap died. It was quite tragic. It was Gil who found his body, lying at the foot of the cliff. It seems he'd fallen in the darkness, though there have been rumours it wasn't an accident. You know how talk goes in a small town. Always rumours. Whatever the truth of it, Gilbert was greatly upset. I've sometimes wondered if that might be the reason he disappeared. I've no real idea, though. I seemed to have lost touch with my son long before he left,' James finished sadly.

Justin's brow furrowed, trying to think himself into Gil's shoes, but found he was as much out of touch with his friend as James Martin. 'Might he have gone to London?' he offered, without much hope.

'We considered the possibility and sent Robert—you remember Robert, I'm sure—he's as true a servant as you could hope for. We despatched him to London to make discreet enquiries the week Gilbert vanished, but not a sound or sign did he gather. After two fruitless weeks of searching, we called him home. It was a hopeless task.'

The more Justin considered what James had told him, the more puzzled he grew. Gil was the best of fellows, but he'd never been the most adventurous of spirits. As boys, it had always been Justin that led the way: building dams, scrumping apples, climbing every one of the estate's five oak trees. Always Justin who thought up the pranks that landed them in trouble. He hadn't seen his friend for three years, but when they'd last met, he'd thought Gil more sober than ever. Hardly a man liable to kick up his heels and disappear without a word.

'I imagine you've tried the local doctors,' he said tentatively, fearing that his friend had come to harm in some way, but unable to say it directly.

'I've checked with every doctor in Sussex,' Mr Martin said grimly. 'I've even visited the mortuary, but not a sign of him.'

There was a rustle of silk and a faint trace of perfume: Caroline had stepped down from the carriage and walked back to them. 'You must help us, Justin.' Her eyes were large and frightened and the appeal went straight to his heart.

'Mrs Martin, you know that I'd do anything to help, but—'

'You must find him,' she said, her voice cracking. 'You must find Gilbert.'

Her husband wrapped a restraining arm around her. 'You cannot ask the impossible of our young friend,

Caroline.'

'If anyone can find our son, Justin can.' And she turned back to the carriage, her eyes already beginning to fill with fresh tears.

Justin shook his head. He felt enormously weary. His father's sudden death had shocked him far more than he'd thought possible. He'd felt guilt, unbearable guilt, that somehow he'd shirked a sacred responsibility. And the guilt had only grown when he'd arrived home and found Chelwood in the most wretched disarray, a rascally bailiff having taken advantage of Sir Lucien and enriched himself at the expense of the estate. If he were to put Chelwood to rights, weeks of work lay before him, even with a new and trustworthy man in charge.

And if that wasn't bad enough, he'd learned this minute that his dearest friend had gone missing without a trace. Had vanished into the air as though he were a magician's accomplice. What was going on? Whatever it was, Caroline Martin expected him to find out.

'Take no notice of my wife,' James said. 'She is naturally distraught. Of course, you can't be expected to begin looking for Gilbert, with your own life in such turmoil. Please forget what she said, and forgive us for intruding so badly on a day when *your* grief should be paramount.'

For an instant, Justin had forgotten his father, forgotten Chelwood, forgotten even his beloved regiment. He'd been remembering his dear friend and all they'd meant to each other. And in some strange way the image of the girl he'd just met had become tangled in his mind with the image of

Gil. But why? It made no sense, but nothing about this day made sense. Miss Ingram was one complication he could avoid and he'd be sure to. There had never been space for women in his life and certainly not now; it was Gil he must think of.

'I doubt I'll be successful, Mr Martin, but I'll do my damndest to find your son,' he said firmly.

Chapter Three

Lizzie felt fortunate that the rain had held off, the black rolling clouds travelling swiftly westwards, but in their place the early October sky was left bleached, an eerie half light pervading the world. It seemed the large congregation, that only minutes ago had poured from the ancient church and through the ivy-covered lych gate, had been carried away on the wind. Not a soul was visible as she and Mrs Croft left the shelter of the Citadel, the small hilly enclave of houses and lanes that clustered around St Mary's, and walked down the hill towards the estuary. Lizzie wondered if Justin Delacourt was still talking in the churchyard or whether he, too had disappeared from the world. He was an attractive man, she conceded, but his curt, uncivil manner had ruffled her. Yet, she felt intrigued.

'Who were those people, Mrs Croft?' she asked. They were battling their way along the river bank against a now furious wind. 'I mean the people who greeted Lord Delacourt so warmly—almost as a long-lost son.' And when her companion gave no answer, she added doubtfully, 'He *is* Lord Delacourt, isn't he?'

'Not quite.' Mrs Croft allowed herself a smile. 'You have elevated him. When his father died, he became Sir Justin, though I imagine he prefers to be Major Delacourt. And those people, as you call them, were the Martins.'

'They seemed to know him very well,' Lizzie reiterated.

'They own Five Oaks, the estate that adjoins Chelwood Place. Justin ran tame there for most of his childhood. The Martin family were very good friends of Sir Lucien and the two sons were the closest of companions, always playing together or learning with the same tutor.'

'He is lucky to have such good friends at this sad time.' Lizzie hoped she might encourage the older woman to talk. Mrs Croft could be annoyingly discreet, volunteering only the most superficial of news.

'They'll have much to say to each other—sadness aplenty to share, I make no doubt.'

The tone was vague and the comment a little cryptic, but when Lizzie dared to look a question, she was met by brisk dismissal. 'It can be of no interest to you, child.'

But it was of interest to Lizzie, or at least Justin Delacourt was. 'I gather Sir Justin is in the army.'

'Indeed, and wishful to remain a serving officer, it seems, though I am not sure how practical that will prove.'

'How long has he been a soldier?'

'It must be some six years. He has done very well, though he joined as an enlisted man. In the Light Dragoons, I believe. He wanted no favours, but his natural leadership has seen him rise through the ranks very quickly. That and this dreadful war England has been fighting these past ten years.'

Lizzie was silent, thinking of her father who'd fought that war and was still fighting it. She hadn't seen him for three years and the last occasion was one she wished not to remember. It was on her account that he'd been given compassionate leave to travel back to England. Even now, she blushed, remembering her disgrace.

She wrenched her mind away from the unhappy thought. 'Soldiering must suit him,' she said.

'Why would it not? Lucien, himself, was a splendid soldier until he was persuaded by that woman to sell out. Harangued into submission, more like.'

The old lady seemed to realise that, for once, she had said too much and finished brusquely, 'I've no doubt his son will be careful to avoid the same fate.'

The wind by now was even fiercer, blowing directly from the sea and howling so loudly that it was impossible to speak more. Lizzie's bonnet was almost torn from her head and she quickly untied its ribbons and held it tightly to her chest. She'd been entranced during her first few days in Rye to be living so close to water, but after several bouts of inclement weather, she'd begun to wish that Mrs Croft's house was situated in the small town's medieval centre. The remnants of Rye's fortifications protected the Citadel's narrow, winding streets against all but the worst weather, but Brede House was open to a battering from every direction. To the south, the English Channel roared its might, and to the north lay marshland and an even harsher landscape.

Today the path home seemed longer than usual and Lizzie had several times to support her companion as they battled to stay upright. Below them, the river stretched a restless grey, every inch of water rucked by the fearsome gale into ridges of cold, foaming white. It was as though the sea had lost its way and come calling. Wave after wave of water hit the shingled mud with a fierce power, then retreated with a roar, dragging to itself everything in its path. Above them, gulls competed with the cacophony, dipping and calling in tempestuous flight, unsure it seemed whether to rejoice in the wild beauty or take shelter from its dangers.

They had gone some half a mile along the coastal path when they heard a faint noise coming to them on the wind. Both ladies turned, clutching their skirts against the oncoming blast. A carriage had stopped on the Rye road, running parallel to the path, and a figure was striding towards them.

'Mrs Croft, please forgive me.' Justin Delacourt arrived, only slightly out of breath from having battled the wind at running pace.

Lizzie saw the surprise in her employer's face at Sir Justin's sudden appearance. Both of them had thought him on his way back to the Chelwood estate.

'Please forgive me,' he repeated. 'You should not be out in such weather. I was most remiss in allowing you to slip away in that fashion.'

Lizzie was conscious that his gaze was trained on the old lady's face. Deliberately so, she was certain. She appreciated his concern for Mrs Croft, but not that he was again choosing to ignore her.

He appeared not to notice Lizzie's glare and went on with his apologies. 'I fear I was so taken up with talking to the Martins, that I forgot to ask you to drive with me. I'm a little late, but please allow me to offer you a seat in my carriage.'

'How kind of you,' Mrs Croft murmured. 'But really there's no need. We have only a short way to go.'

'You have at least another fifteen minutes to walk and, in this weather, that's far too long. Allow me to take you home.'

'My companion...' Mrs Croft began '...you are in your curricle, I think.'

He shot Lizzie a swift glance and then looked away. She was a servant in his eyes, she thought, and could be comfortably discounted. But it was Mrs Croft she must take care of. Gently, she nudged the elderly lady towards the hand Justin was extending. Her employer, though, still hesitated.

'I'm sure Miss Ingram is hale enough to finish the walk on her own,' Justin said in an even tone. 'If not, of course, my groom can dismount.'

'Surely not—a groom to relinquish his seat!' Lizzie was unable to bite back the words. 'That would never do!'

Henrietta Croft looked uncomfortably from one to the other, bewildered by the animosity slicing through the air.

'Naturally, you're welcome to travel with us, Miss Ingram. Perkins will not mind walking the short way to Brede House.'

'And nor will I. As you say, I'm hale enough.' Lizzie turned to her employer. 'Go in the carriage, Mrs Croft,' she said warmly. 'You're finding this weather very trying and should reach home as soon as possible.'

Justin gave the old lady an encouraging smile, but she was shaking her head. 'I think it best I continue my walk with Elizabeth. She will take good care of me, you can be sure.'

But still he lingered, forcing Mrs Croft to speak firmly. 'You have many calls on your time, Justin, and I'm sure you must wish to return to Chelwood as soon as you can.'

He was dismissed and turned back to the road and the waiting Perkins but, as he walked away, Lizzie's voice carried tauntingly on the wind. 'It must be arduous, don't you think, Mrs Croft, being such a brave soldier *and* owning a large estate?'

~

Within a short while, they were turning into the drive of Brede House and its avenue of trees, where the wind blew less strongly. The respite allowed them both to regain their breath and Lizzie to regain her temper. She began to feel ashamed of her outburst and wished she could forget the wretched man, but annoyingly he was filling her mind to the exclusion of all else.

'Do you know which regiment of dragoons the Major serves in, Mrs Croft?'

'You ask a vast amount of questions, young lady.' Henrietta had not appreciated the small drama and evidently wished to speak no more of Sir Justin. 'What possible interest can Major Delacourt's regiment have for you?'

'My father is also a military man,' Lizzie responded, a hot flush staining her cheek. Any mention of Colonel Ingram always raised this peculiar mix of pride and resentment. 'He is even now in the Peninsular and has been for very many years.'

'I had no idea, Elizabeth.' Mrs Croft spoke more kindly, as they reached the house and a maidservant struggled to open the door to them. A final gust of wind found its way between the trees and literally blew them into the entrance hall. 'You must take tea with me, my dear. It's the very thing to warm us and prevent our taking a chill.'

Henrietta divested herself of coat and hat, located the missing umbrella still in the hat stand, tutted a little, and then led the way to her private parlour. Lizzie was soon perched on the edge of the satinwood sofa, unable to relax completely. It was not her first invitation to this sanctum, but always she felt awkward. It wasn't only that the parlour lacked air and was stifling in its warmth, or that the furnishings were depressing—Mrs Croft refurbished frequently, though always in brown. It was the fact that, as a companion, Lizzie was never quite sure where she belonged. Governesses must suffer the same problem, she thought. Educated gentlewomen forced to live within the restrictions of polite society, yet also at the beck and call of an employer. One day greeted as a friend by those who came to the house, while on another wholly ignored. It made life difficult, since in truth you belonged nowhere.

'And where is your father at this moment, my dear?'

'To be honest, I've no idea. The last news we received at the Seminary was months ago, just after the battle of Vitoria. He sent a message to Bath to say he was still alive and well.'

A two-line message, she thought unhappily. That was all she warranted, it seemed. Now if she'd been a boy... how many times had she dreamed of being able to follow the drum along with her father, instead of the tedious life she was forced to lead?

'I'm sure that very soon there will be more news,' her employer said comfortably. 'While you're living here, you can be certain that Clementine will send on any messages she receives.'

'I'm sure she will,' Lizzie said dully.

It was lucky, of course, that Clementine Bates had a weakness for military men, since Lizzie knew for a fact that Hector Ingram had not paid her school fees for many a long year, and it was out of charity that Clementine had allowed her to remain at school as a pupil teacher. Her father's charm seemed to suffice for whatever was owing, but it left his daughter having to live her life at Clementine's behest. And right now her behest was for Lizzie to suffocate in a small coastal Sussex town looking after her cousin, a lady four times Lizzie's age.

'It must be very upsetting for you,' Henrietta continued, 'not seeing your father for such a long time. But there's always the possibility that he might be granted leave. Now that would enliven your days a little, would it not?' She sipped delicately at her tea and smiled at the young woman sitting across from her.

It was hardly likely, Lizzie thought, that her father would come to Rye. But something else had occurred to enliven her days. Sir Justin had arrived in her world and he offered an enticing challenge. He was aloof and ungracious, arrogant even, but she hoped she could persuade him to unbend. Men were not usually slow to fall for her attractions and Lizzie didn't see why he should be any different. It was not the most worthy of ambitions, she confessed, but there was little else in Rye to excite her. Mrs Croft was a dear, kind lady, but their life at Brede House was wholly uneventful. And after all, she'd been sensible for a very long time, hadn't she?

Chapter Four

The next morning when Lizzie pulled back her bedroom curtains, a hazy sun greeted her. The storm had subsided and the world outside looked inviting. If her employer had no immediate need of her, there might be time to snatch a walk. As luck would have it, Mrs Croft had a visitor that morning, an acquaintance from the congregation at St Mary's, and was looking forward to a comfortable cose with her. A companion's presence wasn't always welcome, Lizzie reflected, and it would be a good time to make herself scarce.

She'd expected her life in Rye to be hedged around with petty rules and restrictions, and it was true that the work could be monotonous. But when Mrs Croft required no attendance, she seemed happy for Lizzie to spend her precious hours of freedom as she wished. For the most part, they were spent walking by the river or meandering quiet lanes in the surrounding countryside. This morning, though, Lizzie had in mind a particular ramble, and it was perhaps best the old lady knew nothing of it.

A casual comment to Hester, Mrs Croft's maidservant,

gave Lizzie a clear idea in which direction she should walk and, after a hasty breakfast, she set off towards the Guldeford Ferry. This small boat service was the quickest means of crossing the river to the marsh opposite. Chelwood Place, apparently, was a mere three miles away, across the river and lying to the left of the marshland. Like so many estates locally, it was famous for the wool it produced, and Hester had warned her that if she found her way there, she might well have to walk through fields of sheep. But sheep didn't bother Lizzie.

Setting out from Brede House, she found the sky a misty autumn blue and the sun growing stronger by the minute, but she knew from painful experience that the weather could change rapidly. Only a few days ago, she'd begun her walk in brilliant sunshine, only to be turned within minutes into a veritable sponge by rolling, wet clouds. Thick mists could descend at any time, the small ferry and several crossing points on foot being all that separated Rye from the marsh.

This morning Lizzie had risked a light costume, but decided to take a protective cloak that she could abandon once she arrived. She was intent on looking her best and had selected from a meagre wardrobe her second best gown, a dress of primrose floret sarsnet. It was a trifle old-fashioned, bought for her by Colonel Ingram as a peace offering before he returned to the Peninsular, but she had tried to bring it up to date with a trimming of French flounces. With a bright yellow ribbon threading her chestnut curls and a primrose silk reticule, painstakingly made over the last few evenings, she thought herself presentable. She hoped she could persuade Sir Justin into thinking so, too.

The ferry proved as dirty as it was ancient, and she spread a handkerchief across one of its grimy seats before lowering herself carefully onto a broken plank. The ferryman gave her a disdainful glance, spat over the side, and turned to the shepherd who had followed her on board. Their muttered conversation in an impenetrable dialect filled the short journey, but Lizzie was happy to be ignored: she was on another adventure.

Once on the other side of the river, she found the path to Chelwood without difficulty. As Hester had explained, it skirted the marshland and travelled in a semi-circle inland. Beneath this morning's high blue skies, the marsh looked benign, but here and there the wooden structures marking a sluice gate rose starkly against the flat landscape and from a distance looked for all the world like a gallows. There was something primeval about this world, something deep and visceral and, brave though she was, Lizzie was unsure she'd want to venture into its depths. She was glad that Chelwood lay at its very edge.

An hour's brisk walking brought her to the gates of the mansion. They were immense, a rampart of black iron decorated with several rows of sharp-tipped spikes. They were also resoundingly locked. The lodge keeper's house lay to one side and she wondered if she dared lift the knocker and ask to be admitted. But what reason could she give for her visit? To stroll casually up the carriage way towards the house and 'accidentally' bump into Sir Justin was one thing, but to demand admittance on a formal visit when no invitation had been issued was quite another.

Possibly, there was a second way into the grounds, an entrance less thoroughly guarded. Veering left, she began to push through the deep grass that grew around the perimeter wall, walking until her small boots were sodden with dew, only to be disappointed. There appeared to be no other way in. The estate wall was as old as the iron gates, and here and there crumbling, where large stones had come loose and in places fallen to the ground altogether. It gave footholds in the masonry for anyone daring enough to climb, and Lizzie stood for a while calculating whether she could manage the ascent without damaging either her dress or her limbs. She would have to, she decided. She hadn't donned her second best dress and come all this way, merely to turn around. And for some reason, though she'd no idea why, there was a need in her to meet Justin Delacourt and speak to him alone.

She chose a section of stonework that was crumbling more quickly than elsewhere and would offer more footholds. Hoisting up her petticoats around her knees, she reached up and began to climb, hand over hand. It was fortunate the lane that abutted the wall was narrow and lonely; it would have been mortifying to be caught showing her stockings. She gained the top of the wall and perched there for a while, recovering her breath, but then saw to her dismay that a long drop lay in store. The inside of the wall had not succumbed to the elements as badly, and there were no footholds and no easy path to the ground. Lizzie took a deep breath, closed her eyes, and jumped, landing awkwardly on her ankle and bruising her shins. But at least she was in Chelwood.

A pain shot through her foot, but she couldn't stop to worry. It was still early and she wanted to catch Justin before he left the house to begin the day's business. She'd already wasted too much time. Gazing around her, she saw she'd landed in a thicket of trees that appeared to be part of a larger spinney. The undergrowth was lush and uncut and straggling branches obliterated her view. Pushing past the trees, one after another, she attempted to find a path, but there seemed always to be another row of trees to negotiate.

Then the first drops of rain fell. She'd been so busy clambering over the wall, she'd not noticed the blue sky disappear and a menacing black take its place. The few drops soon became a downpour and then a torrent. She pulled her cloak tightly around her, sheltering her hair beneath its hood, but in a short while she was wet to her skin. The ground beneath her began to squelch ominously, and she was dismayed to see the lower part of her dress, as well as her boots, become caked in mud. How could she accost Sir Justin looking such a fright? There was no hope for it: she would have to abandon her adventure and return to Brede House as best she could.

But Lizzie was lost. The spinney seemed to stretch for miles and she had no idea of the direction she should take. She could only hope that she'd come upon the main drive winding its way through the estate, then hurry back to the gates and beg the lodgekeeper to let her out. She was bending down to loosen a twig tangled in her skirts when she felt something hard and unyielding pressed into her back. Through the downpour, a voice sounded in her ear.

'Right, me lad, let's be 'avin' yer. Yer can disguise yerself all yer wish but yer ain't gettin' away. Not from Mellors. Chelwood Place ain't open fer poachers—not now it ain't.'

Lizzie tried to turn and show her face. There was a gun to her back, she was certain, but if this man knew her to be a woman, surely he'd lower the weapon and allow her to go.

Evidently, though, he was taking no chances. 'Keep yer back to me.' He prodded her angrily with the weapon. 'I knows yer tricks. Now walk!'

'But—' she started to protest.

'Keep quiet and walk. By the sound of it, yer but a striplin'. What's the world comin' to, eh?' And Mellors tutted softly to himself while keeping his weapon firmly levelled.

Lizzie had no option but to walk. She could sense the tension in the man and feel the hard pressure of the shotgun in her back. She doubted he would use it if she tried to escape, but she couldn't be sure, and dared not take the chance. For minutes on end, she was forced to march ahead until they were out of the spinney and walking over smooth lawns towards the driveway she'd been seeking. A gig was drawn up outside the front entrance—precisely as she'd imagined. Sir Justin would be leaving at any minute and, in her plan, she'd seen herself trip up to the front door just as he appeared. Looking a picture of primrose loveliness, she would launch herself into some story of having become lost and wandered on to his land by accident. He would wonder how he could ever have ignored such a delightful girl and would immediately set about pleasing her.

That was the fantasy. This was the reality, her feet oozing mud, her hair dripping water, and far from tripping up to the front entrance, she was being frogmarched towards the rear of the sprawling mansion. Taken to the servants' quarters, she thought—at least she would be spared the humiliation of meeting Justin Delacourt face-to-face.

Poking Lizzie in the back, the man prodded her forward down a long passageway to a large, airy kitchen at its very end. The room was bright and homely, smelling of baked bread and fresh coffee, and Lizzie realised how hungry she was. Her tiny breakfast seemed an age away.

'Look 'ere, folks,' the man said gleefully, 'look what I've caught meself.'

The cook was just then taking newly baked cakes from the oven but, at the sound of Mellors' voice, she stopped and looked around. The scullery maid on her knees paused in her scrubbing, and the footman held aloft the silver he was polishing.

'You best put that gun down,' Cook said crossly. 'Master won't like that thing in the house.'

Mellors did as he was told, but was unwilling to give up his glory quite so quickly. 'See 'ere,' he repeated, and pushed Lizzie into the centre of the room. 'Take a look at me very first catch. There'll be plenty more of 'em before I'm through.'

The cook sniffed at this pronouncement and the

footman allowed himself a small snigger. Wearily, the scullery maid began on her scrubbing again.

Lizzie stood in their midst, dripping puddles onto the flagstones, her cloak still wrapped around her, the hood still covering her head. Anger at this stupid man coursed through her veins. It wasn't his fault that she was drenched, she conceded, but to be treated so disagreeably and then made a fairground exhibit, was too much.

She pushed back the hood on her cape and shook out her damp curls. The cook, the maid, the footman, once more stopped what they were doing, but this time gawped at Lizzie, open-mouthed. Mellors, busy looking for string to bind his victim's hands, turned round, surprised by the sudden, ghastly silence. Even in her present state, Lizzie looked lovely. What she didn't look was a poacher.

'What *have* you done, Mr Mellors?' Cook rubbed the flour from her hands with a satisfied smile on her face. It was clear the bailiff, or whatever he was, was not a popular man among his fellows.

Lizzie was swift to use the moment to her advantage. 'How dare you!' Her voice quivered with indignation. 'How dare you treat a lady in such a wicked fashion!'

Mellors looked bewildered, but still managed to stutter a reproof. 'But yer wuz poachin', miss.' Failing to see the absurdity of the situation, his obsession was all-consuming.

'Poaching! Are you completely witless? Do poachers normally come calling in a muslin gown?'

There was more sniggering from the footman and the

unhappy bailiff hung his head a little lower. 'No, miss, but—'

'And if I am a poacher,' Lizzie continued inexorably, 'where are my tools? Do you think I've hid them? Perhaps you would like to search me for the odd snare?'

The footman guffawed at this idea, until Lizzie's indignant stare silenced him. 'And where, pray, are my illegitimate spoils? Why be a poacher and end empty-handed?'

'You could 'ave 'idden the stuff, miss,' Mellors tried desperately.

'Hidden? Upon my person perhaps? You are ridiculous.'

'Mebbe you warn't poachin' then, but you wuz still trespassin',' he continued doggedly.

'I'm no trespasser, you scurvy man.' Lizzie drew herself erect, making up in dignity for what she lacked in height. 'I'm here to call upon Sir Justin Delacourt.'

Mellors shifted uncomfortably. His master's name evidently gave him pause, but it seemed he would not yet own himself beaten. 'So what were yer doin' in the spinney? It ain't ezackly usual for Sir Justin's visitors to come that way.'

For an instant, Lizzie was flustered, and she saw a small, sly smile creep over Mellors' face. There was no alternative—she would have to behave shamelessly.

'I met Sir Justin for the first time yesterday,' she said in a low voice, 'but I was deeply moved by his sadness. I had not the opportunity then of speaking to him of his father, and I came here today only to pay my respects. I meant well, but look how I've been treated!' She began to sniffle slightly and managed to squeeze several teardrops from her eyes.

'There, there, my pet,' the cook weighed in. 'Look what you've done, you clumsy oaf!' She turned to Lizzie. 'Come here, my dear. You need looking after, not berating. Poor lamb, you're wet through.'

Lizzie coughed artistically. 'I meant no harm, ma'am. You see, I was so touched by the funeral, I merely wanted to say how sorry I was.' A few more tears trickled down her cheeks without robbing her of one mite of beauty.

Mellors and the footman looked on askance, but the scullery maid clasped her hands to her breast, drinking in the romantic possibilities.

'I am soaked to the skin,' Lizzie continued, her voice barely audible, her hands clasped together. 'I've been in these clothes so long that I shall likely die of pneumonia.'

Her sudden terrified wail startled her listeners into action. There was a general fussing and clucking as the cook and the scullery maid took her to their bosoms, and Mr Mellors protested his innocence, and the footman was sure that a fit young woman would not contract pneumonia from just one soaking.

'What the deuce is going on here?' Sir Justin strode into the kitchen and, in an instant, the uproar ceased, to be followed by a strained silence.

'Perhaps one of you would care to explain this mayhem and tell me why I've been ringing for coffee these last ten minutes, but had no answer. Do I employ you to serve me or not?' His beautiful voice held a new severity.

All of a sudden, he became aware of Lizzie, abandoned in the middle of the room, and still dripping ceaselessly onto the floor. An expression of blank amazement replaced the frown on his face.

'Miss Ingram?' he queried. 'Can it be you?'

'It can.' She gave a saucy smirk at the bailiff and, since there was nothing left to lose, announced boldly, 'I have come to call on you, Sir Justin.'

Chapter Five

J ustin remained motionless, stunned by the vision before him. Elizabeth Ingram was the last person he expected to find in his kitchen, and to find her dripping and mud-stained was astonishing.

'How came you here, Miss Ingram?' He almost stuttered the words.

'At the point of a gun,' she said bitterly. 'You should not complain that your servants are tardy, Sir Justin. One of them at least is a little too eager.'

'What do you mean?'

'Your bailiff—I think that's what he is— believes me to be a poacher!'

Justin looked even more stunned, his hand ruffling his halo of hair. 'Mellors?' he queried, hoping for enlightenment, and was immediately subjected to the bailiff's impassioned defence.

'The lady wuz in a cloak, Sir Justin,' Mellors protested. 'She 'ad her back ter me and in the rain, I took her fer a boy.'

'Then I fear you may be in need of spectacles.'

The other servants cackled joyfully at this sally, but Mellors' face took on a truculent expression. 'It were an easy mistake to make, Sir Justin. We've 'ad a spate of poachin', you knows that. You told me yerself to be extra vigilant.'

'Vigilant, yes. Foolish, no. You'd better wait for me in the office – I may be some time... And take that gun with you.'

The man slumped to the door, still ruffled. 'She wuz trespassin' for sure,' he managed as a parting shot.

Justin Delacourt turned impatiently to face his audience, who seemed caught in a trance and had barely moved since he entered the room. 'You may forget the coffee, but make sure that tea is ready in the library in ten minutes.' His tone was even more severe, and his servants speedily resumed their chores.

Striding across the room to the hanging line of brass bells, he sounded one vigorously. 'My housekeeper, Mrs Reynolds, will be with you shortly, Miss Ingram. She will escort you upstairs, so that you may...um...tidy yourself. When you've finished, ask her to bring you to the library.'

He accorded Lizzie a brief bow and, without another word, walked through the door and strode to the library. What the devil was the girl doing wandering in his grounds? Was Mellors right when he said she was trespassing? She must have been, otherwise why hadn't she called at the lodge and asked the porter for admittance? And how had she got in? The lodge gates were the only entrance to the estate, a fact bemoaned for years by servants and masters alike, but nothing had ever been done to improve the situation. And nothing would be done now, since there was precious little money for refurbishment.

But Miss Ingram. He'd been stunned at the sight of her, and not just because she had no place in his kitchen. Even in her sodden condition, she looked lovely, her soft brown eyes wide with indignation and her fiery curls already drying to a glossy mass. He hoped her gown was not completely ruined, since he thought it likely that her wardrobe was not extensive. Until the dress could be laundered, Mrs Reynolds must find a replacement from one of the many wardrobes scattered across the house. It would probably not be to Miss Elizabeth's taste, but then she should not have come calling in a downpour, or more accurately she should not have come trespassing. He would have some questions for that young woman.

But it was at least half an hour before he could pose them and, when Lizzie slipped quietly into the library, all desire to question her fled. Her skin, still luminous from the rain, was blooming with health, and her dazzling hair had been marshalled into some kind of order.

It was the dress, though, that mesmerised Justin. A deep blue of the finest silk, years out of date, but showing the girl's shapely figure to splendid effect. He almost gasped. His mother had worn that dress and she, too, had been beautiful. In form at least, he amended, for there had been nothing beautiful about Lady Delacourt's nature. But what had possessed the housekeeper to alight on that particular gown? Justin could only imagine that a young Lavinia had been the same size as Miss Ingram, and this was one of the few dresses that fitted his unexpected guest.

And fit her it did, lavishing its care on every curve. A lace shawl was draped across her bosom—just as well, Justin thought, or he'd be too distracted to talk. His mind juddered to an abrupt halt. How could he think in that manner of a girl he hardly knew? He was shocked at himself. It was the evil influence of his mother—she trailed immorality, even in the clothes she'd left behind.

'Come in, Miss Ingram.' His throat had become very tight. 'Come in,' he repeated, and gestured to the table. 'Alfred has brought tea and there are fresh baked madeleines. I hope you'll partake of some or Cook will be disappointed.'

Lizzie did partake and with gusto. Justin thought he'd never seen a young lady so happy to eat, and the sight was strangely pleasurable. When she became aware of his eyes on her, she said simply, 'I had hardly any breakfast, and walking in the rain has made me ravenous.'

It was not exactly the response a Society miss would have given, but then Miss Ingram was hardly a Society miss. She was a hired companion, who spoke confidently, and looked good enough to eat herself. In short, she was a conundrum.

'Walking was not all you were doing, I think,' he said gently.

She flushed a little and looked defiant. 'No, it wasn't. I was being marched across your estate at the point of a gun.'

'But why were you in the Chelwood grounds?'

He noticed her slight hesitation. 'I became confused,' she said, 'and lost my way. Then that clunch of a bailiff found me and took me for a poacher.'

'You must excuse Mellors. He is new and very eager to be seen doing a good job.'

'He hasn't exactly covered himself in glory this morning,' she responded, munching her way through a third madeleine.

'Let's talk about you,' Justin said, determined to bring the conversation back to where he wanted. But it wasn't easy when she was sitting so close and looking more lovely in his mother's gown than ever Lady Lavinia had. He tried to focus his mind. 'The only way into Chelwood is by the lodge gates and you didn't come through them. How did you get into the estate? And why?'

The question was bluntly put since he'd given up any pretence of subtlety. He couldn't play word games, not while his body was reacting so treacherously.

'I climbed the wall.' Lizzie's defiance was marked. 'And as for why, because it blocked my way.'

Justin looked at her, amazed. 'Do you normally scale walls if they're in your way?'

'I don't normally meet them. Most people don't feel the need to live behind locked gates.'

She had quite neatly turned the tables on him, but he attempted to recover. 'My bailiff considers that locking the gates acts as a deterrent to law breakers. But then he's unused to adventurous young ladies.' As I am, he thought. The idea of any woman in his mother's tight little circle, lifting one elegant foot to that wall, was laughable.

'Adventurous? Do you think so?'

'Few ladies of my acquaintance would hurl themselves over ten feet walls.'

'I didn't exactly hurl myself—and your friends must be sad company.'

'Acquaintances,' he corrected. For some reason, he didn't want her to think he was part of the *ton* society he so despised. 'But you're right, they lack courage! They would never make a soldier!'

'*I* would—it's what I've always wished for.'

Justin was once more startled. He'd meant the remark as a pleasantry only. She looked up and saw his face. Then laughed. 'Don't worry! I know that a woman can't join the army, but I'd give anything to do so. To be in Spain at this moment, to know the camaraderie, the excitement, the thrill of victory.'

'Victory is not assured,' he warned. 'We've lost almost as many battles as we've won, and it's only recently that the tide has turned.'

'I know. At Badajoz and Vitoria.'

He was intrigued. 'You have followed the war closely?'

'My father is fighting in Spain,' Lizzie said simply.

'Your father?' Her name had had a familiar ring, he remembered, when Mrs Croft first introduced her, but he'd taken little notice. He'd been far too concerned with her beauty to think of anything else, and far too disturbed by his response to it.

'He's not by any chance Colonel Ingram?'

'He is.'

She was transformed, her face alight, her smile glowing. It was clear her father was a hero to her and why should he not be? Justin knew him by repute as a very brave man.

'You've met him?' The words were almost breathless and the plate of madeleines pushed to one side.

'Once. I met him only once. It was after Vitoria. His regiment was taking over from mine and I was about to leave. I'd just received news of my father's death and knew I had to return to England immediately.'

'And how was he?' Lizzie was all eagerness. 'After the battle, he wrote only two lines to say that he was alive.'

'He appeared well, but I was with him little more than an hour.'

'That's one more hour than I've known.' Her voice had become shadowed and her liveliness lost.

Justin refilled her cup and wondered if he should say more. At length, he asked, 'When did you last see him?'

'Some three years ago.' She jumped up from her chair and wandered to the window. 'You have a vast estate here.'

It seemed she no longer wished to talk of her father. What had happened three years ago, Justin wondered? He found himself wanting to ask, wanting to know more of her, but good sense reasserted itself. He must keep the conversation to trivialities.

'Most of the estate is given over to sheep farming, though we've acres of parkland—excellent for riding—and a thriving kitchen garden.'

'Everyone farms sheep here.'

'That's because it's profitable, especially now that taxes have been reduced and we can export to France without a huge levy. It's put the smugglers out of business,' he joked.

'There are smugglers here?'

Lizzie had turned back from the window, her eyes wide and her voice humming with excitement. The girl's vitality was entrancing, but she had a raw energy that could easily lead her into trouble. Another reason, if he needed one, to keep his distance.

'The smugglers have long gone,' he said firmly. 'Once the taxes were rescinded, smuggling lost its profit and therefore its attraction.'

'But it can't only be wool that was smuggled.'

'Spirits and tobacco, I imagine. Perhaps even tea. But members of the last gang were hanged years ago and the Preventives are now everywhere along the coast.'

'The Preventives?'

'Excise men. I'm afraid it's unlikely you'll come upon an adventure.'

Her face had fallen and he had to stop himself smiling at her disappointment. 'You must find life as a companion a trifle slow.'

'Mrs Croft is very kind,' she said quickly.

'But still a lady in her eighties. Why did you take such a post?'

The more he spoke to her, indeed the more he looked at her and felt her charm, the more odd it seemed.

Lizzie's response was tart. 'Possibly because I don't own an estate like Chelwood.'

He could have kicked himself. She had evidently to earn her own living: no doubt Ingram was in debt and unable to help. Most soldiers he knew were in debt, since much of the army had been unpaid for months.

'I'm sorry,' he began, wishing away his crass comments. 'That was a stupid thing to say.'

'There's no need to apologise, Sir Justin. I find military men in general are quite blinkered. They see only the narrow world that is theirs and nothing of the world outside, which at times can be as difficult as any military campaign.'

'I'm sure it can.' Justin could find nothing better to say, but to his own ears he sounded indifferent, even condescending.

When Lizzie spoke again, her voice was a little too bright. 'I must leave you in peace. The rain has stopped at last and I should return to Brede House before it begins again. If you would ring for your housekeeper, I'd be much obliged. By now, my dress should be dry.'

'Nonsense. I'll make sure your gown is returned clean as well as dry, but in the meantime I'll drive you back to Rye. The gig is at the door and you can be home in minutes, rain or no rain.'

She looked for a moment as though she might refuse his offer, but then thanked him very prettily and walked to the door.

Neither of them spoke as they drove the five miles back to Brede House, but Justin was acutely aware of her warm body sitting snug beside him, and of the slightest trace of jasmine filling the air. He tried hard to subdue his feelings, but failed miserably; his sharpened senses relished her very nearness and he could only thank heaven that the journey was brief. There was no space in his life for a woman.

Women were the very devil—he should know that better than anyone—and could ruin the best of men's lives. From a young age, he'd steered clear of entanglement despite others' best efforts, and he was not about to let a girl he'd met by chance destroy his peace of mind. She was a mere acquaintance, not even that.

It seemed, though, that Lizzie Ingram was refusing to play the part he'd assigned her. She had given him no clear answer as to why she was wandering in the grounds of Chelwood, and Justin suspected that her trespass had been deliberate. That she had come looking for him. If so, alarm bells should be ringing. She was dangerously beautiful.

But that wasn't all... the attraction he felt went much deeper. There was an ardent soul behind those deep brown eyes and, even in the small time he'd been with her, he'd found himself tumbling towards its bright sun. The thought made him crack the whip and the surprised horse immediately picked up its pace. He must curb such fancies, he chided himself. Elizabeth Ingram was no more than a shadowy presence in his life and must remain so. He had sufficient problems already.

Chapter Six

Lizzie bid a prim farewell to her escort at the entrance to Brede House. Crunching her way along the gravelled drive, she was careful to hold her head high and not look back at the carriage. Justin was just a little too alluring. What a pity that Piers Silchester did not exude the same attraction since, as Miss Bates was fond of pointing out, he was everything Lizzie should want—loyal, loving, stable. The trouble was that she didn't want it, or at least not enough.

Instead, she seemed continually drawn to men who offered her fleeting excitement. From bitter experience, she knew the military was an exclusive world—a world in which women had no part. Justin Delacourt was most definitely a soldier, a gentlemanly one, but nevertheless a soldier. He lacked understanding of the cramped lives women were forced to lead, knowing nothing of the narrow horizons that bound Lizzie. It would be years before *he* settled to any kind of humdrum life and, in the meantime, female company merely signified to him a little pleasantry, a little dalliance.

Why was a woman's life so very difficult? A small sum of money was all it would take to give her independence, but even a little money was beyond Lizzie. Still, a companion's life, for all its limitations, had to be better than marriage to Piers. Gentle soul though he was, he was also the dullest of the dull. He'd been the choice that Clementine Bates had offered: marriage to Piers Silchester or companion to Mrs Croft.

Lizzie couldn't blame Miss Bates. She knew herself a liability, a loose cannon prone to fire in any direction. It must have been a blessed day for Clementine when she learned from her shy music teacher that he hoped to make Miss Ingram his wife. But when Lizzie proved reluctant, Miss Bates' patience had run out.

She would have to marry one day, Lizzie supposed. Just not yet. And when she did, she dared not lose her heart to an adventurer—doubtless, Piers would be the lucky husband. He was the most dependable man she knew and he worshipped her. In his eyes, she was a goddess. When she tried to imagine Justin Delacourt as a fellow worshipper, the thought made her laugh aloud.

She wondered if he even found her attractive. He'd certainly stared at her, long and hard, when she'd entered the library wearing that dress, his ever-changing eyes shading from light to dark as his glance held. Goodness knows why, since the garment was the frumpiest thing imaginable. But he'd stared nevertheless, and not in a pleasant way. In the bedroom, Mrs Reynolds had confided that the gown had belonged to Sir Justin's mother, someone she called Lady

Lavinia. Her tightened lips suggested to Lizzie there was something odd about the woman.

Was she dead? If so, why hadn't the housekeeper mentioned the fact, especially since Sir Lucien had only just died himself? And if she wasn't dead, then where was she? The dress was old-fashioned, it was true, but Lizzie saw immediately that its material was richly luxurious and that it was beautifully made. Lady Lavinia must at one time have enjoyed wealth, enjoyed being spoilt, enjoyed being adored. Perhaps *she* had been made a goddess. If so, it was unlikely to have been her son doing the adoring. After that first amazed stare, Justin's face had registered a dour distaste.

Lizzie had reached the front entrance of Brede House, and was about to raise the cast iron anchor that served as a knocker, when the door flew open and a figure dashed past her, nearly pushing her to the ground. It was a female form, wild-eyed and seemingly distraught. She had a brief glimpse of a face before the woman started down the drive at the most tremendous pace. Lizzie looked after her in astonishment. It was Mrs Martin, she was sure, the woman she'd seen in the churchyard. Why was she visiting Mrs Croft, and why had the visit upset her so badly that she'd tossed aside all vestige of propriety?

Lizzie walked into the hall and saw that the drawing room door had been left ajar. Advancing cautiously into the room, she spied the remnants of tea scattered across the small occasional table that was used when visitors called—a plate of uneaten macaroons, a teacup tossed on its side. Seemingly, it had been a social call. But what kind of social call ended with a desperate flight? Or, for that matter, left the hostess prostrate? Mrs Croft was slumped into one of the armchairs, her hand to her forehead, as though nursing a sick headache.

'Mrs Croft?' she said gently. 'Are you feeling unwell?'

At the sound of her voice, the old lady stirred and, seeing Lizzie's anxious face looking at her from the doorway, attempted to pull herself upright.

'No, my dear, I thank you, just a little tired.' Her voice was barely above a whisper. 'Socialising at my age can be a little trying, you know.'

Her employer evidently had no wish to dwell on what had happened, and Lizzie wondered if she should leave the matter. It would probably be as well for her to escape now, before Mrs Croft recognised the outdated dress she was wearing. But she could not leave the old lady in such a mournful state.

'I saw Mrs Martin,' she mentioned quietly. 'She passed me as I came through the door. She seemed very upset.'

Mrs Croft looked down at her feet and uttered the deepest of sighs. 'I'm sorry you were witness to her distress. Caroline is grief-stricken and her behaviour at the moment is unpredictable.'

'But why? I mean why is she grief-stricken?' The question sounded harsher than she'd intended, and Lizzie tried to make amends. 'I'd not realised that Mrs Martin was so attached to Sir Lucien.'

'Not Sir Lucien, my dear,' Mrs Croft said gently. 'It's her son that she mourns. She has lost Gilbert.'

'Lost as in dead?' Lizzie queried, wide-eyed.

'Lost as in lost. You might as well know, since it's now common knowledge. Gilbert Martin vanished some months ago and his parents have been unable to trace him. No-one seems to know a thing about his disappearance.'

'How strange. And how sad. But why was Mrs Martin so distressed? She could have received nothing but comfort from you.'

'I'm afraid not. I could not give her what she wanted. She asked me to intercede with Justin Delacourt. Beg him to put all other concerns to one side in order to search for her son. I told you, did I not, that Gilbert Martin was the closest of friends with Justin?'

'You did. And she was upset with you because you said no?'

'I cannot bother Justin at a time like this. He lost his father only weeks ago, and has been left an estate that is teetering on ruin. It will take him an age to put right, and I know that he is desperate to return to his regiment.'

'Couldn't she ask Sir Justin herself—if he's so very close to the family?'

'She has already asked him for help, but she wanted me to add my voice to her pleas. I could not, in all honesty, do that. Justin has more than enough to contend with. If he has promised to help in the search, he will do so—he is a man of his word—but it must be on his terms and at a time of his arranging.'

'And that's not what Mrs Martin wants?'

'No, indeed. Justin must drop everything. I'm afraid that she is slightly unbalanced at the moment. Her son was everything to her. He was a late child, you see, a delicate boy, or so Caroline always maintained. His disappearance has sent her spiralling into an abyss and none of her friends' advice or her husband's care has been able to prevent it.'

'I'm sorry you've had such an uncomfortable afternoon, Mrs Croft.' Lizzie felt genuine concern for her employer, the old lady's pallor testifying to how badly shaken she had been. 'Can I bring you some water perhaps, or fetch down the footstool for you to rest more easily.'

'No, but thank you for your kind thoughts, Elizabeth. I shall sit here a while and listen to the river. It's nearly high tide—I can already hear the waters lapping in the distance. It's a most soothing sound and is sure to restore me very soon.'

Lizzie took her cue and slipped out of the room and up the stairs. Once in her bedroom, she swiftly changed her dress, then stood at the open window and listened to the same water slapping against the small, stony beach which lay beyond the garden. Taking up her sketch pad, she began to draw, but not the river snaking below nor the clouds busily filling the sky above. She drew a face, one she'd studied well and recently. When she'd finished, she was pleased with her portrait—the strong, lean cheek bones, the eyes steady and appraising, the hair a wild halo—though she was not so pleased with herself. She should cast Sir Justin from her mind.

He'd fascinated her from the outset and his curt indifference when they'd first met had only sharpened her interest: he was an invitation, an enjoyable prospect to lighten the dull days ahead. But this morning it had taken only a very little time in his company to realise her mistake. He was far too attractive, certainly too attractive to treat lightly, and if she were sensible, she would keep her distance. Lizzie looked down at the paper on her knee. What on earth was she doing, drawing portraits of the man? She took the page and tore it neatly in half, dropping it in the nearby waste bin. He was a footloose soldier and she must forget him. Instead, school herself in time to appreciate the estimable Piers.

There was a soft knock on the door and Hester came in carrying fresh bedding and towels.

'Is mistress feeling any better now, Miss Elizabeth?'

'She is resting. She wished to be left alone.'

'She shouldn't be put under that kind of strain, not at her age she shouldn't.'

'Mrs Martin was very upset.'

'Mebbe. But that ain't no excuse for upsetting an old lady like she's done.'

Hester had been with Mrs Croft for years and had a fierce loyalty to her mistress. She knew everything that happened in the house, and no doubt in Rye itself.

A thought wormed its way into Lizzie's mind. 'Have you heard anything of her son's disappearance, Hester?'

She shouldn't be gossiping with a maidservant, but she knew why she'd been tempted. It seemed that she wasn't yet willing to forget Justin entirely, and Hester might provide some small piece of ammunition in any future tussle with him. As so often, Lizzie was choosing not to be sensible.

The maid appeared unwilling to answer and looked fixedly down at the carpet.

'You have heard something, haven't you?' Lizzie prompted.

'A little, miss. It's probably nothing and I shouldn't be saying it, but Mr Gil was fair taken with that gypsy woman, and I've been wondering if she had anything to do with his going away.'

'A gypsy woman?' Lizzie tried hard not to sound eager, but her nerves were tingling. Could there be a real adventure here?

'She weren't truly a gypsy. But she didn't seem to have a proper home. And she mixed with some queer company— still does for that matter.'

'So she's still in Rye? Who is she, Hester?'

'Goes by the name of Rosanna. A right heathen name, if you ask me.'

'Rosanna who? What's her last name?'

'There's no other name, leastways none that I know of.'

Lizzie thought hard. It seemed incongruous that someone of Gilbert Martin's standing should have made such a woman his sweetheart. But under the influence of love, men could act completely out of character and contemplate the wildest of actions.

'And Gil Martin was walking out with her?' she prompted, hoping that was the right term.

Hester snorted. 'He weren't doing that—walking out, I mean—not too boldly, leastways. He daren't be seen with her, but everyone knew he was fair gone.'

'Why didn't he want to be seen?' Lizzie was sure she knew the answer, but was keen to keep the maid talking.

'With a no-good woman like that and him a gentleman!'

'I understand.' Lizzie nodded her head sagely. 'I imagine his parents have no knowledge of Rosanna.'

'I wouldn't think so, miss. Reckon he'd have kept mortal quiet about that particular friendship.'

'But when it became obvious that he was missing, surely someone must have mentioned the girl to them?'

Hester drew herself up to her full height. 'Folks round here don't gossip,' she said firmly. 'Least, they don't gossip to the gentry. Mr and Mrs Martin are well respected— nice people—and no-one would want to hurt 'em by telling 'em such a thing. Not when their son wanted to keep it secret.'

Lizzie shook her head, but kept her thoughts to herself. She had seen Caroline's face, desperate with grief, and for an instant had shrunk before the intensity of its pain. What must it be like to lose your only child and not know what had happened to him? Surely, it would be better to risk distressing the Martins if it meant solving the mystery of their son's disappearance? But evidently Rye was a close-knit community, and secrets were secrets and had to be kept.

But not by her. A tantalising idea hovered into view. She might be able to help Mrs Martin—didn't the poor woman deserve whatever aid she could offer?—and at the same time, irritate Justin Delacourt. Lizzie had been left feeling flustered and gauche by their encounter while he... he'd been a little too smooth, a little too in control. It would be good to disturb that infuriating calm.

Justin had been charged with the onerous duty of finding his friend and he'd need every small clue he could lay his hands on. And Lizzie had one. And not a small clue at that. A very big clue. She would dangle it before him, tease him with it, and at the same time edge Caroline a little closer to finding her son.

Chapter Seven

The will had been read with few surprises, since except for several small bequests to servants and close friends, everything had been left to Sir Lucien's son. The lawyer from London had come and gone, leaving Justin to distribute the gifts his father had bequeathed. A beautifully tooled calf-bound volume detailing the delights of Sussex and Kent was one of them. The book was destined for Mrs Croft, in remembrance of the happy hours she and Sir Lucien had spent poring over its expensive illustrations.

His father had left a handwritten note, asking Justin to deliver the gift to Henrietta personally, and the dead man's request caused his son to sigh. It would mean a journey to Brede House and a possible encounter with a young woman he'd hoped to avoid. Mrs Croft left the house infrequently these days, and how to get the book to her without meeting Miss Ingram presented a problem. Justin turned it over in his mind for several days without finding a solution, irritated with himself that he had so little control over his feelings, he was shirking a visit to one of his father's oldest friends.

Since the lawyer's departure, it had rained incessantly and when, on the third morning, he woke to a cloudless blue sky, it seemed a sensible time to go in search of the old lady. Mrs Croft was sure to have kept within doors the last few days, but hopefully she'd be unable to resist the promise of such glorious weather. There was a chance she would walk along the river path towards the town and he could take her up in his carriage and present the precious gift to her there and then.

First, though, he must keep his word by visiting Five Oaks. He steered the carriage through the Chelwood gates into the autumn lanes and was at once enveloped in a world of glorious colour: coppiced trees fountained upwards and linked arms to create a cavern of russet foliage, while here and there patches of sunlight pierced the canopy and speckled gold across all they touched. It had been cold overnight, but waves of sun-warmed air were already radiating off the land and chasing away all but the finest veils of mist.

Despite the difficult morning ahead, Justin was feeling more optimistic than he'd been since the dreadful news of his father's death had reached him. It must be the beautiful weather, he thought, for little else had changed. The estate was still in desperate need of renovation, his friend was still missing, and his regiment still awaited his return. Yet some kind of magic was being weaved, since his heart felt unaccountably light as his horses sped him on his way.

At Five Oaks he was greeted with great affection, waved

into the sunny drawing room and plied with refreshments. Relieved that no mention was made of the task Caroline Martin had laid on him, Justin talked animatedly of the various schemes that he and Mellors were devising to set Chelwood to rights. After half an hour he rose to take his leave, and it was only when he reached the front door that he remembered Sir Lucien's bequests.

'I almost forgot!' He delved into the old carpet bag he'd unearthed from the hall chest at Chelwood. 'The will has now been proved and I've several gifts to distribute. My father wanted you both to have his collection of old maps. I have them here.' He brought forth several rolls of crinkled cream parchment.

'How very kind of Lucien,' James responded warmly. 'He knew my interest in the history of the area. But would you not wish them to remain at Chelwood? I remember them decorating the walls of his study there. It would seem a better resting place for them.'

'His study is now mine, Mr Martin, and is covered in schedules for the advancement of the estate. There is even the odd illustration of a rare pig! My father knew how much you would value these—far more than I—and I hope you'll accept them as a small remembrance of him.'

James clasped the younger man's hands in his. 'I'd be honoured to have them, Justin. They will be accorded pride of place in my own study.'

Justin hesitated. He had yet one more gift for Five Oaks, but he was unsure how to introduce it. Caroline saw his hesitation. 'What is it, Justin? You have something more?'

'Mrs Martin, please forgive my clumsiness. I should never perhaps have brought this with me, but I'm legally bound to carry out the provisions of the will.'

The Martins were looking at him, puzzled expressions on both their faces. He drew from the bag a small, carved wooden object. 'It's a native Indian curio that my father purchased when he was serving in America—'

'And it's for Gilbert?' she finished for him.

Yes,' Justin admitted, not knowing how to proceed.

'How very kind of your father to remember Gil's collection. Of course, you should have brought it.' Her voice had only the slightest tremor. 'But will you do one thing for me before you go and take it to Gilbert's room?' Her voice was cracking now. 'You know where it is. You know where he kept his collection.'

Justin sprang forward, relieved to be doing something. 'I promise to find the perfect place for it.'

He was past the waiting couple and up the stairs before Caroline's tears began to flow. He felt angry with himself that so far he'd done nothing to help the Martins. He'd been too busy with estate matters and, he told himself crossly, too busy with the girl. True, she'd taken up only a little of his time at Chelwood, but simply thinking about her had wasted precious hours. He'd not daydreamed like this since he was a boy and he needed to snap out of it.

Gil's room was just as its owner had left it, just as Justin had seen it the last time he'd visited: bedclothes uncreased, cushions plumped, fresh paper on the desk and a newly sharpened quill and pot of ink in the writing tray. The mirror reflected the same pictures, the mantelshelf held the same ornaments. He remembered being here three years ago, laughing and joshing with his friend, twitting him over his ever growing collection of native artefacts. *You need to travel, Gil,* he'd said, *and not just in your mind.*

He strode over to the large wooden display cabinet that filled one corner of the room and opened its two glass doors. The shelves were already full and it took time to find a space into which he could fit his father's small offering. The top shelf seemed a little less crowded and he reached up to it, shuffling several objects closer together. There appeared to be some resistance towards the back of the shelf and, with some difficulty, Justin reached across and pulled out a sheaf of papers that had been taped to its underside.

Immediately, he saw they were part of a private correspondence. He shouldn't look at them. They were Gil's. He went to tape them back and, by accident, caught sight of the subscription which headed the first page.

My darling.

'My darling?' Surely not. Surely not Gil. Justin was no ladies' man himself, but Gil was even less of one. He could not recall a single instance when his friend had shown the slightest partiality for any woman. Justin took the papers over to the desk and flicked through them. They continued in the same vein. *My darling, My sweetheart, Dear heart,* followed by protestations of love and longing that the writer would soon be with his beloved forever. Justin's eyes scrolled to the bottom of each page. There was no doubt.

He had recognised his friend's hand, but a vague hope that Gil might have penned the letters for someone else died when he saw the unmistakeable signature.

But to whom had his friend been writing? There was no clue. And he'd not sent the letters, so what did that mean? Judging by the dates, he'd written them day after day, one after another, but had never sent them. It was a further puzzle. Almost as though Gil had been leading a double life that nobody, least of all his parents, was aware of. What had James said—that he no longer knew his son?

Justin sighed. The letters didn't advance his search one iota—indeed, they complicated it—and they wouldn't help Caroline in her misery. The only thing to do was to fit them back into their hiding place and forget he'd ever read words meant for another. Who that other was, Justin had no idea and probably never would. He was certain, though, that the unknown had nothing to do with his friend's disappearance. Gil had been gone for three months and, if he'd eloped with a sweetheart, he would have confessed his wrongdoing by now and been reunited with his family. Perhaps a little in disgrace, but nevertheless welcomed home with love.

No, there was no sweetheart, Justin decided. It was simply wishful thinking on his friend's part. If there had been a real woman, she was a distant figure only, and Gil had been worshipping from afar, lacking the temerity to approach her. Instead, he'd written letter after letter, finding a release for his emotions, but saying nothing to anyone. How lonely he must have been, Justin thought, to have fallen in love with a dream, to have confided his deepest feelings to a few sheets of paper.

The letters had been an unwelcome discovery, and he was tempted to drive directly home, but chided himself for a cowardly choice. He would drive in the direction of Brede House, he decided, and hope to catch sight of Mrs Croft taking her usual walk along the river path that led to the town. As he neared the entrance gates , he saw the skirts of a much younger woman disappearing towards Rye. It was Lizzie Ingram, straw bonnet masking those glorious chestnut curls, and a basket swinging from her hand. Henrietta must have sent her to do the marketing, a little late in the day, but most fortunate for him. He could visit the house now without fear of meeting the girl.

As soon as he entered the small parlour looking out towards the river, he saw that Mrs Croft was not in the best of spirits. But her forlorn expression gave way to a welcoming smile when she saw him and, getting to her feet with some difficulty, she came forward to clasp his hand.

'How lovely to see you, Justin. And how kind of you to spare a few minutes of what must be precious time.'

He felt a twinge of guilt, but said as convincingly as he could, 'It's always a pleasure to see you, Mrs Croft, and today especially—I have come on a very particular mission.'

She looked enquiringly at him and, in response, he withdrew the leather-bound book from the carpet bag.

'I've come to bring you something I think you'll treasure. Sir Lucien thought so at least. Here.' And he handed her the soft calf-skin volume.

She smoothed its cover with a gentle touch. 'So many happy hours,' she murmured. 'Hours that have gone. Friends that have gone.'

Justin struggled to know what to say. His hostess appeared more unhappy than he'd ever seen her, and he cast blindly around for words of comfort. But he need not have worried. As he delved deep to find a cheering sentiment, the door opened abruptly, and Lizzie stood on the threshold.

Chapter Eight

Lizzie smiled saucily at him. 'Sir Justin! I was wondering who could have come calling and in such a very smart carriage. Is it new? And how heavenly to drive out from Chelwood on such a day!'

'Good morning, Miss Ingram.' He'd stiffened at the sight of her, but managed a small bow, his face bereft of expression. 'The day is certainly beautiful and you're dressed for walking, I see. Were you perhaps thinking of taking the air? If so, I can recommend the coastal path—it's at its best when the sun is shining and there's little wind.'

Lizzie's smile did not falter. 'What a delightful suggestion! But unfortunately I must engage myself elsewhere this morning. It's my ribbons, you see.' And she pulled from her basket a shining length of jonquil satin. 'I thought to go to Mercer's to match this very lovely yellow, but I'd gone no more than a hundred yards when I realised I'd left my purse behind.'

So that was the reason for her return. Or at least, the reason she claimed. But had she perhaps caught sight of his carriage and made the decision to return to Brede House?

To return and torment him. He'd put nothing past her—her trespass at Chelwood had been shameless. Well, he could be shameless, too, and make it difficult for her to stay.

'I believe the haberdasher closes at noon, and if you're wanting to purchase more ribbon, you'd be wise to set out immediately.'

She was still smiling, an uncomfortably satisfied smile, Justin decided. 'How thoughtful of you, but I'm in no hurry. I find Rye lives at a slow pace and it's necessary to match one's own rhythm to it. Whether I get the ribbon today or tomorrow or the next week hardly matters.'

It was a brazen contradiction, since a minute ago she'd insisted she had not the time to go walking. He felt a growing exasperation, but he could press her no further without appearing blatantly discourteous. His hostess was already looking askance at him. Miss Ingram had decided she would stay at Brede House this morning, and he must make the best of it.

'I've interrupted your conversation,' Lizzie said. 'I'm so sorry.' Her lips curved provocatively. Lips, he noticed, that were full and warm and red.

Justin felt himself growing hot, his thoughts stumbling. Trying to regain his composure, he said in as toneless a voice as he could manage, 'There's no need for apologies. I came only to give my father's present to Mrs Croft.'

'And a beautiful present it is, too,' Henrietta intervened, seeming relieved that the conversation had returned to firmer ground. 'But won't you stay for some refreshment, Justin?'

'Thank you, but no. I must return to Chelwood. There's much to do, as you know. But I'll call again very soon and perhaps then we can talk at greater length.' But only when I can be absolutely sure that Miss Ingram is nowhere in the vicinity, he told himself.

'Before you go, Justin...' the old lady caught at his arm. 'I think I should warn you...' She broke off, unable to find the right words, and then with difficulty, murmured, 'It's Caroline, Mrs Martin.'

'What of her?'

'She is in great distress.'

'I know, Mrs Croft. I'm aware of how much she must be suffering.' Justin gently disentangled her arm from his and began walking towards the door. But she was on her feet and following him, her voice unusually urgent.

'I'm sure you are. How could you not be? I understand she has asked you to aid her in the search for Gilbert. But she has been here, too, to ask something similar of myself.'

Justin stopped in surprise. 'That *you* should aid her? Surely not!'

'That I should add my voice to hers in persuading you to begin your search immediately. I refused, I fear. I know how much work you have before you. And I know, too, that the Martins have tried almost everything to find their son and not succeeded. How Caroline imagines you can perform miracles, I do not know.'

The Martins had said nothing to him this morning of Caroline's visit to Brede House. Perhaps James was ignorant of his wife's call. Or Caroline was ashamed now of the disturbance she'd caused?

Justin pressed the old lady's hand in reassurance. 'Mrs Martin is overwrought— understandably so—and we mustn't be too alarmed if she behaves unusually. But I confess I'm worried she is relying on me so heavily. Gil was, is, my friend, and I've promised to do all I can.' He smiled wryly. 'My promise was well-meant, though I'm at a loss where to start.'

'That's hardly surprising. If all the enquiries the Martins have sent out over these past months have come to nothing, how can you, newly arrived and in the most difficult of circumstances, be expected to fare better?' Henrietta looked searchingly up at her visitor. 'It would not be wrong to forgo your promise, Justin, since it was unfair of Caroline to have extracted it from you. Your focus must be on Chelwood. Caroline must know that and she will soon come to her senses. When she does, she will see what an impossible task she has given you.'

'I can only hope so.' He reached the door as Mrs Croft rang the bell for Hester. 'But I don't want you to be worried by this business. If Mrs Martin should call again, you must refer her to me.'

'I think it unlikely that she will.'

Chapter Nine

A s soon as Hester had escorted their visitor to the front door, Lizzie bounced from her seat. She had been listening to the conversation intently, and now had a plan.

Gesturing to the sun that beamed its way through the parlour window, she said, 'As the weather remains so kind, I think perhaps I will walk to Rye after all, Mrs Croft. As long as you'll be comfortable for an hour? If the haberdasher closes his shop, it won't be for long, and apart from the ribbon, my second best reticule is badly in need of retrimming. I can buy you the new cap you mentioned, too.'

Her employer nodded assent and settled herself wearily back into the armchair. In seconds, Lizzie was slipping out of the front door just as Sir Justin jumped into the carriage's driving seat. He saw her out of the corner of his eye and had no alternative but to offer to drive her to Rye. It was not what he wanted, but for the second time that morning, fortune appeared to favour him.

'Thank you for your offer, Sir Justin, but I prefer to walk. It keeps me fit and healthy. Or hale, as you would say.'

That was true enough, he thought: her slim figure filled the simple sprig muslin in all the right places. He wished he could stop noticing, but it seemed an impossibility.

'There is something I might be able to do for *you*, though,' she said pertly, 'something you might be interested in knowing.'

Her words took him aback and he paused for an instant before deciding, reluctantly, to dismount from the carriage. The reins, though, remained firmly within his grasp—whatever it was she had to impart, Justin had no intention of lingering.

'And what exactly might I be interested in, Miss Ingram?'

'You've been charged with the burden of finding your lost friend. I may have the information you'll need to begin your search.'

He very much doubted it. The Martins had searched high and low. And the whole of Rye knew that Gil was missing and would be on the alert, while Lizzie Ingram had been here but a few weeks. What could she know? It was a ploy to draw him in, he thought, or designed simply to irritate him. She was evidently used to male admiration and his refusal to pay her the necessary compliments must rankle.

'If you can help in any way, I'd be grateful.'

He kept his voice impassive, but couldn't stop himself looking into her face. There was that smile again—provocative, tantalising, teasing him with its promise.

'Do you know of a woman called Rosanna?'

What was this nonsense? 'No, I can't say I do,' Justin

said tersely. 'Should I?'

'Not necessarily, but your friend did.'

'Gil?' He was shocked out of his formality. The thought of the letters he'd read earlier loomed large.

'Yes, Gilbert Martin. Apparently he had a close relationship with a woman called Rosanna. If *I* were looking for him, I'd want to speak to her.'

'That's impossible,' he stammered. 'Who is this Rosanna anyway?'

He had put the letters down to fantasy, nothing more. Now this girl was naming a flesh and blood woman. Was she mocking him or could she really be serious?

'I believe she's a woman of some mystery. She's not exactly a gypsy, but neither does she live a settled life. I'm told, too, that she keeps dubious company.'

'In that case, Gilbert would have had no commerce with her.' Justin's tone was uncompromising, and he made to remount the carriage. His suspicions had disappeared: Gil would never have taken up with such a woman.

'You shouldn't dismiss her so lightly. I've no doubt this Rosanna is fascinating to men, and even those with the highest morals, like your friend, might well have been captivated by her attractions.'

'I know Gilbert Martin and, if you'll forgive me, the idea that he'd become embroiled with such a woman is a complete hum.'

Lizzie took a deep breath, drawing herself up to stand ramrod straight, her eyes flashing a clear challenge. '*I* will forgive you, Sir Justin. But will the Martins?'

Chapter Ten

Justin watched her as she began to walk, basket in hand, along the winding drive towards the Rye road. He wanted to run after her, ask her for more details, ask her for some kind of evidence, but it was clear he would get nothing more. She must know she had dealt him a blow and he was sure she was enjoying it. She had said just enough to torment him, but not enough for him to discount the news entirely. The notion of Gil in an intimate relationship with any woman was astonishing enough, but with a woman such as Lizzie Ingram had described, it had to be impossible.

Yet there were those letters. They may never have been sent, but they could have been written to a real woman. Reading them this morning, he'd been so astonished that he'd decided on a fantasy sweetheart, but was that because he still saw Gil as the boy he'd been and not the man he'd become in Justin's absence? Or was it, perish the thought, that it was easier to assume that nothing could explain his friend's absence, and there was therefore nothing to investigate?

If he'd once been tempted to think so, he couldn't any longer. It wasn't only the letters to Rosanna, if such they were, but the fact that the woman kept dubious company. If Lizzie were right, that had to be significant. He guessed she had quite deliberately thrown that piece of gossip into the conversation in an effort to intrigue him or, more probably, annoy. But that didn't mean it was untrue.

There was no hope for it, Justin thought heavily, he'd have to explore further. For the next day or so, Mellors would have to carry on alone with the work at Chelwood, at least until he'd disproved the suspicions that Elizabeth Ingram had planted in his mind. He'd made the Martins a promise and he must do his best to fulfil it.

For a good half a mile, Lizzie danced along the river path, elated by the fact that she'd confounded the infuriating Justin. His expression, when she'd mentioned his friend's involvement with the mysterious Rosanna, had been dumbfounded. How satisfying! He deserved to be put out of countenance. It was clear to Lizzie that he had set out to visit Brede House, hoping she'd not be there.

The minute she'd remembered leaving her purse on the bedroom chest, she had turned back and seen his carriage draw up at the gates to Brede House. It appeared to linger there, seeming unwilling to commit to any particular direction. But then, the horses had made a swift turn into the driveway, as though relieved of a burden. In that instant, Lizzie had realised that *she* was the burden. Justin Delacourt had wanted to avoid her, and when he'd seen her in the distance on her way to Rye, had taken advantage of her absence.

At church, Lizzie had thought him snobbish, too high in the instep to acknowledge a humble companion, but after her visit to Chelwood Hall, she'd had to revise that view. He'd treated his uninvited guest with courtesy and without condescension. So why was he so desperate to escape her presence, choosing to visit Mrs Croft in secret? Did he feel uneasy in the company of young women? She thought it unlikely. As a soldier, he must have had dealings with plenty over the years. Was it then a particular woman, Lizzie Ingram, that he found unnerving?

She hoped very much that it was so. It would only be fair, since each time they'd met, she had felt similarly unnerved. In church, she'd been captivated by his wonderful voice, driving with him from Chelwood she'd not been able to stop her skin from prickling in a most peculiar fashion and, just now, standing so close, the look of him, the warmth of him, had sent each and every small fibre tingling within her. The fact that she possessed crucial information had kept her mind steady, but it had been difficult to maintain a calm exterior while her body was responding so disturbingly. She'd been almost glad to see him regain the driving seat and set his horses in motion.

But not glad that he'd rejected so completely what she had told him. He'd not believed her or, more likely, had not wanted to believe. He'd refused to accept that his friend was capable of falling in love with a low-born and possibly impure woman. Why was Justin so stubborn? He might know his friend, but she knew women better and, if this Rosanna had set her sights on Gilbert Martin, Lizzie had no doubt that she'd succeeded. And surely it was right that Mrs Martin was told of anything that might lead to her son?

The elation Lizzie had felt slowly drifted away, as she walked on into the town, and was replaced by a strong sense of irritation. Why were men, why were soldiers, so blinkered? She'd thought the information gold dust and yet Justin Delacourt had dismissed it without a thought. It would serve him right if *she* followed up the clue she'd unearthed.

Her mind began to buzz. No, she told herself, she must forget whatever mad thoughts were stirring. Embrace the calm of the river, that today was flowing smoothly with hardly a ripple breaking its surface. It was no use, though: her thoughts had broken loose and she couldn't curb them. She had imagined Rye to be a staid town, yet in the last few days adventure had beckoned from every quarter—the talk of smugglers, the disappearance of a local gentleman, a secret love affair with a mysterious woman. Adventure beckoned, so why not grasp it? Find out who Rosanna really was, what she looked like, what she knew. Justin Delacourt had no intention of finding out, so why shouldn't she?

When she reached the haberdasher's, she found the shop still open but crowded. Until Mr Mercer was free to serve, she riffled through the buttons and ribbons that he'd laid out for display in long wooden trays. An elderly customer in an unfashionable poke bonnet was at the counter, making an anxious choice of a length of silk organza for her granddaughter's first party dress, and all the time maintaining a mumbled commentary on the high cost of the material.

'Prices have risen, Mrs Cartwright,' the shopkeeper was saying, a trifle tight-lipped. 'I make little enough profit as it is.'

'I'm sure that's so, Mr Mercer,' the woman agreed, her tone placating, 'but I can't forget the time—you, too, I'm sure—when we could buy the most beautiful silks from France for next to nothing.'

He looked warningly at her and she caught his glance. 'Don't mind me, I'm an old woman. I realise those days are gone and best forgotten. We must be glad the law's no longer broken with impunity.'

Lizzie didn't think she looked particularly glad.

A younger woman, weighed down by the heavy pannier she carried, cut across the conversation. 'We *should* be glad that Rye's no longer a den of thieves,' she said emphatically. 'People can walk through the town freely now without fear.'

There was a murmur of agreement amongst the several women standing behind her.

'You've only to think of what the Mermaid used to be, to know that's so!' exclaimed a red-faced woman, looking every inch a farmer's wife and perspiring quietly at the back of the waiting line.

Her words loosed a torrent of condemnation from the other women. 'They say the Mermaid has a hidden cellar and secret passageways to other inns in the town—no wonder it's been a villains' haunt for so long!'

'And still is, I reckon. Have you seen those men, lordin' it up, sittin' in the window, as bold as brass as though they own the town?'

'It's not just the men!'

'No, indeed. Have you seen that woman—'

'She shouldn't be mentioned in decent society.' The elderly customer patted the brown paper package Mr Mercer had handed her, as though seeking reassurance. 'We must protect our young folks.'

Lizzie's hand had stopped on the brocade she was fingering. She'd been engrossed by the conversation as it see-sawed between members of the group. The person they'd just spoken of, could that be Rosanna? It had to be: a woman who consorted with a gang of desperate men and who outraged society. She'd been right, Lizzie thought—there was an adventure here and she couldn't resist its siren call.

Abandoning any desire to buy yellow ribbons or trimming for her reticule, Lizzie slipped out of the shop. As she closed the door behind her, the haberdasher was continuing to complain of high prices and the women to lament the moral threat to their town.

They had mentioned Mermaid Street and Lizzie knew where it was. She'd noticed the signpost when attending services at St Mary's, but Mrs Croft had always refused to walk that way to the river and had warned her of setting foot in the street. But curiosity burned too brightly now and she hurried up West Street towards the church, then swerved left, winding her way around the churchyard to arrive at the top of the infamous road.

Its cobbled length fell steeply towards the river, and she could see in the distance a cluster of small boats bobbing on the incoming tide. Some way down on the right hand side, an old black and white Tudor building raised its head. The Mermaid Inn! A few carts rumbled their way over the cobbles making for the quayside but, except for Lizzie, there were no passers-by. It was as though the population of Rye had chosen to put this particular street into quarantine.

Lizzie kept to the left hand side of the street, her face shadowed by the brim of her bonnet, but her eyes surreptitiously keeping watch on the other pavement. Soon she had drawn nearly opposite the tavern and slowed her pace to a crawl.

She saw them immediately. A sizeable group of men, roughly clad in stained leather jerkins and sitting at a downstairs open window, pint pots in their hands and their heads wreathed in noxious clouds of smoke. They lazed at their ease, making an untidy circle around a table scattered with empty tankards and remnants of food. And amid this detritus—was that a pistol, she could see?

Lizzie tried to look more closely. It *was* a pistol, in fact several pistols, and they looked to be cocked and ready for use. Her knowledge of firearms was limited, but a cocked gun meant it was loaded and she was in the direct line of fire.

She knew she should scurry down the hill as fast as her legs could carry her, but instead she couldn't stop looking.

They were the ugliest collection of men, Lizzie thought, bearded and unkempt and most likely, unwashed.

One man in particular she noticed. He was not in any way flamboyant and, at first, he hardly registered. But there was a stillness about him that drew the eye. A malevolent stillness. His hair was tow-coloured, his eyes lightless, but his brows thick and black. He had the look of an other-worldly creature, an avenging demon. It was a hauntingly evil face.

At that moment, a voluptuous figure swam into view and Lizzie was so stunned by the woman's appearance that her feet seemed to grow roots and anchor her to the ground. The woman *was* flamboyant. Her hair was black and her eyes even blacker. She was beautiful, Lizzie thought, beautiful in a bold, brazen fashion. Miss Bates would have called her a hussy—or worse. She was wearing a red dress, the material so thin you could almost see her naked skin beneath, and so tight that it left nothing to the imagination. As Lizzie watched mesmerised, the woman placed the tray of tankards on the table and began to sway in and out of the chairs, stroking the men's beards and leaving light kisses on their foreheads. Her kiss for the tow-headed man seemed to linger. This had to be Rosanna.

Lizzie swallowed hard. She should have nothing more to do with this. Walk on, she told herself. Walk to Brede House and forget you ever witnessed this little tableau. It had danger written all over it.

But there was a spirit of devilment in her, a thirst for the uncommon, that was too strong. If she could only get Rosanna alone, she might discover exactly what had happened to Gil Martin, for one thing was very clear: this woman was the enchantress Lizzie had predicted. She most definitely could have enchanted Justin Delacourt's friend. But into what?

Chapter Eleven

It was several days before Lizzie walked into town again. Mrs Croft had been badly upset by Caroline Martin's visit, more than the household had realised at the time, and she needed constant attention— first from her doctor and then from both Hester and Lizzie. But as the old lady gradually recovered her spirits, her interest in the world returned and, with it, the desire for new books to read. A branch of the circulating library had been set up the previous year in small premises next to the George Hotel on Lion Street, and Lizzie was despatched on a mission to find reading material for the recovering invalid. It proved a difficult task, since Mrs Croft was a voracious reader and over the months the library had been thoroughly plundered. But eventually, after an hour of searching, she secured two volumes she thought might satisfy her employer.

She was glad to leave the stuffy air of the library behind and feel again the sea breeze blowing off the river, though disappointed to see how fast the light was fading. She'd hoped to use this visit to further the plan she'd decided on, but it was October and each day brought with it an earlier dusk—Lizzie could almost feel the sky growing sullen. She would have to hurry to get back to Brede House before darkness fell.

The image of Rosanna still teased her, though, and on her way to the river path, she dared once more to walk down Mermaid Street. This time the inn's window was closed against the cold air and there was no sign of any of the men she'd seen before. Lizzie was swept by a strange mix of regret and relief, and walked swiftly down the hill towards the track that would lead her home. A flash of red caught her eye. A dress—disappearing into the warren of narrow paths that branched from the bottom of Mermaid Street into what she'd learned was the poorest part of the town.

A red dress! Who else wore such a garment? The figure ahead was Rosanna's, she was almost sure. But she had little time to go after her—it was growing darker by the minute and Lizzie knew she should be on her way to Brede House. That was the sensible thing to do. But she'd never been sensible, she thought ruefully, and set out to follow the woman's swaying figure.

Reaching the end of Mermaid Street, she saw a glimpse of red vanishing around the next corner and hurried in pursuit along the narrow lane. Past the *Ship Inn*, avoiding several of its already drunken clients, then, still shadowing the figure ahead, she turned left into an even narrower thoroughfare. Every kind of dirt and rubbish had been strewn across the bare earth that constituted a path. Carefully, Lizzie picked her way along the filthy lane, sending up thanks that she had worn her stoutest boots. A row of mean cottages lined either side of the narrow byway, and a cacophony of noise accompanied her every step: doors were banged almost off their hinges, cooking pans crashed into china sinks, angry curses flew through the air.

A faint glimmer of candlelight shone from the uncurtained windows, but the sky above was thick with cloud and offered no trace of moon or stars to leaven the inky night that was falling so swiftly. On a half-ruined wall, Lizzie spied the silhouette of a ragged black crow. The bird perched spectre-like, emerging out of the shreds of mist now stealing ashore from the river. An omen of desolation. But she couldn't turn back. She was close to her quarry, so close she must keep going. If she could discover in which of these houses Rosanna lodged, she would brave the inhabitants and ask to speak to the woman. Courage would surely be rewarded.

But when Lizzie reached the end of the street, she came to an abrupt halt. A crossroads confronted her and she'd no idea which direction to take. The red dress, that had been a beacon shining the way ahead, had disappeared into thin air. She could have cried with vexation. She must choose one of the tracks that faced her, but which? As she hesitated, a figure stepped out of the shadows behind her and she felt an iron grip close around her arm. Her heart somersaulted.

'You should go no further, Miss Ingram.'

Her mind blurred at the sound of the familiar voice.

'What!' She tried to twist herself around to face her

captor, but remained locked in Justin Delacourt's hard grasp.

'You are hurting me.' She was breathing fast, more from the shock of his sudden appearance than from any pain he was inflicting.

'Forgive me, but I had to stop you from venturing any further into this den of villainy. We must retrace our steps immediately.'

'I'll leave as soon as my business is finished, and not before,' Lizzie said angrily.

Indignation had replaced the initial shock and her limbs no longer trembled. She was so close to her goal and no-one was going to stop her, certainly not the man who'd shown contempt for the information she'd brought him.

But Justin Delacourt had other ideas. 'You will leave now,' he said simply, his tone implacable. 'Place your arm on mine and we'll walk to the end of the street as calmly as though we were out for an evening stroll.'

'But—'

'No "buts". We are being watched and, if I'm not mistaken, we could be attacked at any moment. It's a fine opal ring that you're wearing, and I'd not the forethought to remove this handsome timepiece from my jacket.'

'I can't leave yet. There's something I must do.' Lizzie's protest was half-hearted. His hand was still firm on her arm, and she knew he could make her do exactly what he wanted.

'Enough,' he commanded. 'Whatever your mission here, you must abandon it. Now take my arm and together we will walk very slowly away.'

She had no alternative but to do as he wished. She felt the sinews of his arm against hers, and his hand guiding her firmly towards the broader streets that ran upwards to the Citadel and eastwards to the bustling port. She'd been so focussed on her mission that meeting Justin in that unlikely place had come as a thunderbolt, and suffered an even greater shock when she realised she could be in immediate danger. The minute she'd spied that red dress, her quest had been all-consuming, and she chided herself for her foolishness in blithely ignoring the possibility of attack.

Walking together, they retraced their steps until they stood at the bottom of Mermaid Street once more, the coastal path lying ahead of them. Lizzie felt braver now, brave enough to disentangle her arm and throw out a challenge.

'Thank you for your escort, Sir Justin, though I'm unsure what right you have to determine where I walk.' She knew he had acted with good sense, but some demon in her refused to acknowledge it.

'I have no right, Miss Ingram. Simply a wish to save you from unpleasantness. You should not be walking in that area and particularly not at nightfall. There are more villains to the yard than you can shake a fist at.'

They stood facing each other, the river below them snaking its way blackly to the sea. Here and there, when the clouds parted, licks of silver danced across the water's surface but, on the far bank, the marshy plain lay flat and dark, crouching like some latent beast ready to strike. Lizzie shuddered involuntarily.

'Allow me to escort you home.'

'Thank you, but there's no need. The path is straight and I know it well.'

'I hate to contradict a lady twice in one evening, but I consider there is every need. Please take my arm again and I'll see you safely back to Brede House.'

Something in his voice made Lizzie do as he asked. Something in her wished to do it, to feel his warmth as she walked beside him, to feel the comfort of his being near.

For a long time, they kept an easy silence, until Justin suddenly asked, 'Why *did* you venture into that part of town?'

'I lost my way.'

'Really? You have a habit of losing your way, it seems.'

She was grateful the dusk hid her flushed cheeks. 'Why were *you* there?' she countered.

'I'll come clean,' he said engagingly. 'I was looking for the woman you called Rosanna.'

'So you did believe me!'

'It wasn't a case of believing or not believing. You gave me information and I felt duty bound to follow it up.'

'And what did you find?'

'A great deal—and yet at the same time, nothing.'

Lizzie's mouth hardened into a severe line. 'You're deliberately setting out to bamboozle me,' she said coldly.

'Forgive me, Miss Ingram, that's not at all my wish. I discovered that Rosanna is an intimate of several unsavoury gentlemen, who are suspected of having formed a new smuggling gang. Also that an excise man—presumably on their trail—fell to his death just before Gilbert Martin disappeared. The death was recorded as an accident by the magistrate. It's how all these things fit together that mystifies me, and makes me feel I've got nowhere. It would seem, though, that Rosanna could be the key.'

'I told you so,' Lizzie said triumphantly. 'And if you'd not stopped me this evening, I would have discovered just what she knows of your friend's whereabouts.'

'You were not lost after all?' he teased. 'But again, I must disagree. The woman you were following had melted away, disappeared into any one of those buildings. If it's some consolation, I lost sight of her at the same time as you. There are boltholes aplenty in that wretched quarter, and you would never have found her.'

They had reached the drive of Brede House and come to a halt, facing each other. 'And you might well have had your throat cut in trying,' he said.

'Aren't you being a little melodramatic?' She tried to shrug off his warning, but her voice was shaky.

In the clouded light, his expression was solemn. 'I'm the last person in the world to cry wolf, Lizzie, and when I tell you that you were in great danger, you must believe me.'

She was charmed by the way in which her pet name had unconsciously slipped from him. That's how he thinks of me, she thought— as Lizzie, not Miss Ingram.

He captured her hands in a firm grasp. 'You must never go to that part of the town again. Promise me.'

His touch was making her feel light-headed. Or was that simply fatigue? Whatever it was, Lizzie struggled to make her argument. 'Then how are we to discover the truth? I'm certain that Rosanna lodges in one of those houses. We must find her and question her.'

'*We* are not going to find her. You must leave this investigation to me.'

She pulled her hands from his. 'You are so used to giving orders, Sir Justin, that you think to command women as though they were soldiers.'

'I doubt I could command you.' His smile was laconic. 'And didn't you express a wish to be a soldier? That involves taking orders, you know.'

She tossed her head in annoyance, and had begun to walk towards the house, when he grabbed hold of her arm to detain her. 'Tell me, whatever possessed you to go searching for the woman?'

'You made me very angry when you refused to believe me,' Lizzie returned candidly. 'I decided to show you how wrong you were.'

'If I admit to my fault, will you promise to let the matter lie?'

She looked at him thoughtfully. 'It wasn't only that I wished to prove you wrong. It was an adventure as well.'

He raised his eyebrows at the confession. 'And that's important?'

'I thought it might enliven my life a little.'

'It would certainly do that. But I can't imagine that adventure can be so important that you'd deliberately walk into danger.'

'You can't imagine it because your life is one long adventure. Mine has been spent in a Seminary. Think of it—the whole of my life in a girls' school, and in Bath of all places.'

'It sounds a trifle dull.' There was sympathy in his voice, but edged with caution.

'It was abysmally dull.'

'And you were at the school because your father was serving abroad?'

Lizzie nodded.

'But had you no female relations to care for you? What of your mother?'

'My mother is dead... but you needn't worry,' she said, seeing the concern in his face. 'I was a baby at the time. I remember nothing of her.' She fingered the band on her finger. 'I've only this opal ring to remember her by. An elderly aunt looked after me until I was seven and then she died, too. Perhaps I have that effect on people.' Despite the joke, she couldn't prevent a note of wistfulness entering her voice.

'And then?' he prompted.

'And then my father placed me at the Bates Seminary for Young Girls, and there I've stayed ever since—with a few exceptions,' she said unguardedly.

'And what exceptions would they be?'

'I did try to escape.'

'Tell me.' Justin leaned back against the iron gatepost, clearly entranced.

'When I was nine, I packed my most treasured possessions in a large handkerchief and started to walk to Bristol. I must have seen an illustration of Dick Whittington. Bristol isn't that far from Bath. Though perhaps a little too far when you're nine,' she added.

He burst out laughing. 'I would imagine so. What happened?'

'I got as far as Tiverton. It's a small village where everyone seems to spend their time watching everyone else. Anyway, the local beadle caught me and wouldn't let me go until he'd made enquiries. Of course, he found out where I'd come from and I was duly returned to Miss Bates.'

'And how did she respond to your bid for freedom?'

'She was kind, I think. At least not too cross—not as cross as when I tried to join the travelling circus.' Lizzie saw the astonishment on his face. 'I didn't actually want to join them, but they were on their way to Southampton and it seemed a good opportunity.'

'Does Miss Bates by any chance sport white hair?'

'She does—but I'm sure she had it before ever I came on the scene.'

'I don't share your confidence. But why this desire to get to the coast?'

'I wanted to reach Spain,' she said simply. 'In fact, the first time I wanted to get to Canada—my father was still there after he fought in the American War. Later, it was the Peninsular. Canada or Spain, I had little idea where either country was. I just wanted to find my father.'

'And the circus was your last bid to travel abroad?'

'Oh, no.' She was abruptly downcast. 'But that's all history.' Lizzie had no intention of disclosing that particular episode. It was too shameful.

The breeze had picked up as they talked and she shivered a little from her inadequate clothing.

'Here.' He removed his jacket. 'How ungallant of me to keep you talking while you are slowly freezing to death.'

'Now that *is* melodramatic,' she said shyly, 'but thank you.'

He sheltered her with his jacket, pulling her very slightly towards him as he did so. She felt her face brushing against his chest and the sound of his heart on hers. His hands lingered on her shoulders, then stretched themselves towards temptation. She felt the lightest touch. Fingers stroking her neck and slowly tangling themselves in the strands of hair falling loose from her bonnet.

For a moment, the clouds parted and a fingernail of moon floated across the dark arc of the sky, illuminating his golden halo of hair. Everything about Justin Delacourt was beautiful, she thought. Everything. His lips were so close she could see their outline. His mouth hovered and she could almost feel its warmth on hers. She waited, her breath stilled, her body softening towards him.

'Come,' he said brusquely. 'We must get you indoors before you become any colder.'

Lizzie felt a confusion of emotions: anger, humiliation, and deep, sinking disappointment. To cover her turmoil, she turned without another word, and walked down the drive towards Brede House. He strolled silently beside her, neither of them speaking until they reached the front entrance.

'You must leave finding Rosanna to me,' he reiterated. 'I want you to promise.'

It was as though their earlier conversation had continued unbroken, as though the moment of intimacy between them had never happened. Lizzie, left empty and bewildered, nodded her agreement and handed him back his jacket.

'I'll undertake to talk to the woman as soon as I can. You can be sure I'll find out whatever she knows.' Justin's voice sounded a little too hearty.

She took a deep breath and tried to collect herself, tried to pretend his touch had been as unimportant to her as it evidently had been to him. 'That's all very well, but what if she'll not talk to you?' It was a last attempt to save her adventure.

'She will,' he said, grimly.

And Lizzie had to believe him.

Chapter Twelve

Justin woke the next morning feeling strangely unsure. Since he'd joined the army six years ago, for every day of his life and every minute of every day, he'd been certain of who he was, where he was going, and what he was doing. But today he felt decidedly uncertain.

Finding the woman, Rosanna, didn't concern him. It might not be easy, but he guessed that a few greased palms would help track her down and similar largesse might get her talking. He didn't believe Rosanna would lead him to his missing friend, but if the woman could add anything to the sketchy picture he'd so far managed to construct, it would be worth the effort. If he could pass on to the Martins the slightest piece of new information, he would feel better.

And it would demonstrate to Lizzie Ingram that he'd fulfilled his promise. She was the reason he was feeling insecure. How stupid —a girl he barely knew, a girl he'd met only days ago, and a wayward one at that. She'd thought nothing of wandering at dusk into the worst part of town and all in the name of some unspecified adventure. Her childhood exploits had made him smile, but she could have come to serious harm last night and that wasn't so amusing. It wasn't amusing either that he'd come near to kissing her. No wonder he'd woken this morning feeling decidedly uncomfortable. What had possessed him to get so close?

He was honest enough to admit that she had got under his skin from the moment he'd first seen her, but that, if anything, should have made him more circumspect. Instead, having rescued her from the danger of Rye's back streets, he'd pushed them both towards a greater danger. Even as he'd felt the touch of her breath on his cheeks, he'd sensed her body soften towards him and seen her full lips raised to his. The image returned with devastating clarity: it was enough to send a man crazy.

Is this what had happened to his dear father? Had he experienced such overwhelming desire that he'd thrown his whole life into chaos—his career, his family, his estate— in order to satisfy it? And what had been the result? Nothing but disillusion and bitterness.

Justin had grown up with his father's pain and sworn, when he was little more than a child, that he would never, ever, follow in Sir Lucien's footsteps. So what on earth had he been doing last night? A moth singed by the flame, he chided himself, unable to resist the auburn curls, the dark brown eyes, the saucy smile—above all, the smile. It was a novel experience and he didn't like it. It made him restless and impatient, when his whole concentration should be on returning Chelwood to a secure footing before he returned to his beloved regiment.

This morning he abandoned any idea of eating breakfast and went instead to the estate office. Mellors was already there and greeted him with a gloomy face.

'Beggin' your lordship's pardon, but I've been goin' through the account books fer the last few years and the estate's losin' money by the month. We don't charge proper rents, Sir Justin, that's the nub of it. There's some tenants paying what their grandfathers did. We must raise our rents, there's no help for it.'

Justin turned away from the stack of ledgers hugging the table. 'I've no wish to bleed my tenants dry, Mellors.'

'Nothin' like that, sir. Just a modest increase, I'm thinkin'. It'd be more than justified. There's farmers over Hawkshead livin' high while we can't afford to mend the stable roof.'

'So what do you suggest?' Justin's voice expressed all the weariness he felt.

Remorse was still biting deep: he felt sure his father had died from worry. Sir Lucien had died alone while his only son was a thousand miles away, happily ignorant of Chelwood's problems. If only he'd not stayed away so long, if only he'd known how burdensome the estate had become to an increasingly frail man.

'We need an inventory, sir. That'll be the ticket. An inventory detailin' the rents for every tenant, the size of their farm and the general state of repair.'

'There's no inventory?' Justin was shocked to think that he'd not even considered the possibility.

'There were one, years ago.' Mellors scratched his head. 'Leastways, I believe so. But happen it's been lost and not replaced. Seemingly, Sir Lucien wasn't one to worry too much about paperwork.'

'No, indeed. And no doubt it accounts for many of our troubles. You're right—we need to know what rents the whole estate is earning. There may even be tenants who are behind with payment, but I've no idea.'

'So I can begin work on a new schedule?' Mellors looked more hopeful than he had for days.

'Yes, make a start now. But I don't want to worry people.' Justin's brow creased into tiny furrows. 'My father may not have been good with paper, but he was respected and well-liked. I don't want that to change.'

'Reckon we should call a meetin', sir.' Mellors warmed to his theme. 'Explain our difficulties and tell them how the estate can't afford to rent out farms at sums that have been around for a hundred years or more. Prepare them for the changes, as it were.'

'I suppose we'll have to. But so far, I've had no time to meet my tenants and I'd rather it wasn't my first encounter with them. Perhaps we could offer a more sociable occasion before we talk business? A chance for me to get to know at least some of them. Years ago, in the autumn, I remember my father used to throw open the doors of Chelwood to celebrate the harvest and the year gone by.'

Justin's face shadowed for a moment. Those evenings had ceased when his mother had abandoned Chelwood for good and Sir Lucien, alone in the great house but for his young son, could no longer face people's curiosity.

'It'll be expensive,' the bailiff warned.

'You sometimes have to spend money, Mellors, to accumulate it. And it need not be wildly expensive. We're in mourning for Sir Lucien and that will preclude any extravagant entertainment—a simple buffet perhaps, a little champagne even, some pleasant music. We could invite some of the townspeople, too. Well-wishers that I've not had time to visit.'

Mellors' gloom was back, but his lugubrious expression only made Justin more determined. 'Yes,' he said with conviction, 'a meeting of town and country will be an excellent way to celebrate my father's life and mark a new beginning. Before you start on the inventory, draw up a list of those we should invite. Make sure that you include the Martins—and Mrs Croft.'

And, of course, her companion. Was that why the idea had such appeal? That he could bring Lizzie Ingram to Chelwood again?

There was a very good reason, Justin assured himself, a perfectly legitimate reason, for the evening's entertainment. And naturally he couldn't omit Henrietta Croft from the guest list. And where Mrs Croft came, so did Miss Ingram. It was really quite simple. Having settled the matter to his satisfaction, he turned to the sheaf of papers his architect had left him for the renovation of the west wing. One day, he might even have the money to carry out the ambitious plans.

~

The Chelwood celebration was to be held the following Friday evening and Justin was eager for the day to arrive. More eager than he'd ever been when his father had presided over similar gatherings. He checked the arrangements constantly. Had Mellors booked the string quartet travelling all the way from Canterbury? Had Cook ordered additional titbits from the most prestigious caterer in Tunbridge Wells? Would his butler bring up as much champagne from the cellar as the sideboard would hold? His staff tried to smile through the barrage of commands, though with increasing difficulty, and it was only a sudden remembrance on his part that saved an outright rebellion. He must go to Rye—he had a woman to find! And he needed to find her before Friday evening.

As Justin had suspected, it took only a short time and several sovereigns before he was face-to-face with Rosanna, though as soon as he met the woman, he knew he'd not need to pay her to talk. Rosanna would always be happy to speak to a gentleman, more than happy to speak to a good-looking gentleman, who bore a military title and dressed in expensive superfine. She was beautiful, Justin thought, if you liked that kind of ripeness, and he could well understand that her sultry attractions might render men malleable clay.

She tried flirting with him, subtly at first and, when he proved unresponsive, more overtly. Justin had no intention of succumbing to her charms: he'd sought her out only because he had questions he needed answering. But he was to be disappointed.

Yes, she had known Gilbert Martin, though only as an acquaintance. He'd been friendly with the excise man—the man who'd so tragically fallen to his death. It was all very sad. The last time Rosanna had seen Mr Martin had been a chance meeting in the market place, but the encounter had been unremarkable and she remembered nothing much about it. Like everyone else in the town, she'd been shocked to hear of his friend's disappearance, but had no idea what might have become of him.

Patiently, Justin put the same questions to her several times, but her response was always the same, her eyes unwavering, looking frankly into his. He would get no further, he could see, and could do nothing more but bid her a courteous farewell and walk away. He doubted she knew anything but, beneath her seductive exterior, he sensed a sharp mind at work and, if she did possess information, she was not about to disgorge it. Lizzie would not be pleased to find the trail had gone cold, but there was little more he could do.

Chapter Thirteen

Mellors had been commanded to deliver invitations for the Friday entertainment to the outlying farmers on the estate, while Justin had undertaken to call on the townspeople who were to be invited. Brede House was next on his list, and he found Mrs Croft sitting quietly in her armchair, her book cast aside.

'How good to see you, Justin, and thank you for your kind invitation. A gathering to celebrate Lucien and Chelwood? It seems most fitting.'

'So you'll come?' He wished he didn't feel so anxious to hear her reply.

'I would love to, my dear, but these last few weeks I've been feeling my age—I'm getting old, there's no denying it—and I would find an evening party a little too tiring.'

Justin could not quite conceal his disappointment and she said quickly, 'I'm sure that Elizabeth would be happy to be my representative. She is such a lively young woman and she must find this place a little slow. But perhaps I've spoken out of turn and you were not intending to invite her?'

'I couldn't invite you without your companion,' Justin said gallantly, 'but will Miss Ingram be happy to leave you and come alone?'

'I am well enough on my own. In fact, I enjoy the solitude. Another sign of old age, I fear. But Elizabeth can take Hester for company, if you're happy to send your carriage for them both.'

'Naturally, I'd be delighted to send Perkins.'

'Good,' Henrietta said, surprisingly brisk. 'You'll need to ask Elizabeth yourself, of course. I believe you'll find her walking in the cove. She has been working very hard this morning, taking down and rearranging an entire wall of books for me, but she is an indefatigable walker.'

His smile was wry. 'So I've noticed.'

Justin walked through the long, narrow garden that separated Brede House from the river. The leaves had turned russet, small heaps of them scattered across the pathway, gathered there by the wind that funnelled upstream from the Channel. Picking his way through the crackling fronds, he passed the stone folly that overlooked the river—it had been built years ago by a sailor nostalgic for the sea—and reached the wicket gate that led directly to the water.

Unhooking the gate, he scrambled down the worn, wooden steps to the small cove lying sheltered beneath the cliff. He remembered playing here with Gil many years ago. The cliff was riddled with caves and there'd been a game of dare they'd played for the whole of one long summer—who could travel furthest through the caves and towards the sea before the tide turned. Some of the caves had been so low and narrow, they'd had to wriggle their way through, while others were wide caverns, stunning in their immensity.

Sometimes, they'd travelled so far that they 'd almost reached the sea before the sound in their ears became a warning to turn back. One day, they'd been so intent on exploring that they'd not heard the sound of waves drawing near until their boots were suddenly leaking water. They'd ran and wriggled their way back through the chain of caves, terror in their hearts, and arrived at the cove with the river already lapping at their feet. They'd never played that game again, Justin reflected.

Lizzie was on the shingle beach, standing by the river's edge. The rocky outcrops on either side of the cove glinted in the late autumn sun and she'd raised her hand to shade her eyes as she looked across the quick flowing river to the marsh beyond, almost black in this newly intense light. Beneath her shawl, she was wearing a simple muslin dress that hugged itself tight to her trim figure, and her hair this morning hung free around her shoulders. His heart did a small flip. He wanted to reach out and touch that hair, to feel his hands tangle again in the softness of those auburn curls.

He cleared his throat and she looked around, surprise on her face. 'Forgive me, Miss Ingram, I'd not meant to startle you.'

'You may startle me at will.' She smiled at him, a warm, welcoming smile, and he felt again that small insistent pulse. 'You have news for me, Sir Justin?'

'*Some* news,' he said cautiously. 'But first, tell me how you've been since your adventure. I feared you might have caught cold from our evening walk.'

She laughed aloud. 'You must think me a very weak creature.'

'I'm glad to hear you've taken no hurt—I'm hoping you'll be willing to brave the night air once more. I'm hosting a small celebration at Chelwood this Friday evening and wished for both yours and Mrs Croft's attendance. She tells me, though, that she no longer feels able to manage a late entertainment. Perhaps I might persuade you to come alone?'

'You wish me to come to your party?' Lizzie sounded surprised.

'It's not precisely a party. A small gathering only. To celebrate the end of the harvest and the year that's passed. I've invited a number of my tenants and a few townspeople and local gentry. For many years, my father hosted a similar event—and I felt it right to reinstate the tradition.'

'It seems a thoughtful way to honour Sir Lucien.'

It warmed Justin that she'd recognised the deeper meaning of his gesture.

'He was a good man and much admired,' he said, staring fixedly at the fast flowing river. 'He deserved a longer life.'

'You loved your father greatly, I think.'

'How could I not? He was my rock, the dearest person to me in the whole world.'

'People don't always love their parents.' Lizzie appeared

to hesitate. 'I imagine your feelings for your mother are quite different.'

He was taken aback by her perception and a tinge of colour stole into his tanned cheeks. 'You are frank, Miss Ingram. Is my distaste so very evident?'

'I wore her dress at Chelwood,' she reminded him, 'and your face told its own story.'

Justin allowed himself a small sigh. 'It's true my mother spread little joy. She was not a happy woman.'

Lizzie gave him a quick glance before venturing to ask, 'Has she died?'

'As good as—dead to Chelwood, at least. She left the house fourteen years ago and never returned.' Except once, he reflected, but he'd not think of that.

'Where did she go?'

'Everywhere and nowhere. Mostly London, living with whoever was her latest... friend.'

Lizzie's eyebrows shot up at this matter-of fact-statement.

'You'll hear the stories soon enough,' he continued. 'I'm surprised you haven't already. It speaks volumes for Mrs Croft's discretion!'

'All Mrs Croft ever told me was that your father was forced to give up soldiering. If I remember rightly, her words were severe: *Sir Lucien was harangued into submission by that woman.* I think for the moment she'd forgotten she was talking aloud.'

His lips twisted. 'Mrs Croft spoke truly. My mother always got her way.'

The tide was coming in now and pushing the river

further up the deep channel it had furrowed over centuries. Lizzie's slippers were in grave danger of drowning and she moved quickly back from the water's edge to perch herself on one of the many rocks that enclosed the small bay. Patting its warm, flat surface, she gestured to him to take a seat beside her, her curls glinting in a sun that had settled low in the sky. A few stray tendrils of hair had blown across her cheek and Justin itched to smooth them back into place. Somehow he forced himself to keep his hands locked against the rock's hard surface.

'You've not called on your mother since Sir Lucien's death?'

'Why would I wish to? I've made it my business to avoid her and the rackety set she runs with.' Hardly to be wondered at, he thought, after the most humiliating experience of his life. 'In truth, I rarely think of her. And at the risk of sounding callous, over the past few years my life has been so crowded it's been easy to forget she was ever my mother.'

Lizzie nibbled at her lip. 'You've been in Spain a long time and involved in the bloodiest of conflicts, but now that you're in England...'

'It makes little difference. I'm determined my mother has no further opportunity to spread discord. She is the one person who will not be attending the celebration! The people here know the worst of my family and won't speak of her.'

Lizzie drew a slow circle on the rock with her finger. 'You might find the party more discordant than you expect.'

He looked slightly bemused and she murmured, 'You've invited *me* to Chelwood.'

For a moment, he was caught unawares. He wouldn't find it comfortable to have her beneath his roof, it was true. On the contrary, it would be delightfully uncomfortable. And though he should be fighting such thoughts with every ounce of his will, he couldn't but relish the feeling. Lizzie was looking quizzical, waiting for him to speak. Please God, he'd not betrayed his thoughts.

'I'll stand out like a sore thumb among the wealthy farmers and the local gentry,' she explained. 'I'm a servant, Sir Justin.'

So that's what she had meant!

'You're a companion and that is very different,' he countered.

She was insistent. 'For many, a companion is synonymous with a servant.'

'Perhaps,' he had to concede, 'but for a very few only. Far more will welcome your being there. The Martins, for instance. I'm on my way now to Five Oaks with their invitation.'

'You have news for them?' Lizzie's eyes sparkled, turning almost amber. Her eagerness to carry on the adventure was a delight and he hated that he must disappoint her.

'News that is no news, in fact. I hope, though, they'll welcome the little I have discovered.'

'You've found Rosanna!' Her cheeks were flaming with pleasure and Justin couldn't stop looking at her. 'You've found Rosanna?' Lizzie repeated a little unsurely.

With a huge effort, he pulled his thoughts back to the business in hand. 'I did find her and spoke to her, but...' his strong fingers reached out and covered Lizzie's hand, '...but I fear I discovered little. Rosanna knows nothing of Gil's disappearance. She admits to knowing him, but only very slightly. He was a pleasant gentleman, she said, and they would exchange a few words when they met, but that was all. The last time she saw him was on market day when she bumped into him by chance. They spoke for just a few minutes, and she never saw him again.'

Lizzie was quick to disentangle her hand, jumping abruptly to her feet. She stood facing him and her expression was scornful. 'And you believed her?'

'I must believe her.' Justin had got to his feet, too. 'I can see no reason for the woman to lie. And she confirmed something that James Martin had already hinted at—that Gil had made a friend of the excise man who died, and that the man's death had upset him greatly. She wondered if Gil had been affected so badly that his disappearance was the result.'

'So although she knew your friend only slightly, Rosanna could discern when he was greatly upset and likely to fall into a megrim?'

He felt irritated at Lizzie's evident distrust. 'I imagine the excise man dying so brutally was a topic of conversation in the town for some time. And Rosanna could have exchanged words about it with Gil. Perhaps he told her how upset he was. He was never a person who could hide his feelings.'

Lizzie turned away from him, her shoulders hunched angrily.

'Why can't you accept what she says? I put the same questions to her two or three times and always received the same answer.'

She was facing him again, looking straight into his eyes, her expression unwavering. 'Rosanna is lying. I can't believe you were taken in by her.'

'Why are you so sure she is lying? I'm a good judge of character, Miss Ingram, and I can assure you I was not taken in by her.'

'We're not talking of character here. We're talking of a beautiful woman, who no doubt fluttered her eyelashes, smiled sweetly, and spoke softly.'

Justin flushed angrily. 'That doesn't necessarily suggest she is a liar.'

'It does suggest, though, that you've been duped.'

'I resent that accusation.'

He did not take kindly to having his word challenged and felt an overwhelming impulse to shake the truth into her. He had no interest in Rosanna, seductive as she was. He had no interest in any woman. No, that was no longer true. He *should* have no interest in any woman, he corrected himself. He couldn't be completely certain that Rosanna had told him the truth but, with no other option, he must believe she'd spoken in good faith.

'Resent it by all means, but you are badly misled,' Lizzie declared. 'Rosanna has wound you round her small finger, as she does all the men of the town. She has told you a pack of lies. Of course, she knows more than she's saying, but you were too besotted to make her tell you. She has deceived you.'

'You are entitled to your opinion.' His voice was sharp with suppressed anger. 'But I've done what I promised and can do no more.'

'You disappoint me, Sir Justin. I had thought you a more resourceful man.'

He would have liked to grab her there and then and show her just how resourceful he could be, but he had himself under control now, and his tone was deliberately measured. 'I'm sorry to have disappointed you, Miss Ingram, but I trust you'll still feel able to come to Chelwood on Friday. I'm happy to send my carriage for you.'

'Please don't concern yourself,' Lizzie said icily. 'If I wish, I am quite able to get to Chelwood by myself.'

His response matched hers in rancour. 'Naturally, you are. How stupid of me! For the moment, I had forgotten your last visit.'

And with that, he turned on his heel and, without another word, strode towards the wooden steps.

Chapter Fourteen

Lizzie stared sightlessly at the water eddying in small circles at the riverbank's edge. She was angry and disappointed. Disillusioned, too. Justin Delacourt had been blind to the woman's obvious duplicity. He'd allowed himself to be duped! Within minutes of meeting Rosanna, he'd succumbed to the woman's flattery; at the first flutter of her eyelashes, he'd capitulated. He was no more subtle than that. No more reliable than any soldier Lizzie had ever met, no more dependable than the father who'd abandoned her. Had she really allowed herself to think that, just possibly, she'd found a man who measured up to her dreams? A man who was daring and brave, yet steadfast and trustworthy, too? If so, she'd been more foolish than she'd believed was possible.

She turned to make her way back to Brede House, feeling out of sympathy with the whole world, and needing to walk off the anger ripping through her. A long, long walk, she thought. But she couldn't leave the house, not when Mrs Croft was in her room and taking a late afternoon nap. When the old lady woke, she would need Lizzie's services.

But she was far too restless to take up a book or settle to her drawing, yet somehow she had to relieve her stifled feelings, or she'd burst. She would attack the parlour! Hester had cleaned it that very morning, but that seemed not to matter. Grabbing a cloth and feather duster, Lizzie began ruthlessly to scour and polish the furniture. With every vigorous lunge, she imagined her fists to be pounding a row of military chests, with every swish of the feather duster, she was decapitating a line of soldiers. The more she cleaned, the more furious her movements, so that she became a whirl of activity filling the small room. Several ornaments wobbled beneath her hand and nearly fell from the mantelshelf, but when she snatched up the tray left from Mrs Croft's nuncheon, the china slid dangerously to one side and her employer's favourite teapot toppled down onto unyielding floorboards, where it broke into small pieces.

Lizzie was brought to a sudden halt, and was standing aghast at the carnage when Mrs Croft came slowly into the room.

The old lady blinked, surprised into stating the obvious. 'You have had an accident, my dear.'

'I'm so sorry, Mrs Croft. I thought to get the parlour sparkling for you, and look what I've done.'

'Accidents always happen, my dear. I'm sure you were trying to help.' Lizzie had the grace to feel ashamed. 'Get Hester to clear the pieces before we sit down, will you?'

'There's no need to bother Hester. I can easily clear it myself.' She began to shovel the sad fragments into the dustpan. 'I know you loved this teapot, Mrs Croft, and I promise to replace it as soon as I can. If you can tell me where it came from?' Lizzie could only hope it was not an heirloom or so expensive that it was beyond her purse.

'You mustn't worry yourself, Elizabeth. The pot is of no value. I believe I bought it last year from a stall in the market. It has been a good pourer, but I'm sure I must have a dozen other teapots in the cupboard.'

'Maybe, but this one was your favourite and you must allow me to buy you another,' Lizzie said firmly. 'Tomorrow is market day and, if you'll excuse me for just an hour, I'll get there bright and early and return with an exact match!'

~

She was in the town before ten o'clock the next morning, still feeling shamefaced at her outburst. What was it about Justin Delacourt that made her so angry? It was perhaps better not to question herself too deeply, since she had an uneasy suspicion that she wouldn't like the answer. She must simply put him out of her mind, she decided. He was not the man on whom to pin her dreams. There never would be a dream man, and Miss Bates was probably right when she'd advised Lizzie to think sensibly about the future and settle for a secure life with someone she could depend on.

The market was already in full swing as she turned the corner of West Street and found herself outside the white frontage of the George, the oldest coaching inn in Rye. Farmers had gathered inside to do business, and a chatter of conversation filtered through the open windows and onto the street. Lizzie hurried past, her eyes fixed on the line of stalls stretching into the distance, trying to locate where she might begin to look for china.

She was amazed at the bounty on display. Dozens of wooden trestles groaned with every conceivable fruit and vegetable, and several stalls outside the baker's shop sported unsteady piles of flat breads, selling for a bargain price. And everywhere mounds of clothes: men's, women's, children's, of every hue and style, tumbled together and spread on linen sheets to protect them from the dirt and damp of the cobbles.

The smell of roasting meat floated in the air and, mixed with that of sweetmeats, making Lizzie feel slightly nauseous. Several people were already eating, she noticed, seated on upturned barrels or using them as makeshift tables.

The market snaked right into Lion Street and she followed the line of stalls until, at last, at the quieter end of the thoroughfare, she came to those displaying china. Wandering slowly from stall to stall, she picked a cup up here, a saucer and plate there, looking for the elusive pot. There were numerous teapots certainly, but none that seemed a match for the one she'd so carelessly destroyed.

She turned and wandered back the way she'd come, passing on the opposite side a street artist, perched precariously on a folding stool. The man was vociferous in his invitation to the crowd to have their likeness drawn, but Lizzie refused his offer. She could draw her own likeness if she had a mind. In pausing to walk around his seated figure, though, she discovered a stall she hadn't seen before, half-hidden by the artist's solid form. She noticed the pot immediately and pounced. It was the twin of the one she'd broken.

Lizzie was about to ask its price from the stallholder, when a small ripple ran through the crowd. Almost a frisson of nervousness. The buzz of chatter dwindled to nothing and the stallholder's attention was lost. He was no longer looking at Lizzie, but in the direction from where she'd come. She followed his glance and her eyes opened wide.

It was Rosanna, her voluptuous curves gowned this morning in bright emerald silk, and her ample bosom sporting a neckline so low she was almost unclothed. The dress was downright indecent, Lizzie thought. No wonder the crowd was holding its breath.

But it was the man with Rosanna that took all of Lizzie's attention—one of the group she'd spied days ago at the window of the Mermaid Inn. The tow-headed man, the man with a face that spoke wickedness. Rosanna was clinging to him, gazing dotingly into his eyes, occasionally lifting her head to press her lips against his. People instantly made way for the couple, as arm in arm they strolled leisurely along the pavement towards the High Street, looking neither to left nor right. Reaching the bottom of Lion Street, they disappeared from sight, and an audible sigh flowed through the crowd. A communal gasp as everyone once more began to breathe easily.

Lizzie turned to the stall holder. 'Who was that?'

'Them's folk yer don't want to know, miss.'

'Everyone else seems to know them.'

'That woman ain't fit for decent society.' The man spat disparagingly onto the cobbles.

'And the man?' Lizzie persevered.

The stall holder lowered his voice. ''e's a bad lot, a very bad lot. Name of Thomas Chapman. That's all yer need to know.'

It meant nothing to Lizzie. 'Is the name of Chapman important then?'

'You're a furriner, I take it. You keep clear of all the Chapmans, believe you me. Them's a bad lot,' he repeated.

'But how?'

'You're a persistent one, ain't you, missy. That man's grandfather was George Chapman, *the* George Chapman, but no doubt yer never heard of 'im?'

'No,' she said, bewildered.

His voice dropped again, almost to a whisper. 'Gibbeted he were, on Hurst Green.'

Lizzie stared.

'Shocked yer, 'aven't I? But he were part of the worst gang ever. Notorious they were. The Hawkhurst Gang—a bloodthirsty lot, cruel and violent. They terrorised this part o' the world fer years and George, well 'e murdered a revenue officer who were doing 'is duty. Then 'e paid the price.' His tone expressed satisfaction.

'So George Chapman was a smuggler?'

'Told yer, didn't I? One o' the Hawkhurst gang.'

'And this man?'

The stall holder spat again. 'Like father, like son. Or in this case, like grandfather.'

'Thomas Chapman is a smuggler!'

The man hastily shushed her and looked warily around. 'Never say that. Remember, them's that arsks no questions ain't told no lie—*watch the wall, my darling, while the Gentlemen go by!*'

'The Gentlemen are smugglers? But I understood there was no smuggling here. Not any longer.' She remembered what Justin had told her. 'There are Preventives along the coast, isn't that right?'

The man snorted. 'What use are a few Preventives against that band of cut throats? There are two revenue cutters.' He held up his fingers. 'Two between 'ere and Poole! Last week *The Stag* were 'ere and we won't see that ship again for nigh on a month. Plenty of time for the mice to play, wouldn't you say?'

'But there are revenue men on shore. Excise men? I heard there was one based in Rye until a short time ago.'

A frightened look crossed the man's face and he hastily took the teapot from Lizzie's hand, wrapping it in string and brown paper. She wanted to ask him more, ask what he knew of the dead excise man, but his face told her he would say nothing. He might even refuse to serve her if she persisted in her questions and send her away empty-handed. She passed over the coins he'd asked for and turned for home.

Her mind was teeming. From the first time Lizzie had set eyes on Thomas Chapman, she'd known he was bad through and through. Every nerve in her body had told her so. And now it appeared that Rosanna was a friend of his—far more than a friend by the look of it. She was no longer simply the woman who brought the men their beer at the Mermaid Inn. She was Thomas Chapman's lover. She must know what happened to the excise man, Lizzie thought and, more to the point, she *must* know what had happened to Gilbert Martin.

But what was Justin's friend doing with a woman, who so evidently was another man's lover? Had he not known of the relationship? He couldn't have done, and Rosanna had taken him for a fool. It was the only explanation. Gil Martin was a wealthy young man and ripe for the plucking. No doubt she'd played him cleverly, encouraged him in his infatuation to shower her with gifts, and expensive gifts at that. She would get precious few from Thomas, Lizzie was sure. But what a tangle! Rosanna was in thrall to the evil Thomas while Gilbert was in thrall to her.

Lizzie walked swiftly back to Brede House feeling vindicated. She'd been right and Justin Delacourt had been wrong. But it hardly mattered now. It appeared his friend had fallen into the clutches of a desperate gang of men and, wherever Gilbert Martin was, he needed rescue. Justin must be told. At the moment, he knew nothing of Rosanna's connection to this terrible gang, and why would he? He'd been abroad for years and, since his return to Rye, his days had been spent at Chelwood. As for servants' gossip, he was not the man to listen to it.

Justin needed to know what she'd just discovered—the

happiness of the Martin family depended on it—but how was she to alert him to the danger his friend faced? After their quarrel, he was unlikely to visit Brede House in the near future. She could write to him, telling him what she'd found, but would he even read her letter? They were hardly on speaking terms, after all. And, if he did read the letter, would he believe her? Past experience was not encouraging. But, if Gilbert were to be saved, Lizzie had to urge on Justin the need to act immediately. Despite promising herself she would keep away, she must go to Chelwood, she decided. There was no other option.

Chapter Fifteen

'I hope you'll feel able to go to Sir Justin's entertainment, my dear.' Her employer fixed Lizzie with an anxious gaze, as the young girl poked the fire into a comforting warmth. 'Hester can accompany you, so you'll not be travelling alone.'

Mrs Croft was settled for the evening in her favourite chair, but something was marring her contentment, Lizzie could see. She had been speaking of Chelwood, as she often did, though always in relation to Sir Lucien, her mind taking pleasure in wandering the byways of the past. It saddened Lizzie to see the way the old lady's world had narrowed so drastically with age, and the ability to look forward had been overtaken by the enjoyment of looking back.

'I would like to go to Chelwood, Mrs Croft.' Lizzie excused herself the small, white lie.

Her employer's face cleared. 'That's excellent news, Elizabeth. I was worried you had decided not to attend, and I feel that good manners require at least one of us to be there.'

'It's my gown that's been the problem,' Lizzie said. Another white lie. 'It's sure to be a grand affair, despite Sir Justin being in mourning. I'm concerned that the only dress I have that's at all suitable for an evening party will look shabby in such a gathering.'

The old lady leant forward, her face warm and her eyes alert. 'If that's your only concern, I may be able to help you.'

Lizzie looked puzzled. Was Mrs Croft about to double her wages? Somehow she didn't think so. And surely she couldn't be suggesting that she donated one of her own gowns? Lizzie was a fine needlewoman, but the stiff taffetas and voluminous skirts of the old lady's generation would defeat even her dexterity.

'My granddaughter—' Mrs Croft broke off, finding it difficult to continue.

Lizzie was astonished. She'd not known there was a granddaughter or even that Mrs Croft had once been married. Really, she'd hardly considered the matter. And, if she had, she would have imagined the 'Mrs' to be a simple courtesy title, since Henrietta had always appeared to her a natural spinster.

'I had a granddaughter,' the old lady tried again. She paused for a moment, and with an effort gathered herself together. 'She was most fashionable in her time, you know. My dear Susanna.'

Her eyes filled with unshed tears and she hurried to finish what she wished to say. 'Of course, the gowns Susanna left are no longer fashionable, but their materials are not so very different from those young women wear today, and they have maintained their colour and texture extremely well. I know you to be most adept with a needle, so if you'd care to take a look…'

Lizzie was touched. Mrs Croft had lost a loved grandchild, but borne her sorrow in silence. She would like to have asked what unkind fate had destroyed the old lady's happiness, would liked to have expressed her sympathy, but she knew instinctively it would not be welcome. Instead, she said in her most practical tone, 'That's most kind of you, Mrs Croft. I would love to look.'

'Then you must go to the room at the very end of the corridor in which you have your bedroom. There you'll find a large wardrobe. It's unlocked. You may take what you wish.'

Lizzie thanked her profusely and made haste upstairs. If she was to remake a dress for tomorrow evening, she would have to work swiftly. The oak wardrobe was exactly where Mrs Croft had directed. A strong smell of rose petals flooded the room as she opened the door. Faced with a row of gowns, all carefully protected by linen covers, she took them down one by one, and ran a practised eye over them.

As the old lady had promised, they were beautifully cut, though now unfashionable. The materials, though, were lustrous. She guessed that Susanna must have possessed much the same colouring as herself, since virtually every dress was a perfect complement for her hair and complexion. At the bottom of the cupboard, she found a large bag spilling over with lace trimmings and spools of ribbon. The wardrobe was a treasure trove.

After a good thirty minutes of unpacking and repacking, Lizzie had chosen her gown. It was a shimmering eau-de-nil silk, with a matching lace trim at the hem. She found a spool of deeper green ribbon that she could fashion into love knots as trimming for the waist and sleeves. It was fortunate that Susanna appeared to have been a good deal taller than her, allowing Lizzie to lift the waist and cut the skirt to a much narrower shape. The puff sleeves and bodice required no alteration.

The gown must have been chosen at a time when the stiff skirts and petticoats of an earlier age were starting to be replaced by the freedom of current fashions. Once the skirt was cut to size, there would be sufficient material left to fashion a matching reticule. Excitedly, Lizzie bore her trophies to the parlour wishing to thank her benefactress, but Mrs Croft was already slumbering by the fire and Lizzie thought it wrong to disturb her: the sight of the dress might provoke painful memories.

Leaving her employer to sleep, she made her way to the kitchen where a large scrubbed wooden table was perfect for the intricate cutting she must do. She found Hester drowsing by the open stove and a sudden, odd wave of impatience took hold of her. What was she doing here, a young girl in a house of sleeping women? Once she'd settled this business with Justin Delacourt, Lizzie told herself, she must take hold of her life and drift no longer.

With an impetuous sweep, she cleared the table, rousing Hester as she did. The maid blinked herself awake and, intrigued by Lizzie's plans for the dress, found a new store of energy. She set to work with vigour, helping to unpick the seams, fashion the love knots and finally drape yards of silk over Lizzie and pin the gown to exactly the right shape.

'The dress will look some lovely, miss,' she opined, 'once you've done all the fancy stitching.'

'I hope so or I'll have wasted some very expensive material! Mrs Croft's granddaughter had excellent taste, even though her dresses are a little dated now.'

'She did that, miss. A lovely lady was Miss Susanna.'

'She never married then?'

'Bless you no. She were too sickly ever to marry. Her mother died giving birth and it was two to one the baby would follow. But the little mite survived—just. And it were thanks to her grandmother's care.'

'What happened to her father?' It was the inevitable question for Lizzie.

'He disappeared, thinking both his wife and child had perished. Mrs Croft sent looking for him, but he never came back.'

'So the baby lived here?'

'All her life. She was the mistress's angel. So close they were.'

'But she was always sickly, you say. Poor Mrs Croft to lose her so young.'

'She were sickly it's true, but if it hadn't been for that man...'

'What man?'

'We don't talk about it, miss, not in this house.'

'You have just this minute talked about it.' Lizzie had pricked her finger from inattention and she sounded tart. 'Who was he?'

'Nobody knew. He were a stranger. Appeared one evening in the garden. Scared the daylights out of Miss Susanna when she went to call the cat. She doted on that cat.'

'But how could that have led to her death? Did the man attack her?'

'Not exactly. But her heart was weak and seemingly when he jumped out at her in the dark, it faltered and then stopped.'

'How very dreadful. And she didn't live to identify him?'

'All Miss Susanna could whisper was *a man*. I heard her myself, since I'd run out into the garden when I heard a scream. *A man*, she said, *a man* and *behind me*.'

'And was there no investigation?'

'There were nothing to investigate, miss. Just a few words from a dying girl who everyone knew to be sick.'

Lizzie thought it the saddest story she'd ever heard and her respect for Mrs Croft rose. To lose your daughter in childbirth was dreadful, but then to lose the child you'd raised and loved in her stead was truly terrible. Lizzie determined she would make this dress a garment of which Miss Susanna could be proud, sewing furiously for hours, until by midnight she was ready to try on a rough *toile*. Both women held their breath as Hester slipped the gown over Lizzie's shoulders and stood back. The dress was a perfect fit.

~

She worked late into the night and for most of the next day, but by seven o'clock that evening she was dressed in a fashionable new gown and ready to leave. Since she'd refused the ride in Justin's carriage, it would take them at least an hour to walk to Chelwood Hall. Hester had tried to persuade her to retract her decision, but she'd been resolute in refusing. She was no longer angry, but felt a heavy disillusion. To think that Justin Delacourt had been led by the nose—and by such a woman! Lizzie was going to Chelwood only because she had compelling news, she told herself, and she was doing it for the Martins' sake, not for Justin's.

Nevertheless, she couldn't help but feel a tremor of excitement. This was the first party she had attended in Rye, indeed the first party she'd attended alone and without the eagle eye of Miss Bates watching her every move. The first time, too, that she'd dressed just as she wished.

While she waited for Hester to collect her cloak from the scullery, Lizzie studied her image in the mirror, anxious that no crease marred her gown and no smudge spoilt her complexion. She felt a quiet satisfaction: she would be the equal of any woman there. The maid had helped tame her luxuriant curls into the popular Roman style and glistening ringlets now cascaded from a carefully arranged topknot. A string of pearls wound its way in and out of the ringlets and Lizzie had artfully feathered a few stray tendrils of hair to frame the perfect oval of her face. The slightest blush of rouge to her cheeks—Miss Bates would certainly not have approved—and a smear of rose salve to her lips, completed her toilette.

She twisted the opal ring on her finger, thinking of the mother she'd never known, and hoping *she* would have approved and thought her daughter beautiful.

'You look lovely, miss. A real picture!' Hester seemed as delighted as Lizzie with the result of their hard work.

She wasn't delighted, however, with the tramp along country roads. At this hour of the day, there was no possibility of taking the ferry which would have shortened the journey considerably. From the outset, Lizzie set a spanking pace, with the maid dawdling a little in the rear. She'd ignored Hester's advice that she wear boots until they reached the Hall and had donned the flimsiest of evening slippers. After half a mile, the slippers—so beautiful, so elegant—began to pinch, and gradually grew more and more painful. By the time they had covered another mile, Lizzie could barely walk.

'There now, miss, didn't I tell you? We'll never get to Chelwood at this rate,' Hester scolded.

'We will.' Lizzie's tone admitted no argument. 'And why are *you* complaining—you have boots to walk in.'

'And whose fault is that,' Hester muttered. 'If we ever get there, it will be a miracle and we'll be so dirty, we won't be worth setting eyes on.'

Their progress was becoming slower by the minute. The lane they were following was heavily used by farmers' vehicles and they were forced to zigzag from hedge to hedge in an effort to avoid the worst potholes and, here and there, patches of deep mud. When a cart coming from the opposite direction rounded the bend a little too quickly, they found themselves stranded in the middle of the track, with a horse thundering down on them.

The driver managed to bring the beast to a sudden halt, missing them by a whisker.

'It's Mr Jefferson, ' Hester exclaimed, her bonnet knocked slightly askew.

'Well, what have we here?' The farmer's face broke into a wide smile. 'Two damsels in distress!'

Lizzie's lips tightened and she started to walk on, but was stopped by Hester clamping a fierce hand on her arm. 'We're in a little trouble, Mr Jefferson. The carriage we ordered never came and, as you see, we've been left to walk in our party clothes.'

Lizzie gaped at the maid's dishonesty, but before she could contradict her, Mr Jefferson had jumped down from his box and was moving bales of hay around in the back of the open wagon.

'We can't have that, can we, me dears?' he said over his shoulder.

In a few minutes, he'd arranged the cart to his satisfaction and held out his hand to Lizzie. 'There now, ladies, your carriage awaits. Seats fit for a queen, I swear. And where might you be wanting to go?'

'Chelwood Hall, please,' Hester said quickly, before Lizzie had time to protest.

The farmer propelled Lizzie upwards into the wagon and onto the nearest hay bale where she sat fuming at her own stupidity. Why on earth had she insisted on wearing the slippers? Now she must suffer the indignity of travelling in a hay cart. Hester had no such qualms. Smiling contentedly, she took a seat beside Lizzie as the cart lurched forward and once more began its swaying progress. In less than half an hour they were clip-clopping up the drive to the entrance of Chelwood Hall.

As they drew near, Lizzie could see the house ablaze with light and hear the sounds of distant music, its faint ripples escaping into the night. She felt herself freeze. She'd wanted to bid the cart farewell before anyone caught sight of her, but if she could hear music singing through the air... the mansion's huge oak front door must be wide open!

It was, and standing there, Justin Delacourt himself. Naturally, he would be, she thought bitterly. He'd evidently positioned himself to greet his guests as their carriages pulled to a halt, but he would not have been expecting such an arrival. Lizzie was mortified.

She tried not to look at his splendid figure walking towards her, and failed. He was dressed in the deep blue jacket of the dragoons, gold buttons gleaming, and a white silk sash crossing his chest. Tight grey pantaloons clung to a pair of muscular legs, and on his feet the lightest of evening slippers. For a moment, the image of another uniformed soldier floated across her vision and Lizzie felt a great lump rising in her throat.

But not for long. She looked again at the fine, sensitive face and her father was forgotten. A golden halo of hair and a pair of smiling eyes were quickening her heart and sending her stomach twisting and turning in an alarming fashion.

Justin came level with the cart and she was sure he must be struggling to keep his face straight, but barely a quiver ruffled his polished tone. 'Welcome to Chelwood, Miss Ingram.'

He helped her down from the vehicle, carefully brushing the stray straws from her cloak. 'I'm delighted you've been able to attend our small affair. You must come in and meet my other guests.' He turned back to the maid. 'Hester, you'll find a ready welcome in the kitchen, I believe.'

Hester bobbed a curtsy and Lizzie, unable to say a word, found herself steered expertly towards the open door and the flagged hallway.

Chapter Sixteen

'You must have had an uncomfortable ride, Miss Ingram. I wish you had sent a message. My carriage was entirely at your disposal.'

'Thank you. You're most kind, but really how I travel is of little account.'

She was an extraordinary girl, Justin thought. Most women would have been close to hysterics if they'd been discovered in such a predicament, but she was brushing the matter aside as though arriving on a hay cart was a daily occurrence.

He tried once more to break the sheet of ice wedged between them. 'I hope you weren't too cold. We're well into autumn now and the evening air has a chill.'

'On the contrary, I found it most invigorating.'

Her tone remained curt and he knew himself unforgiven. 'Here, let me take your cloak. One of the footmen can banish any lingering straw.'

Lizzie glared at him, but allowed him to slip the cloak from her shoulders and hand it to a waiting servant. He saw her snatch a quick glance at the long, ornate mirror that hung to the right of the door and give a small smile. Relief that her beautiful silk gown had come to no harm perhaps, and that she still presented a creditable appearance?

To Justin, she was more than creditable. He stood behind her, the two of them gazing at her reflection in the mirror. She looked lovely, utterly lovely. The eau-de-nil silk of her dress shone lustrously and skimmed her body in the most enticing fashion, setting off to perfection the soft cream of her skin. Beneath the light of burning candles, her chestnut ringlets flashed sparks of fire, enough to warm a man's body through and through, Justin thought.

He must stop right there. Surely a military man could discipline himself sufficiently to control such hazardous feelings? He straightened his shoulders and offered his arm into the drawing room, where an ever increasing buzz signalled the champagne was working its magic.

Lizzie made no move, but remained standing at arms' length, a defiant expression on her face. 'I will play at being your guest, Sir Justin, but I've come tonight for one reason alone—to pass on crucial information.' Her voice was cold and clipped.

Justin felt scorched. For a moment, he'd been caught in a dream: an enchanting young woman, lissom and lovely, emerging from out of the night and here for him alone. But in a few words, the dream had folded: Lizzie had come only to resurrect a tiresome quarrel.

He felt himself begin to bristle, as he remembered their conversation in the cove. She'd been wrong to accuse him of weakness and she was wrong now. He'd not been weak, simply pragmatic. He had Rosanna's measure, he was sure, and no amount of flattery or fluttery, had influenced him.

Gil had been mooning over a woman, it was clear, and if by any chance that woman had been Rosanna—he still found the idea ridiculous—adoration from afar was all there had been. Gil was too timid to embark on a full-blown love affair and would never have been close enough to Rosanna for the woman to know anything useful about his disappearance. He knew his friend, and Lizzie Ingram did not.

Lizzie's brow puckered. She had thrown down a challenge and he could see she was waiting for his response. Ignoring the provocation, he said, 'I hope, Miss Ingram, you'll be happy to meet some of our neighbours and perhaps enjoy a little music. The Cheriton Quartet are reputed to be excellent musicians.'

'I'm sure they must be, but I've not come for music. As I said, I'm here for quite other reasons.'

Justin groaned inwardly. The evening was heading for trouble: it was like swimming towards submerged icebergs, with the tip of their next quarrel hovering just above the water line. He didn't want another argument with this lovely girl, but it seemed inevitable, since what could she possibly know? Some trivial snippet of gossip she'd gathered from her last trip into town? While all he wanted was to take her in his arms and kiss away this whole worrisome business.

'I understand you're here with information,' he said in a level voice, 'but for the moment, I must make myself available to welcome any late-arriving guests. As soon as I can, I will come to you.'

He was not going to escape, so better to advance immediately into enemy territory. Once all the guests had arrived, the quartet could be formally introduced and, with everyone engrossed in the musical recital, it should be easy to extract Lizzie from their midst. She deserved a hearing after braving the hay cart, and the least he could do was listen.

She thanked him crisply and allowed herself to be escorted into the adjoining room. It had been simply decorated for the occasion with posies of wild flowers lining the buffet table and branches of greenery hung from the panelled walls. Nothing too festive or fancy, Justin had told his people, and thought they had managed well—a fitting backdrop to celebrate his father's life and work in a community he'd loved.

Hovering on the threshold of the drawing room, he saw that nearly every pair of eyes had come to rest on Lizzie, many of them warmly admiring.

'Allow me to introduce you to some of our neighbours,' Justin said, feeling a stupid pride that he had the most beautiful woman in the room on his arm. For the moment, he forgot they were hardly on speaking terms.

One or two of the younger men hastily broke off conversations and began to advance towards them, but before they could reach their goal, James Martin was there, bowing low to Lizzie and tapping Justin's arm in a friendly fashion.

'You must introduce me, Justin. This is a lady I've not

yet met, but feel I most definitely should!'

'Miss Ingram, this is Mr James Martin, our very good friend and neighbour at Five Oaks. Mr Martin, Miss Elizabeth Ingram—she is staying with Mrs Croft at Brede House.'

'So you're quite used to being beaten and battered by the elements, Miss Ingram? What a house that is. I wonder that Henrietta can bear to live there still, what with the weather and—'

Justin cut in. 'I must return to my post at the door, but would you be kind enough to escort Miss Ingram to the buffet?'

'It will be my pleasure.' James Martin executed an elegant bow. 'Caroline is already enjoying your hospitality, Justin.' He gestured towards the long dining table which had been set up against one of the panelled walls and was crammed with every variety of savoury and sweetmeat. 'Come with me, Miss Ingram, and meet my wife.'

Justin Delacourt had not introduced her as a companion, Lizzie noted. Was that because he was ashamed of inviting a servant to his party, or was it a show of delicacy towards her feelings? She had tried very hard to remain cold and reserved, but it was difficult to stop herself from falling back under his spell. For long moments, Justin's gaze had never left her and she'd known herself admired. She wanted him to admire her, wanted him to desire her as much as she desired him. Such inconvenient feelings. But they were ones she was unable to lose, even after the fierce anger he'd engendered in her. Just the touch of his body as he'd escorted her to the drawing room had made her heart beat erratically.

And it was the strangest thing, but she felt secure with him. Felt herself relaxing into safety whenever he walked beside her, as though he offered a haven, a pair of arms in which she could rest. And that made no sense. In fact, it was plainly stupid. Justin was exciting, and safety and excitement did not mix. Piers Silchester was security, and Lizzie was hard put to recall one exciting moment she'd spent with him.

Piers could be relied on, though. Justin Delacourt could not. Hadn't he let her down in succumbing to Rosanna's charms? And how long would he be any part of her life? Once he'd put Chelwood Hall to rights, he would leave the district, return to Spain and to the war. It was inevitable. He might look admiringly at her, but to him she was simply a pretty object, an item to appreciate before moving on.

James was guiding her towards the buffet table and towards his wife. Lizzie wondered if Caroline Martin would remember seeing her, from the time she'd rushed wildly from Brede House. She hoped not. The conversation was going to be uncomfortable enough. James was a charming man and no doubt his wife was equally charming, but Lizzie would have preferred to talk to someone else. In the light of what she'd discovered recently, it would be difficult to gloss over the dreadful suspicions filling her mind.

Caroline came towards her, a gentle smile on her lips. Lizzie saw with relief that she'd not been recognised. A small relief only, she thought, finding herself scrabbling to make polite conversation with a woman whose heart she knew must be breaking beneath the social mask she forced herself to wear.

Yes, Lizzie said, she was enjoying living in Rye. She found the countryside pleasant and the sea air invigorating. Mrs Croft was a dear lady and a kind employer. Lizzie would love to visit Five Oaks and there was no need for the Martins to send their carriage for her. She was a keen walker. And, who knows, she might meet Mr Jefferson and his cart—though she kept the latter thought to herself.

'Can I get you some food, Miss Ingram? A glass of champagne?' James was at her side.

'Just the champagne, thank you.'

She couldn't eat, not while she had this information gnawing away at her, not while she was in the company of the Martins. It was fortunate that just then Caroline's attention was claimed by an acquaintance she'd not seen for some while and, for the moment, Lizzie felt she could relax.

While James busied himself fetching the champagne, she looked around. A mixed gathering of people were clustered beneath the drawing room's three fabulous chandeliers, enormous crystal constructions, that tonight blazed with the light of a hundred candles. She'd not seen this room on her previous visit and thought the space stunning. A bank of arched windows to the rear of the house looked out on acres of rolling lawn, while another bank of windows in the opposite wall gave on to the gravelled carriageway, winding its sinuous path through flowering shrubs and ancient trees.

Between the two sets of windows, there were oak panelled walls, beautifully carved, and smothered in intricate pattern: fruits and flowers and what looked to Lizzie like *fleur-de-lis*. Hadn't Mrs Croft told her that Delacourt was a French name? Such an old family, it seemed. They must have come from Normandy and were still living in the place where they'd first landed.

In each corner of the room, the carving became even more elaborate. Snakes, Lizzie was sure, coiling themselves around wooden pineapples and through wooden palm leaves. Which Delacourt ancestor had travelled beyond Europe? She'd hardly spoken to Justin of his family, yet she felt impelled to know everything about them. And that was stupid, too, since once she'd spoken her piece, she would walk out of Chelwood's front door and never come back.

James Martin was steering his way around the knots of chattering people, holding aloft two glasses of champagne. Lizzie was dismayed to see that he was not alone, but accompanied by a fresh-faced young man, eagerness writ large on his face. And behind him, more young men appeared, as though the fetching of the champagne had signalled a barrier being lifted. It was the last thing she wanted: she had no wish to attract attention, no wish to be forced into rebuffing advances. Tonight was too important.

At that moment, the first strains of violins and cello reached them, and the young men came to an abrupt halt. A lifeline, Lizzie thought.

'We should take our seats, Miss Ingram. The recital is about to begin.' Caroline had returned, and was shepherding her towards three rows of chairs that had been laid out in the shape of a semi-circle.

In front of the chairs, a playing space had been created, and a temporary dais erected for the quartet and their music. Glass in hand, Lizzie slid quietly into a seat on the edge of the furthest row. The news she was carrying had begun to feel more and more onerous as the minutes ticked by. She was desperate to unburden herself, and watched anxiously as Justin made a short speech welcoming his guests to Chelwood and introducing each member of the quartet by name.

Now, she thought. Now is the time. But then, inexplicably, he disappeared. Lizzie felt crushed, but could do nothing except settle herself to listen, though her mind was everywhere but in the room.

Chapter Seventeen

Ten minutes into *Air from a Suite in D*, Lizzie felt a strong hand on her arm. Slipping noiselessly from her seat, she followed Justin into the hall.

'I thought it best to wait a while before we talked,' he said, walking to the far end of the flagged passageway and stopping outside a room that Lizzie remembered well. 'We shouldn't be disturbed here.'

The library looked much the same as it had done the day she'd trespassed at Chelwood. Why had she been tempted to do such a foolish thing? Because her vanity was so great that she couldn't bear to think a man she admired had refused to admire her? Lizzie felt ashamed at her shallowness and hoped she'd was a better person now. Certainly, she'd been amply punished since—with every one of their encounters, she'd fallen further and further under Justin's spell.

A fire had been lit in the immense stone grate and its heat was ferocious. She was temporarily stunned by it and stepped as far away from the hearth as she could.

'We could walk on the terrace if you prefer,' he offered.

'I've a shawl here if you need it.'

Touched by his thoughtfulness, Lizzie responded with more grace than she'd managed earlier. 'I'd like that very much. The moon is so bright this evening, it will light our footsteps.'

Once through the long doors that led on to the terrace, the sultry heat of the library was left behind. Justin shook out a sumptuous length of Norwich silk and draped it around her shoulders.

'The shawl is your mother's?' Lizzie ventured to ask.

'It is. It seems she has her uses after all—her dress, her shawl.'

'She certainly had a taste for the luxurious. Her clothes are still elegant all these years on.'

'They are clothes befitting a beauty. A diamond of the first water, or so I'm told.'

'Lady Lavinia must have had many admirers.' Lizzie scolded herself. She should not be prolonging the conversation. She should say her piece and leave.

'Dozens, though she treated them with indifference.' Justin seemed as unwilling as she to confront the troublesome business between them. 'My father was one of her most ardent and felt himself lucky that he was the man ultimately to win her. As it turned out, he was anything but lucky.'

'But surely, when she married, she must have been in love with Sir Lucien?'

A sardonic smile lit Justin's face, encouraging Lizzie to make her case. 'If she were the beauty you say, she could have married the most prestigious of titles and become the mistress of a vast estate. She could even have become a duchess! Plenty of beautiful women did. Instead, she chose to come to Rye. There must have been a very good reason.'

'There was, but it wasn't love. She was certainly a beauty, but she didn't *take*—I think that's the phrase—so that when Sir Lucien met her she was already in her second season and without an offer to her name.'

Lizzie frowned. 'Not a single offer? But I always understood that acclaimed beauties made splendid marriages. Are you sure you have it right?'

'Quite sure. I heard it from my old nurse. She didn't share Mrs Croft's discretion alas, but she did know everything there was to know about the inhabitants of Chelwood Hall. She put my mother's failure down to her waspish nature. Even the most adoring of men will baulk at living with a termagant.'

'But not your father.'

Justin couldn't stop the sigh that had been building. 'It was my father's misfortune to fall deeply in love with her. Lavinia's younger sister was due to be presented the following season and I imagine my mother was desperate. Bitter that her beauty hadn't won her the matrimonial prize she thought she deserved, so that when my father made his offer, she accepted. The Delacourt name was an ancient one—the family came over with William the Conqueror—and I suppose that counted for something.'

'I'm impressed! But surely the family must have liked the match, or they'd have intervened.'

'The family was, is, very small—just my father and grandfather at the time. My father was a grown man, he'd been a soldier for years and my grandfather a semi-invalid. He was hardly going to question his son's choice.'

'And how did he like his new daughter-in-law?'

'He didn't. They were forced to live together at Chelwood while my father served abroad, and it proved intolerable. Sir Lucien never blamed my mother but, as I grew up, it became clear to me that she'd pressured him greatly to sell out and return to Chelwood. The army was his life, but he gave it up for her. For nothing, as it turned out.'

'But Lady Lavinia must have been glad when your father returned to live at Chelwood?'

'Intermittently glad, perhaps.' Justin tried to be honest. 'My grandfather died a few years into the marriage and my father inherited the title. For a while it kept my mother content, and naturally she loved the money he lavished on her. She spent whatever she liked and the estate suffered for it. Even in those days, it was a struggle to keep things going. But she found life in Sussex tedious. Rye is a small place and the spread of gentry in the county very thin. Lavinia craved company and when she'd done her duty by producing an heir, she chose the fun and gaiety of the capital.'

'And your father? Did he go with her?'

'It wasn't a choice. He had the estate to run and would never have been happy living in London. He agreed to her staying with friends. But the visits grew longer and more frequent and the times she returned to Chelwood fewer and shorter. Then they stopped altogether. That's when the lovers began.'

He saw her soft brown eyes darken with shock. He shouldn't be telling this tale of unhappiness to such a young woman, and one he barely knew.

'Shall we walk?'

He offered her his arm and, side by side, they strolled along the terrace, its flagstones washed by moonlight and the faintest scent of late blooming roses. Above, the night sky wore an ebony sheen, broken only by a sprinkling of wayward stars.

'You cannot wish to hear more of this, Miss Ingram. Tell me instead how I can serve you.'

But for the moment, Lizzie seemed to have forgotten her mission. 'How was it for you as a boy, living in such a household?'

If she wanted the truth, she would have it, Justin thought. 'I couldn't escape knowing,' he said. 'My mother was the talk of the county. My father, too. One lover followed another until he could stand the humiliation no longer. They were divorced on my twelfth birthday.' Imagine how that felt, he almost said, but bit the words back. 'It was a shameful business. My father took the blame and allowed her to divorce him. Of course, he did. She made a fool of him to the very end.'

'And now?'

'Now she lives in London—though, given her tarnished reputation, somewhat reluctantly, I imagine. But Europe is off-limits and has been since the war began. I believe she has actually married her latest lover. No doubt she was getting a little old for dalliance and eager to strike while her *cicisbeo's* feelings ran high. He is the duke you guessed at and obscenely wealthy, I'm told, so what more could she want? She has money, position and half a dozen estates. She need never be bored again.'

He closed his lips. He must say no more of the woman who had wreaked such unhappiness and wished he'd not allowed himself to say as much. Lizzie Ingram had pierced his armour and he didn't understand why he'd let her do it.

He stopped and turned to her, his face pale and his hair almost silver in the spectral light. 'So, Miss Ingram. The information you have for me?'

Chapter Eighteen

'I'm aware you'll be sceptical of anything I tell you,' Lizzie began stiffly, 'and I wouldn't have courted your disbelief again if I didn't think that what I have to say is important. It could be crucial to finding your friend.'

Justin's expression mixed impatience with a faint spark of interest. 'I hope I'm fair-minded enough to listen to whatever you tell me. If you've truly discovered something that will lead me to Gil, I'll be in your debt forever.'

'It's not gratitude that's needed. It's action,' she returned swiftly. Then in a more conciliatory voice, 'What I'm trying to say is that the situation is urgent. Rosanna—'

Lizzie was sure she heard him tut. 'You don't intend to listen after all?'

'I said nothing,' he murmured. 'Please continue.'

'Rosanna has a lover. Not Gilbert Martin, though I believe he thought himself favoured. She has a lover called Thomas Chapman.' Lizzie saw that the name had some meaning for Justin. 'Thomas Chapman is the grandson of a man who was hung for killing an excise man.'

'Yes, it's an old story.'

'It's not only a story. It's a fact. People here know the Chapmans' history and, by all accounts, his grandson is as violent and cruel as the rest of his family.'

'Forgive me, but what is the connection to Gil? I can't see it.'

'You will,' she said with certainty. 'Thomas Chapman heads a gang of smugglers. I know you believe that smuggling is extinct along this coast, but you're wrong. Ask any of the local people and they'll tell you differently. I've seen the gang myself, sitting in the Mermaid, their loaded guns on the table for all to see. I also saw Rosanna with them, but at the time I thought only that she was the barmaid, nothing more.'

'And now you think differently?'

'She is Chapman's lover—there's no doubt of it. I saw them yesterday at the market, walking boldly, arm in arm, and openly kissing each other.' She flushed a little at the frankness with which she was forced to speak, but Justin appeared to notice nothing untoward.

'Your friend—' Lizzie broke off what she was saying as he began to pace along the terrace.

After a few yards, he turned back, his voice spilling with frustration. 'What has any of this to do with Gil?'

'Don't you see?' she said impatiently. 'Your friend hoped he was Rosanna's sweetheart. No doubt he bought her gifts, showered her with money. He hoped he was the loved one, but her heart belonged to Chapman and still does—and *his* heart is as black as coal. I'm sure that together they used Gil's devotion against him.'

This time her words had an effect. Justin seemed distracted, his hand cleaving a path through well-ordered locks and rumpling its bright strands into dishevelment. 'I found letters,' he began. 'Letters that Gilbert had written.'

Lizzie stared at him. 'This is the first I've heard of letters. Who were they meant for?'

'I've no idea, only that they were written to a woman he loved. Page after page filled with his deepest feelings. I read only a little. I couldn't... but I got the gist. Whoever he was writing to meant a great deal to him, but he didn't send the letters.'

She pounced. 'Which means that he was unsure they'd be welcome. He had doubts about Rosanna—he suspected she loved elsewhere.'

Justin leaned on the walled balustrade and looked out on to the peaceful garden, the bushes of the parterre transformed in the moonlight into a small army of magical soldiers. 'That's pure speculation. We can't even be sure that Chapman and Rosanna are lovers.'

'Of course we can,' Lizzie said scornfully. 'As sure as anyone can be. Even a soldier should recognise passion when it's walking down the road.'

It was his turn to flush. 'I see you've made a study of them.'

'Hardly. I was too nervous yesterday to look at them closely. But so was every other person on the street. People were terrified. Chapman is evil, Justin.' In her excitement, she had called him by his first name. 'I've no idea how far your friend was involved with the gang, whether he was simply pursuing a hopeless love for Rosanna or whether he allowed himself to be pulled into their wrongdoing. But whatever his involvement, I'm convinced that's where you'll find the answer to his disappearance.'

Justin shook his head, trying for clarity. 'I can't believe that Gil would ever do such a stupid thing. Involve himself with a crew of miscreants?'

She stamped her foot. 'Whether he helped them or not, it hardly matters. He's in danger. Surely you can see that? He may have got close enough to discover something they wished to keep hidden. He was a friend of the excise man who died, remember, and not one person in Rye believes that death was accidental. If your friend knew something the smugglers wanted to conceal, then they'd need him to disappear. They may have kidnapped him, may even have carried him over the water to France.'

When he said nothing, Lizzie grabbed his arm. 'We need to rescue him!'

'Who is this *we*? You don't even know him.'

'It feels as though I do. And I'm desperately sorry for his parents. I want to help.'

'Perhaps you have, though I find it impossible to reconcile the man I knew with what you've told me.' Justin looked down at his feet, thinking hard. 'I suppose you may as well know what I learned from the Martins. That a large sum of money has gone missing from the family accounts. They're also missing a necklace, one that belonged to Gil's grandmother.'

Lizzie looked triumphant, but he wasn't quite ready to

concede. 'The information on its own means nothing. The necklace could have been lost anywhere. Gil might not have withdrawn the money.'

'But he did, I'm sure, and spent it on Rosanna. Go to her again,' she urged. 'Use your charm to get her to talk.'

'I have charm? How surprising, but nonetheless very welcome.'

She walked a little away from him, as though priming herself to make an apology. 'I'm sorry that we quarrelled. I'm sorry I doubted you.'

'And I'm sorry I disappointed you, Lizzie. It grieves me to acknowledge that I might have been wrong, but I'll make amends, I promise!'

She liked the sound of her name on his lips and smiled up at him. 'I'll go with you, if you like. We'll confront Rosanna together.'

'You're worried that she'll once more cast her spell over me?'

'I wouldn't blame any man for being entranced by her. She is very beautiful,' Lizzie conceded.

'Some may find her so. My taste is more refined.'

He was looking down at her, his fascinating changeful eyes unusually intent. His hand reached out and with his finger he traced a line down her cheek. 'You are far more beautiful and infinitely more enchanting, you know.'

Lizzie flushed a deeper pink. 'That's poetic talk for a soldier,' she teased.

'When I'm with you, I tend to forget I'm a soldier.' He tipped her chin upwards and gazed into her glowing face. 'You are very lovely and—and I can't stop myself from kissing you.'

He bent his head and his mouth found hers. At first it was a soft brushing of lips. Then his mouth grew harder and his body flexed. His hand was in her hair, tangling her ringlets through his fingers, while with the other he pulled her towards him. She went willingly, her lips still fastened to his.

He kissed her over and over again, longer and more deeply with every kiss, until sheer breathlessness forced them apart. Her dressed was crushed, her hair falling loose, and they stood for a moment looking at each other, dazed, shy. Then his lips were back on her mouth and his tongue delicately probing. Pressed against the stone walls of the house, still warm from the afternoon sun, his body was taut and hers softening in response. She was as lost as he. Nothing had prepared her for this torrent of emotion. Nothing had prepared either of them.

Without warning, the library window flooded with light. A branch of candles was being held aloft and there was the sound of footsteps coming towards the open door. They stood still and silent in the darkness, catching their breath, trying to slow the beat of their hearts.

'It's Alfred,' Justin whispered in her ear. Then at the sight of her bewildered face, 'The footman. His evening duty is to close the curtains and lock the doors.'

'Then we should...' she began, finding it difficult to speak.

'We should.'

'And we should not have...'

'No,' he agreed, 'we should not have. How good an actress are you?'

'I don't know, but shall we put it to the test?' And with her hand on his arm, they walked back into the library, faces schooled into blandness. Alfred looked up at their entrance, surprised to see them.

'I'm sorry, Sir Justin, I'd not realised you were on the terrace.'

'Just taking the air,' Justin said casually. 'Miss Ingram found the heat of the library a little oppressive.'

They walked past him in dignified silence, but once in the hall giggles bubbled to the surface. Like naughty schoolchildren, she thought, feeling lucky to have escaped punishment.

Once at the front entrance, though, Lizzie grew serious again. 'Promise me you'll see Rosanna as soon as you can.'

He took her hands in his and gave them a squeeze. 'You can depend on me, Lizzie. I won't let you down, And this time I'll not be deceived. On the contrary, I've every intention of being the deceiver.'

She frowned. 'I'm not sure I like the sound of that. What do you intend to do?'

'I can't tell you. Consider it a military secret! But don't worry. I'm an excellent strategist and will do only what I have to, and then only if I'm certain it will work.'

'Are you sure you don't need me?' She pressed his hands more firmly. 'I might be helpful to you.'

He laughed, and his eyes shone misty grey in the

candlelight. He looked happier than she had ever seen him. 'You *are* helpful to me, more helpful than you can imagine. But this might be dangerous work, and I'd prefer you to be a million miles away.'

'But—'

'Sometimes, Lizzie, it's the duty of soldiers simply to stand and wait.'

And with that, she had to be content.

Chapter Nineteen

Before she tumbled into bed that night, Lizzie took her sketch pad and pencils to the window seat and drew. It was another portrait of Justin, as handsome as ever, but the eyes were lit with tenderness now, the expression warm and loving. After she'd finished, she sat looking at the face, touching it softly from time to time, even kissing the full lips she'd sketched. She was euphoric, filled with a nameless delight. It wasn't just that Justin had believed her story. Nor that he had trusted her sufficiently to promise he would finish the job she'd started. It was much, much more.

This evening on the terrace, in a magical, moonlit world, she had walked into his arms, felt his lips on hers, and the heat of his embrace warming her skin. She had melted against him, savoured every touch and taste of him—and known herself desired.

Climbing between the sheets late that night, she thought herself too happy ever to close her eyes and, true to her prophecy, she slept only lightly, waking just after dawn when the first streaks of grey light crept through her curtains. It was barely six o'clock, yet she could sleep no more.

What are woken her so early? The first stirrings of unease? The euphoria of last night's lovemaking seemed to have vanished and she felt inexplicably downpin. But why had her mood changed so dramatically?

Lizzie slid from the bed and padded towards the washbasin, beginning to pour water from the china jug. Suddenly she stopped, her attention arrested. She'd succumbed too eagerly to his caresses! That was the problem. She'd been without shame, allowing herself to be kissed in a way that no modest woman should. Her face burned at the thought of the licence she'd allowed. She should not have forgotten that for all his quiet courtesy, Justin Delacourt was a soldier. Soldiers were wanderers, opportunists by nature, and even the most discerning of their company would take what was on offer.

And she had offered herself—openly. She'd always suspected that if Justin kissed her, she would not be able to resist. And she'd been right. Hadn't she slid into his arms, matched him kiss for kiss, pressed herself close to his body and wanted him in a way she had never known before? But it wasn't desire alone that plagued her. She felt a desperate aching for him: for his voice, his smile, his laughter. Lizzie hardly dared put a name to it, but it felt very like love.

It mustn't be. She could not allow herself to love him. Her emotions might be in turmoil, but her mind was clear: in a precarious world, the day would arrive when she must choose sensibly, ally herself with a man who was secure and dependable, a stolid helpmeet for the years to come. But her heart was fearsomely at odds with her head, and if Alfred had not chosen to light the lamps at that moment...

She couldn't believe how imprudent she had been, to have courted disgrace in that fashion! She might have robbed herself of a home, of a job. Of any way of sustaining herself. Miss Bates would never have permitted her to return to the Seminary— not after the mistakes Lizzie had already made.

It was hard, very hard, but to allow Justin Delacourt a place in her heart would be the worst of all mistakes. He might walk the dangerous path with her and revel in their mutual pleasure, but for how long? His allegiance was first and foremost to his regiment and that was where he'd return. His life would continue as always, his future unhampered by a woman, but she would be disgraced forever. Yet how was she to fight these feelings, so dangerous to her well-being? She had only one weapon and that was to keep her distance. She must ensure she was never again alone with him.

Careful not to wake the household, Lizzie washed and dressed and crept downstairs. She would walk, she decided, walk and hope to shake off the thoughts that plagued her. She sped down the gravel drive as lightly as she could, fearing the crunch of heavy footsteps might wake her employer, since Mrs Croft's bedroom was at the front of the house and she was a light sleeper. But she reached the road without mishap and followed it for some way towards Rye. When, after some half a mile, it began to wind its way inland towards the town, she branched off to the left, taking the much narrower coastal path that snaked along the cliff top. Far below, the river had shrunk to a thin, silver thread.

She walked with purpose, pushing disquiet to the back of her mind. Justin had been adamant she should not involve herself further in Gil's disappearance, and she would do as he asked. At the very least, it would create a distance between them. But she was curious about the excise man, who had met his death in this apparently peaceful landscape. The magistrate believed it an accident, the rest of the town did not. Who, she wondered, was right?

When she came upon the spot she'd been told about, it was clear there had been a disturbance. Bushes had been uprooted and lay to one side, sad and withered. A rough patch of earth showed scuffing and stones were piled into an untidy heap, as though feet had gouged them from the ground. It could still have been an accident, Lizzie thought. The man might have lost his footing. It had been raining that day, someone had said, and the cliff top grass could have been slippery. He could have stumbled, grabbing at any bush he could get his hand to, trying to still his fall. If he had, it had been to no avail. He'd toppled over the cliff, leaving a trail of destruction behind him.

Lizzie peered cautiously over the edge. It seemed a very long way down to the shingle beach—no wonder the man had broken his neck. But then she looked again. There seemed to be a ledge about ten feet below her. Very carefully, she leaned out further and, yes, there was a ledge immediately beneath, continuing around the next spur of the cliff. The man would have slipped over the edge rather than fallen, she thought, since his grabbing of the bushes would have slowed him. He would have tumbled to the ledge and no further. A broken bone or two perhaps, but from there he could easily have been rescued.

But he hadn't been. He'd crashed to the bottom. Yet, surely to avoid the ledge, a body would have to be travelling at speed. It would have to be thrown outwards. Lizzie's heart began to pound and blood to thrum noisily in her ears. The excise man's death could not have been an accident!

Even as she stood quaking from her discovery, a murmur of voices drifted on the air towards her. The noise was coming from below and, taking a deep breath, she found the courage to peer over the cliff edge once more. Two men had appeared on the ledge beneath, talking together. She could catch no words, but the conversation was short and sharp. One of them was a rough-looking individual, hair greasily matted, and dressed in patched breeches and a stained leather jerkin. Lizzie recognised him as one of the men she'd seen through the window of the Mermaid Inn. And the other...the other was Justin Delacourt.

She ducked down to lie flat on the grass, hoping she was completely hidden, her mind a frenzy of speculation. What on earth was Justin doing on the coastal path at this early hour and in such dubious company? It could not be simple exercise that had brought him here—he could have walked undisturbed for miles at Chelwood—so why come, and why speak so intently to the unknown man? She was sure their meeting was no casual encounter.

As Lizzie watched, the rough man turned to walk away while Justin began to follow the ledge back, climbing gradually upwards until he regained the greensward and was standing only feet away from her. She held her breath, waiting for discovery. But in a moment, he'd struck out along the path towards the Rye road, evidently on his way back to Chelwood. No horse, she thought, no carriage, and not a servant in sight. He had come to the meeting completely alone. She wondered if he realised the kind of men he was dealing with, the kind of men who could hurl another human being to certain death. He would have to be a fool not to realise, and Justin Delacourt was no fool. So what was behind this encounter?

A dreadful thought lodged in her mind. Was it possible that he'd lied to her, that he'd become entangled in the same mesh as Gil, that he was not as impervious to Rosanna as he'd claimed? It was a crazy idea, yet... he was a soldier and nothing about him was certain, no matter how upright and honourable he appeared. For what did she really know of him beyond his title and his house? Only what her heart told her, and her heart had proved spectacularly unreliable in the past. Hadn't it sent her on a fruitless search for her father and put her in danger along the way?

She hurried back to Brede House, trying hard to forget what she'd witnessed. Whatever the truth of the meeting, it had nothing to do with her, and neither had Justin. She must leave him to solve the riddle of his friend's disappearance and dismiss him from her mind altogether.

In the grey light of an October morning, last night's tryst seemed the most foolish impulse she'd ever succumbed to. It was painful to acknowledge, but their lovemaking was something best forgotten. Justin had probably forgotten it already.

Chapter Twenty

I n that Lizzie was wrong. In the days that followed the party, Justin had ample time to relive the events of that evening. And he did—constantly.

While he walked his estate with the bailiff in the days that followed, discussing the pastures they might fence, the crops they would sow, the improvements they could afford, he thought of little else. He'd lost control of himself that night, been insane to allow things to get so out of hand. Dear God, he'd almost seduced Lizzie Ingram! She was young and heedless, throwing herself impulsively into life and love. But he was not, and he berated himself for his folly. Despite her enticements, he should have been strong enough to remain aloof. Instead, he'd been unable to resist and the control of a lifetime had foundered.

It must never happen again—there was no future in such a liaison, no future for either of them. In a short while he'd be leaving Rye, leaving England, and he had no idea when or even if he'd return. But that was not the crux of the problem, was it? Even if he emerged from this endless conflict unscathed, he was incapable of loving a woman the way Lizzie should be loved. Any feeling he could offer would be a misshapen, half-formed thing—you could hardly call it love—and she deserved a great deal better. But how was he to rescue them from the abyss into which they'd fallen? Since that night, he'd managed to avoid meeting her, but that wouldn't answer for ever. And then what?

It was only the arrival of a letter mid-week that, for a few hours, pushed Lizzie from his mind. Justin read the missive twice over, his anger mounting, then stuffed the sheet of cream vellum beneath the stack of books that littered his study floor. He wouldn't think of the letter or its contents. He'd walk to his furthermost field and check the progress of the men Mellors had hired to hedge and ditch the remaining pastures. In that way, he'd keep his mind a deliberate blank.

He had passed the bailiff's office and was hurrying along the track that followed the boundary of the estate when, rounding a bend in the path, he almost cannoned into Lizzie. Both of them stopped in their tracks and Justin could see she was as taken aback as he. His eyebrows rose in silent query and, just as mutely, she held out the basket she carried.

'It's a pie,' she said, when he'd taken hold of the handle. 'Mrs Croft was insistent I bring it. It's pheasant—your cook apparently has a great liking for Hester's pheasant pie.'

The words were delivered dully as though Lizzie were finding it troublesome to speak, and he thought he knew why. She was regretting their indiscretion as much as he, and he must make this encounter as brief as possible for both their sakes.

'It's good of you to walk so far, Miss Ingram.' He tried for a formal tone. 'And a kind thought of Mrs Croft's.'

'It was her express wish that I brought it,' Lizzie said, making it clear that she'd not come willingly.

Justin tried to keep his eyes averted, but couldn't fail to see that in her green velvet spencer, she looked as lovely as ever. She had tied an emerald green ribbon through her chestnut curls and their bright sheen danced before his eyes.

Fighting to bring order to his wandering mind, he asked, 'Should I take it to the kitchen for you? Or perhaps you'd prefer to give it to Cook yourself?'

'It would help me if you could deliver it. I've a great deal to do at Brede House. Mrs Croft is unwell again and needs constant attention.'

Before he could ask after the health of his father's old friend, Lizzie had turned to retrace her steps. He watched her retreating figure in silence but then, quite suddenly, she stopped and twisted around to face him.

'Who was that man you were talking to by the river?'

For a moment, Justin was bewildered, then enlightenment dawned. 'What man was that?' he asked, deliberately vague.

If he'd thought to distract her, Lizzie was not to be put off. 'It was a few days ago, in the early morning. You were on a cliff ledge and talking together.'

'Yes, I remember,' he was forced to admit, 'but where were you? I didn't see you.'

'I was out walking,' she said shortly. There was a small pause before she asked again, 'Who was he?'

He dare not tell her, Justin decided. He must be evasive. 'No-one you would know, Miss Ingram. But someone who might help me. If you remember, I made a promise I'd get to the bottom of Gil's disappearance.'

His voice had grown strained at the mention of the pledge made to her that night, but Lizzie was not to be deflected.

'You'll not tell me who he is or why you were meeting him?'

'It's far better that you know nothing, Lizzie.' He could not maintain his formality. She would always be Lizzie to him now.

She was staring into the distance with her lips pursed, and he could see she wanted to kick against his refusal to say more. She felt cheated, he supposed, that in some way she'd had her adventure taken from her.

'It really is better this way.' He smiled at her—he couldn't stop himself, despite his vow to remain aloof—and it seemed she couldn't help but return the smile.

'I did wonder...' she began uncertainly.

'You mustn't worry. The man you saw is a means to an end, that's all. Things will turn out well, you'll see.'

She gave a small nod and was making ready to walk on when he blurted out, 'May I escort you back to Brede House?'

What was wrong with him? The words had come instinctively, but what was he doing? He should let her go quietly and be grateful their conversation had been unexceptional, but here he was inviting himself to walk with her.

'You have to deliver the basket,' she pointed out.

He flushed. 'Yes, of course. I had forgot.'

'You could leave it by the hedge. No harm will come to it until you return.'

～

What was wrong with her? What was she doing accepting his escort? He'd not properly explained his meeting with the villainous man, yet immediately she was willing to trust his assurance. It was her heart doing the talking—yet again—and it was telling her that he was too beautiful a man ever to do wrong.

Or, for that matter, to care seriously for her. Hadn't she decided that she must never be alone with him? Yet here she was walking by his side. It was because she'd met him so unexpectedly, she tried to tell herself. He'd startled her, appearing out of nowhere, filling the image she'd held in her mind since they last met. And filling it wonderfully.

They started along the path together, walking in silence, painfully aware of each other. Justin made no attempt to take her arm but she could feel his body close, his step matching hers. He wore what she imagined were working clothes, though he looked smart enough for a parade. His face above the crisp white shirt was tanned and lean, his hair a bright sun in the overcast day. She wanted to reach out and touch: hold his hand, ruffle his hair, smooth his cheek. Madness! One step along that road and she would succumb completely. She'd be a lost woman. She must stop thinking, stop imagining what might be, and start talking. Anything to break the tense silence that had grown alongside their need for each other.

'How does your work at Chelwood go on?' Lizzie asked, her voice sounding uncomfortably thin.

'Well, I thank you.' He was studiously neutral. 'The horrible Mellors is proving worthy of his salary and taking much off my shoulders.'

'Is he still waging his crusade against poachers?' she couldn't resist asking.

Justin gave a wry smile. 'Since that misfortune, he's acted more prudently and, in time, I'm sure he'll make a bailiff of which Chelwood is proud.'

She cast a sideways glance and was quick enough to see his smile fade and a frown take its place.

'But you're worried still?'

'Not about Chelwood. There's a great deal of hard work ahead, it's true, but Mellors and I are clear on what needs to be done to bring the estate back into profit.'

There was a pause before he added abruptly, 'I've had a letter from my mother.'

He shrugged his shoulders, as though by doing so, Lizzie thought, he could shrug away the parent he so disliked.

'You've had unwelcome news?' She ought not to concern herself—it was too personal— but it seemed impossible to stand aside.

'Her husband—the duke I told you of, the one who drips money—has left her. He appears to have found solace in Italy. I can't say I'm surprised. It was only ever going to be a matter of time before the marriage failed.'

'I'm sorry to hear that.'

'So am I,' he said grimly. 'Particularly as her letter hints she may wish to return to Chelwood.'

Lizzie let out a little gasp. No wonder he was so perturbed. He must have hoped his mother's marriage had relieved him of all responsibility for her. But from what Justin had said, Lady Lavinia and Chelwood would seem a poor match.

'I imagine your mother would prefer to stay in her London home,' Lizzie ventured.

'You would think so, but there's a strong possibility that the less than honourable duke will sell it beneath her feet and so render her homeless. There's also the little matter of embarrassment. Having boasted to her cronies of the opulent life she led, it will come hard to confess she's now been abandoned, an ageing woman, and without a penny to her name.'

When he spoke so bitterly, he seemed another person, Lizzie thought. It was clear that whatever Justin had suffered at his parent's hands, he'd neither forgotten nor forgiven. In the face of such hurt, it was difficult to know what best to say and they walked on in silence, the only sound the scuffle of their footsteps on the uneven path.

Eventually, Lizzie plucked up courage to ask, 'Will you allow Lady Lavinia to return to Chelwood if she wishes?'

'I've little choice in the matter. Whatever else she may be, she is my mother and if she's nowhere else to go... She'll have grown frailer with the years and age must command some respect. At least, that's what I've always believed. But it sticks in my craw to have her here.'

'Perhaps it will not prove as difficult as you fear.'

'You are ever the optimist, Lizzie. I wish you were right.'

'But surely the power she once wielded is gone? Your father is dead and can no longer be hurt by her.'

'No, thank God. She can hurt neither of us now. I suppose I must write to her that if she's in distress, she may come, but she's to come alone. No entourage.' The two words chopped through the cool air.

'What kind of entourage does she have?' Lizzie asked, wonderingly. It was a glimpse into another world.

'The horde of banshees she runs with. They will not be welcome at Chelwood—ever.'

'Are they so bad?'

'They are. You have no conception.'

'But once you return to your regiment, your mother would be quite alone at Chelwood. She might be in need of a friend.'

'If she comes here, she comes alone or not at all,' Justin said inexorably.

His intransigence made Lizzie purse her lips again, and catching the expression on her face, he burst out, 'I'm a grown man and there's not a harpy alive who can discomfort me. But I've not forgotten what it was like to be eighteen and at the mercy of such a one.'

'Then let us hope for both your sakes, the duke remains generous,' was all Lizzie could say.

His words had brought home to her in stark fashion how strongly the past was still with Justin, how fiercely he would fight anything that made him vulnerable. It had always been clear to Lizzie that his love of the army made it unlikely he would ever give himself wholeheartedly to love. But she could see now that there was more: for Justin, love was a risk and his fear of humiliation too great. No wonder his transient life as a soldier suited him so well.

Chapter Twenty-One

The ferry was waiting when they arrived at the river, several passengers already on board.

'You should go back to Chelwood,' Lizzie said, stopping at the gangway. 'I can be home in minutes.'

'I offered you my escort to Brede House, I believe,' Justin responded and, following her on to the boat, settled himself on the bench opposite.

With a nod to his passengers, the ferryman cast off, steering his craft out into the river's calm waters. Not a breath of wind touched the river's surface as it meandered a path to the sea, unravelling like a broad twist of beaten metal. Above, the clouds had cleared and the sky seemed enormous, its huge expanse flushed by a warm light, apricot mixed with a cold, bright blue.

It was a short journey across the river and an equally short walk before they reached the gates of Brede House and its avenue of trees. The main entrance remained locked, since no carriages had come or gone from the house that day, but a small wrought iron gate stood to one side and Justin opened it, standing back for Lizzie to pass through. The space was narrow and she could not help but brush against him. A spark, electric in its intensity, surged through her. Then the familiar weakness, her limbs dissolving and her stomach hollow.

She sensed him close behind her. Then his hand was sweeping her curls to one side and his lips were on the nape of her neck, scattering soft kisses. He enfolded her in his arms, wrapping them around her waist and pulling her urgently towards him. Through the muslin of her dress, she could feel the longing in his body and was pierced by an indescribable ache. He spun her around, his mouth hovering over hers.

'Lizzie,' he groaned.

Her lips parted in readiness. She wanted his kiss so much. But she must not. Wrenching herself away, she said in a voice she hardly recognised, 'From here we are in sight of the upstairs windows.' She gestured towards the house. 'Hester or Mrs Croft might look out at any moment.'

His arms dropped to his side and his shoulders slumped. 'Forgive me, Lizzie. I had no right... It's only... that...' His voice tailed away.

They stood gazing at each other, rumpled, breathless, unable to avert their eyes, still balancing on the tightrope of desire.

Then he drew himself upright and said decisively, 'You are right, of course. That was the most foolhardy thing to have done. For my part, dishonourable, too. You must know that I delight in your company, but I've allowed my feelings too much licence and I hope you'll forgive me.'

Lizzie felt dumb, her voice lost; all she could do was bow her head in acknowledgement. At the top of the driveway, they murmured a brief farewell before Justin turned to go. She heard the crunch of his footsteps on gravel, a creak of the iron gate, and then silence.

~

Lizzie hurried to her room, hoping she could snatch a few minutes before Mrs Croft rang the bell. Since her illness, the old lady could be tetchy and, at this moment, Lizzie felt unequal to dealing with her demands. She was still trembling with shock—and the force of their desire *had* been shocking. After their encounter on the terrace at Chelwood, she should have been prepared, but if anything her need for him today had been even greater. It scared her. How long could she fight such overpowering feelings?

And what of Justin? He was as weak as she, it seemed, his hands impelled to touch, his lips to find her mouth. But did he feel more than physical desire? Did his emotions run deeper? Was it possible he could fall genuinely in love? At the thought, a bright glow suffused Lizzie's face. But not for long. Her mind raced on and her pleasure came to a sickening halt. If Justin *were* falling in love, and she could hardly believe it, his love would not endure. It couldn't endure. Not when he knew.

He had upbraided himself for his lack of honour, but what would he say if he knew the things she had done? She'd behaved so very badly. True, she'd been a young girl at the time—but that made it worse. At an age when she should have known only innocence, she'd schemed in the most shocking way, manipulated a man for her own ends, and only by accident had ended the loser. She could never tell Justin her story. It must remain a secret forever. If he knew the depths to which she'd sunk, his love for her, his desire even, would wither instantly. He would no longer wish to know her.

~

When Lizzie woke the next day, it was to find she'd forgotten Mrs Croft had nominated that Friday for the autumn cleaning of the conservatory, a room that lay on the south side of the house. Plants were brought indoors, wicker tables and chairs covered, the light voile curtains taken down and washed, to be replaced by heavier drapes of brocade. The day was filled with activity and by teatime both Hester and Lizzie were extremely tired, since the old lady's instructions were as numerous as they were conflicting.

With some effort, Lizzie had managed to keep her mind on the tasks in hand and only occasionally allowed her thoughts to stray into dangerous territory. So it was with considerable surprise that she found one of the footmen from Chelwood Hall on the doorstep around seven o'clock that evening. Her heart jumped as she saw his outline in the doorway, behind him the sun already setting , turning the sky to a pink marshmallow. It was a splendid evening, an evening for lovers, Lizzie thought, and she dreamed forlornly of spending it with Justin. But it was his footman that was standing at the door, a posy of autumn flowers in one hand and a stiff white envelope in the other.

Hester was fidgeting behind her, shifting from foot to foot, impatient to know what or who had called. Lizzie made haste to thank the man and shut the door. Without a word, she took the posy upstairs, leaving Hester in the hall, her eyes wide with astonishment.

The envelope contained only one sheet of paper and the message inside was brief.

Will you come to Chelwood tomorrow? I would like to show you the improvements I've been making. No need to trespass this time! It was signed simply *Justin.*

These past few days, Lizzie had imagined him to be every kind of man: a thrilling lover who conquered her with his passion, a dashing soldier taking pleasure where he found it, and just yesterday, a blighted man too hurt ever to care deeply for any woman. And now? Now it seemed that he might care, care enough to want her close. The thought made tears prick at her eyes. What she would give to visit Chelwood as his special guest, to eat at his table, to walk and talk with him, to share his innermost thoughts. But she could do none of those things.

If he knew her secret... If she told him the whole story, he might not blame her for a mistake made when she was little more than a child, but he would not condone it. He was a man of principle and she couldn't bear to see the distaste on his face, the same distaste that he reserved for his mother and her friends. She would keep his posy as a memory of what might have been and, though it broke her heart, she would not reply to the invitation.

~

For most of that day Justin had been in a state of chronic indecision, his thoughts wavering this way and that. Yesterday, outside Brede House, he'd once again found himself at the mercy of feelings too powerful to command.

From the moment, he'd met this lovely, lively girl, he'd been intrigued. He'd known immediately that Lizzie was a free spirit. But far more than that. She was his own spirit, his own soul, though he'd tried to dismiss such feelings as fanciful nonsense. He'd told himself she was simply a chance acquaintance, the companion to an old friend, a girl who'd become a stranger once he returned to the fighting and to Spain. Despite her manifold charms, Elizabeth Ingram was a woman like any other, and that in itself was a strong reason to pass her by with no more than a casual greeting.

Yet he'd found himself hoping to meet her whenever business took him to Rye, found himself enjoying their conversations and now, latterly, enjoying a great deal more. It was as though the emotions that over the years he'd so carefully stored away had broken an invisible barrier and were now impossible to recapture.

Only a few days' ago on this very terrace, they'd teetered on the edge of mutual seduction. He'd known Lizzie to be as willing as he and, after that disturbing encounter, he'd told himself it must never happen again. He would avoid her and concentrate entirely on Chelwood. In under a month, he'd return to his regiment and could not afford to be wasting his energy. It was a way of dismissing, or trying to dismiss, the devastating passion she roused in him.

But it had taken only a few minutes at the gates of Brede House, he reflected wryly, for such indifference to ring utterly false. He'd been unable to resist her and the realisation had come to him, there on that carriageway, that he didn't want to. He wanted to give himself to her body and soul. Extraordinary feelings had washed over him, ones he could never have imagined, and the years of bitterness had simply fallen away.

Lizzie was *not* like any of the women he'd known. She was fresh and young and innocent. She was passionate and loving and he wanted her. For the first time he questioned whether he'd been misguided in devoting himself to a life of privation and hardship; whether the camaraderie of the regiment could ever be sufficient to make up for the love he'd hitherto dismissed.

It was as though the premise on which he'd built his adult life was under threat and he had no notion how to respond. All that was clear to him was that he needed to see her again, needed her here at Chelwood. Their parting had been abrupt, both of them overcome by the sheer strength of their feelings. Feelings that had overturned long-held beliefs for both of them. But they'd find a way through, he was certain, a way perhaps to happiness. The decision was made.

He rang the bell and summoned his gardener to the library. Latimer was to pick the choicest blooms from the estate's one succession house and he would sit at his desk and pen the invitation. It proved more difficult than he'd imagined and, after four spoiled attempts, he was forced to settle for the briefest note he'd ever written. He hoped that Lizzie would understand its message.

～

When Alfred returned from Brede House without a response, Justin felt a thud of disappointment. For some reason, Lizzie had been prevented from answering that evening, he told himself, and would send a note on the morrow. But she did not. Nor did she on the next day or the next. He felt betrayed and foolish. Her kisses had meant nothing, it seemed, bestowed without thought, for the pleasure of the moment. She had responded to his embrace, but it was his body, not his heart, that she wanted.

She was no different, after all, from any other woman. For once, he'd chosen to ignore the lesson life had taught him and he was well served. He'd allowed himself to contemplate love, dared to imagine a future lived together. What an idiot he'd been! To think he might have followed in his father's footsteps. That poor man's fate should serve as the greatest of warnings. Justin's mouth set in a forbidding line. If nothing else, he owed it to Lucien Delacourt to save himself. And he would.

Chapter Twenty-Two

Lizzie had not thought it possible to stay so unhappy. But as each morning dawned, her misery, if anything, increased. She longed to see Justin, but knew she must not. She'd not replied to his invitation and now, four days later, he was sure to have given her up. He must feel aggrieved, even angry, and certain never to renew his welcome to Chelwood. Keeping her distance had to be the right course, Lizzie told herself, but why then did every day seem longer than the one before?

For a while Mrs Croft required constant attention but, once her employer began to recover, Lizzie found it impossible to fill every minute of the day. She tried and failed to find solace in her drawing, she read to Mrs Croft—every newspaper and book in the house—then pestered her for extra errands until the poor lady pleaded to be allowed to sit quietly. She attempted to help Hester in her chores, but the maid told her firmly that Lizzie was hired as a companion, not a maidservant, and though she appreciated the offer, the girl was simply getting in her way. Cook was moved to suggest politely that the kitchen was best left to her, after Lizzie had burnt two loaves of bread and undercooked a particularly succulent joint of beef being prepared for Mrs Croft's supper.

Lizzie felt wretched and restless and could attend to nothing for more than a few minutes, dashing from one activity to another without pause. Even walking gave her no cheer. Whenever she ventured out, she was careful to stay this side of the marsh and well away from Chelwood, but with every step she remembered Justin: his smile, his beautiful voice, his strong hands wrapping hers in their warm clasp.

Nights were even worse; she would toss and turn endlessly until, finally, she drifted into sleep, only to wake within the hour. After four dreadful days, she looked at her reflection in the mirror, pale and hollow-eyed, and knew she must do something drastic to rescue herself. She would drink gooseberry wine, she decided, a potent brew kept under lock and key in the kitchen, and follow it by reading until she could no longer see the words on the page. She'd be certain then to fall into a deep and dreamless sleep.

That, at least, was the plan. But either the wine was not as strong as she'd hoped or her reading was too stimulating, since it was many hours before her eyes closed and the book slid slowly from her hands. Two o clock was striking in the hall below when a small sound roused her from the light sleep she'd fallen into. She turned fitfully in the bed. Her covers were bunched into a heap and the book she'd been reading was somewhere wrapped in her pillow. She was lighting the candle to put herself to rights when she heard the noise again. It must be what had woken her. The slightest murmur of voices, the smallest sound of crunching on stone.

Quickly, she extinguished the candle and went to the window. A fingernail of moon floated amid the inky blackness, its muted light revealing only the hazy contours of the garden. For a moment, she watched the silhouettes of trees and bushes, unmoving in the windless air, and cutting through them, straight as any arrow, the path leading to the cove. Had the noise she'd heard come from the garden? She remembered the fate of Mrs Croft's unfortunate granddaughter and quailed, then scolded herself for cowardly thoughts—*her* heart was not weak. What kind of soldier would she make if she jumped at every small sound?

It was time to investigate. Pulling her thick cloak and boots from the wardrobe, Lizzie dressed swiftly, and was down the stairs and out of the back door in a matter of minutes. She was on the path now, the cloak wrapped tightly around her nightdress, and gliding past the stone bulk of the folly. Each step brought her closer to the beach, and with each step the murmurs grew louder. It was the stillest night she'd so far encountered at Brede House. It was why the noise had carried and why she must take the greatest care to move silently so as not to alert whoever was in the cove.

The gate creaked beneath her hand and she held her breath, but the sounds below continued. She crept forward to the head of the wooden stairway and peered into the dark. The river flowed softly, hardly a ripple maiming its surface, and the slither of moon played along the beach. Gradually, Lizzie's eyes adjusted to the gloom and she began to make out figures. Men?

Were they men? If so, they were the strangest creatures. Walking beehives was the only way she could describe them. There were some eight or ten of them dressed in long black top boots, dark tunics and torn leather jerkins, but it was what topped this ensemble that sent a shudder up her spine: on their heads they wore a hive of coiled rope with three small windows cut from the front, two for eyes and one for the mouth. It was a disguise that would ensure the men were safe from recognition, but designed, too, to frighten away anyone unlucky enough to meet them.

Lizzie swallowed hard and tried to look beyond the men to a small boat standing offshore. The vessel showed no lights, but the small slice of moonlight allowed her to make out its shape. The voices she'd heard had fallen silent now—an occasional muttered oath and the sound of water washing around the men's legs was all that reached her. Several of them were wading between ship and shore with what appeared to be barrels strapped to their front and back. Once they reached the beach, they dropped their cargo and returned to the boat for more.

A second group hefted the barrels, one by one, onto their shoulders and crunched their way across the shingle to the foot of the path that climbed steeply upwards from the beach. Lizzie stood on tiptoe, but could see no more than its very beginning, since a tall hedge ran down the west side of the garden.

Then through the clear air, the rattle of harness—there were horses on the cliff above! The illicit cargo was about to make its final journey. Her heart contracted painfully. She was certain this gang of smugglers—they could be no other—was responsible for Gil Martin's disappearance. But where were they taking their haul and might it lead eventually to Gilbert himself?

If only Justin were here... but he wasn't, and she must do what she could. She must follow them, see where they were taking their cargo and, if possible, discover where Gil was being held. If she succeeded, she could send a message to Justin telling him where to search.

The last barrel was being carried up the pathway; she heard the sound of a whip and the slow creaking of carts. Cautiously, she made her way down the garden staircase to the beach. The boat's crew had hauled in its anchor and, with clouds now obscuring what moon there had been, it was barely visible as it made its way downstream to the open sea. The cove was empty and Lizzie raced across the beach to the path that would take her to the cliff top. She dared not let the gang get too far ahead.

But once on the cliff, she came to a dead halt. The men appeared to have vanished and in their place a terrifying luminescence hovered in the air. The tales she'd heard from Hester returned with paralysing effect. The maid was convinced the marsh was haunted and that travellers who lost their way and disappeared had been taken by the marsh witches. Lizzie had given a scornful laugh when she heard the tale but, at this moment, laughing was far from her mind. Had the witches decided to come to town this night? She stood stock still, unable to move.

Then her wits returned and she realised that the shimmering cloud was moving forward in a deliberate fashion, accompanied by the rattle of harness and the sharp, quick step of hooves. Silvery shapes showed faintly against the horizon: the ghosts, it seemed, were pack ponies! The animals must have been painted with a strange, phosphorescent mixture to terrify all that saw them. Newly brave, Lizzie squared her shoulders and began to follow.

Always careful to keep a distance, she walked swiftly in the wake of the convoy. For several minutes, the moon floated free again and she could see from its frail light that ahead were two, no three carts, each one piled high with barrel upon barrel. Black-clothed figures walked by the side of the carts, one or two holding lamps, dimly lit. For some half a mile they trudged along the coastal path, before abruptly swinging right to take a smaller track—one Lizzie had never walked—that wound its way around the base of the town, until it reached a wooden bridge fording the river at its narrowest point. Over the bridge, a bleak flatness loomed out of the dark. They were headed for the marshes.

It was desolate country, the bushes, when they grew at all, bent and crippled by the scouring of Channel storms. It had been windless in the cove, but now Lizzie felt the first chilly gust, cold enough to penetrate her woollen cloak. She hardly noticed, though, since her heart was beating so fast that blood ran warm in her veins.

Here and there a thick mist, feet high, hung like the web of a thousand spiders over dykes that zigzagged across the marsh. The moon had once more disappeared behind banking clouds and she could see little beyond the surrounding darkness. From time to time, she was startled when, seemingly from nowhere, huge sluices reared unexpectedly out of the night. She must keep to the path at all costs, she reminded herself, for where there were sluices there was water as black as pitch.

The carts were picking up speed now and she'd almost to run to keep up. Every so often she lost sight of the dim shapes ahead, but soon she'd hear the trundling of a vehicle on the stony path and see a pinprick of light from one of the small lanterns.

Then the convoy disappeared. Completely. It happened in an instant. Lizzie looked to her right and then to her left, but could see nothing. She strained to catch the clink of harness, but could hear nothing. It was as though the men and their horses had been swallowed by the night's blackness. The clouds above had darkened further and she could no longer see even her feet.

Cautiously, she took a step forward and was relieved to find the path again. She must keep walking, keep searching for the convoy ahead. It could well be close to its final destination and the idea sent her blood thrumming. Perhaps she was near to finding Gilbert, since they must be miles into the marsh by now and this lonely, isolated place would hide a captive admirably. A surge of energy and she began to quicken her pace.

But in an instant she lost the path. Somehow she'd veered into a pool of mud that squelched and sucked around her feet. Hastily, she tried to regain firmer ground, but once more mistook her footing and found herself plunged into icy cold water, her nightdress a floating shroud and her cloak a sodden blanket dragging her downwards. She had fallen into a dyke and plunged knee-deep into water.

Lizzie took a deep breath. She could get out of this. She must get out of it. Overhead, the flap of a soaring bat breaking through the mists caused her to jump and she felt herself sink further into the quagmire. Fear screamed through her, but she told herself that she must keep calm, keep still until the moon swam free of cloud again and she could see her way back to the bank. If only the moon would shine.

But there was nothing to see except blackness, nothing to hear save the tickling bubbles that rose from the mud bed to burst amid the bulrushes. And despite her best efforts at keeping still, Lizzie knew she was sinking further into the mud. She tried again to reach out for the bank, but succeeded only in plunging deeper. Panic triumphed at last and she began threshing wildly in the water, crying out in terror, though there was no-one to hear.

A hand grabbed her arm. She gasped. Could this be one of Hester's marsh witches? How very stupid, but on a night like this anything was possible. The hand was warm and firm and was pulling her to her feet. Hardly able to breathe, she regained the bank. Then she saw it—the horrifying beehive. Her rescuer was a smuggler! He must have been walking at the rear of the convoy and heard her struggles. But the gang was thoroughly ruthless so why had this man saved her? Did smugglers have consciences? More likely, he'd scented an opportunity to make money through kidnap or blackmail. She would be another victim like Gil Martin. At the thought, Lizzie nearly threw herself back into the water.

The gust had become a wind now, rising from the shore and scattering the mist towards the sea and, through the lifting haze, she saw the man take off the dreadful headdress of coiled rope. When the slither of moon sailed into clear skies at last, their two figures stood revealed.

Chapter Twenty-Three

'Lizzie, what on earth!' It was a familiar voice. 'What are you doing here?'

She struggled into speech. 'But you, you're a smuggler!'

'A very bad one, as you see.' The joke made no impression on her. Her worst suspicions had come true. Justin Delacourt had joined this terrifying gang of men.

He seemed unperturbed, though, at being discovered. 'Here—walk with me a little further along the track. It's safer where the path runs well above the marsh.' He took hold of her hand and led her forward. 'We must talk quietly, since the men are not far away.'

'The men? Then you really are a member of Chapman's gang?' She was desperately hoping she'd been wrong.

'A very temporary member,' he said softly. 'I promised you, didn't I, that I'd speak to Rosanna again? But when I'd had time to consider, I thought it unlikely she'd be willing to tell me more. This seemed a better option—to gain the gang's confidence and hopefully discover what's happened to Gil.'

'But becoming a smuggler...' Lizzie was struggling to take in the enormity of what he'd done.

'I couldn't think of another way to gain their trust. Even so, they don't trust me, it's clear. I'm useful to them for the moment, but nothing more.'

'How did it come about?' she asked in a dazed voice.

'I sauntered down to the Mermaid the other evening and let it be known through the rascally landlord that I was bored with life and a trifle resentful. I made out that I'd been forced from the army and had a grudge against authority. I was finding it difficult to settle into civilian life and was desperate for some excitement. Sure enough, when I returned the following night, one of them sounded me out. The gang was looking for a likely man, someone with my height and strength. I told my story again to one of the gang leaders and I must have sounded believable enough, since they recruited me there and then.'

'So that was who you were meeting on the cliff!'

'That was who I was meeting—you can see why I couldn't tell you.'

'But it's so dangerous, Justin.'

'Not half as dangerous as a battlefield, believe me. I had to do it, Lizzie. It was our only chance of discovering what's been going on.'

She heard the 'our' and loved him for it. 'Don't they suspect, though? Suspect your motives? They must know who you are, that you're a man of means, the owner of Chelwood.'

'They know, of course. But they also know I've been

a soldier, and they can imagine that I miss the thrust of battle. I told them that I left the army and Spain under a cloud, and that I was angry with my father for having died so inconveniently. It meant perjuring myself—and I felt very bad about it.'

Lizzie thought for a moment. She imagined Justin could be highly plausible when he chose, yet... 'Taking you into their confidence,' she said, 'still appears a great risk on their part.'

The moon was shining more brightly now, bleaching his halo of hair almost white, and catching the glint of a signet ring as his hand harrowed a path through ruffled locks. Justin smiled down at her, a rueful expression on his face.

'To be truthful, I don't think they would have taken the risk if they'd not had this cargo coming in so soon and in great need of another man. Two of their number have been apprehended by the customs authorities down the coast at Chichester, and they've spoken of others leaving them in a hurry.'

'Gilbert! Do you think they might mean Gilbert?'

The grin had gone and Justin looked much older. 'I suspect that might be the case, but I can't ask. All I've been able to do is join them this night and hope they'll lead me to their hiding place. I've heard them talk of a barn, one they've taken by force from some poor unfortunate who farms in the middle of the marshes, but I've been unable to learn its exact location. I think they're on their way there now and, if they *have* kidnapped Gil, this must be the place they're keeping him.'

'It sounds as though you're still unsure that he's their victim.'

'On the contrary, Lizzie, I think you're right, and poor Gil is their prisoner. Whether he was a member of their gang or not, is irrelevant. One way or another, he learned what they were up to and he knew too much. They would have to prevent him going to the authorities—at least until they've finished their work along this part of the coast. Before they move on, they'll no doubt demand a ransom. But how long they intend to hold him or what his condition may be, I've no idea. All I know is that I must get to him.'

Lizzie's hands flew to her face in a gesture of despair. 'And now you've lost their trail. And it's all my fault.'

'Should I have left you to drown then?' There was laughter in his voice.

She shook her head sadly. 'I should never have followed them. I've ruined your plan.'

He put out a comforting hand and she took it. 'If I moved swiftly, I could probably catch them. But I don't wish to leave you here alone—you're soaking wet and very cold. You need to find shelter immediately.'

He reached down for the small lamp he'd been carrying and held it aloft. 'Dear God, is that a nightdress you're wearing under your cloak?'

'There's no time to explain,' she said hastily. 'You must go, and go now. I can perfectly well find my own way back.'

'No-one's goin' anywhere, me laddies.'

The voice had come from behind them, and together they spun round to face this new threat. Their whispers must have carried across the marsh, Lizzie thought, and one of the smugglers had heard and come to find them.

The man cleared his throat and spat into the dyke. 'Whoever you are and whatever yer game, you ain't goin' no further. You be comin' with me,' and very deliberately he pointed a large pistol at them. There was a loud click as the trigger engaged.

Justin's hand closed on hers and he nudged her leg. She was alert to every hint, but was he really wanting them to flee and with a pistol pointing at their heads?

The man began to move to their rear, all the time keeping them covered. 'Time to march, me lads.'

But as he drew level with them, Justin lunged forward and caught him unawares. He dived at the smuggler's legs and upended him. The man hit the ground with a thud and, before he could get to his feet, Justin had grabbed him by the jerkin and lifted him off the ground. The smuggler fell backwards with a loud splash—he'd landed in the dyke from which Lizzie had so recently been rescued. As he fell, the pistol went off, the bullet travelling harmlessly above their heads and into the air.

'Quick, run!' Justin instructed. 'The shot will have alerted the others.'

They could hear the man wallowing in the water, his arms carving a passage to firmer ground. In no time, he would be on them again. Justin threw the lamp into the dyke and once more they were plunged into darkness. Hand in hand they ran, Justin leading the way along the path Lizzie had walked earlier. Following him blindly, she ran into the night, hoping he knew the marshes a good deal better than she.

They'd run at least a mile before she was forced to stop. Her legs had turned to jelly and a searing pain swept through her lungs, her breath coming short and jagged.

'I can't... You... go on... He'll not find me now.'

'You are quite mad, Lizzie Ingram. You can't think for one minute that I'd abandon you here.'

'But—'

Justin scooped her up in his arms as though she were no more than a child and walked swiftly onwards. They were soon at the bridge and making their way along the narrow path which edged the outskirts of the town, then swinging left again and back on to the coastal path Lizzie knew so well. At her insistence, he set her on her feet and together they made their way down the slope to the cove below Brede House and, finally, up the wooden stairs to the safety of its garden.

'Let's rest here for a moment.'

Justin opened the door to the stone folly and together they collapsed exhausted on the cushioned seat, their hands momentarily entwined. In the turmoil of escape, they had forgotten their estrangement, but slowly the memory came to rest between them. Justin rose and walked towards an old chest which squatted toad-like in one corner. Several neatly folded blankets lay inside.

'Here, take off that waterlogged cloak and let me wrap you in these.'

She felt his hands tucking the warm wool around her,

skimming her body, sending it into tingling alertness. The instant she regained her strength, she thought, she must make her way back to the house.

For some time, they sat in silence. 'Why did you not answer my note?' he asked at length. Lizzie tensed, conscious that she could never tell him the true reason.

'I've been a little busy,' she hedged, and then scolded herself for the feeble response. 'Of late, Mrs Croft has needed my full attendance.' She tried again, but it was hardly an improvement and he swooped on her words.

'How long would it have taken to pen a simple yes or no, I wonder?' His voice was severe and she felt close to tears. Tonight she'd felt herself part of him, sharing the adventure, sharing the peril, impervious to the gap that yawned between them—the fact that he'd no notion of how bad a person she was.

'I'm sorry,' she whispered brokenly.

'Lizzie!' He turned to face her, holding her by the shoulders and forcing her to look into his eyes. 'All I want is the truth. If you find my attentions distasteful, can you not tell me so?'

Her tears began to fall in earnest and she could do nothing to stop them. 'No,' she sobbed, 'I don't find them distasteful. Not at all.'

'Then what is going on?'

With a struggle, she regained sufficient mastery to say in a quiet voice, 'It was discourteous not to have replied to your note and I'm sorry, Justin. But it would not have been right for me to come to Chelwood. It *isn't* right.'

He shook his head, baffled. 'Why this sudden qualm? You've not minded visiting me in the past.'

'That was before... when we were just playing... but now.... you shouldn't know me.'

'What nonsense is this?'

'I wish it were nonsense. If you knew—'

'But I don't know. That's the problem.'

She must put an end to this painful conversation. 'You must believe me when I say that if you knew the truth, you wouldn't wish to be with me.'

He moved closer and, before she could stop him, had put his arms around her. 'Nothing you could tell me would make me wish that.' He gave her a little shake. 'Now, what exactly is keeping you from my door?'

She fixed her gaze on the sodden edges of her nightgown, but made no attempt to disentangle herself. 'I have done a very bad thing.'

'Why don't you let me be the judge of that?'

'It *was* bad. You see, I was most anxious to find my father.'

'And you joined the circus.'

'No. Yes. I did, but this was later.'

He looked questioningly at her, his eyes inviting confidence, and she found the sentences tumbling out, staccato in rhythm and unstoppable. 'It was when I was fifteen. I met this man. He was a soldier, too.'

'Aren't they all,' he groaned.

'I met him at a dance in Bath.'

'I take it that Miss Bates was not your chaperon that night?'

'I had no chaperon. None of the girls were allowed to attend dances—the teachers said we were far too young. But we all knew there was a ball at the Assembly Rooms that evening and that the 11th Foot were on furlough in the town. There would be plenty of soldiers as partners, and all of us were desperate to attend. But it seemed impossible, we were so heavily guarded. Then Sophie Weston bet me I couldn't get there. So I did.'

'Naturally, you did.' Justin sighed. 'It was inevitable. Dare I ask how you got there?'

'I climbed out of the landing window. It was on the first floor and the porch roof was directly beneath. I managed to jump down without harming my best frock or making a noise. Then I simply walked to the Assembly Rooms.'

'That couldn't have been easy. It must have been a fair distance.'

'I wore my boots and carried my evening slippers. It took me an age to get there—the Seminary is on the outskirts of Bath—but I like walking.' She saw him smile and wished it were possible that he'd go on smiling, but her revelations would change everything.

For a moment, Lizzie felt her throat close up. She took a deep breath. 'The journey back would have been easier. Victor-he was the man I met—said he'd take me to the Seminary in a carriage that he'd hired.'

'You should never trust a man called Victor.'

She knew he was joking, but said seriously, 'No, I shouldn't have. But he looked so splendid in his uniform and spoke so convincingly. Victor said that if I wanted to find my father, he'd travel with me, take care of me, keep me safe from harm. If I'd had one sensible thought in my head, I should have known a serving soldier couldn't simply disappear for weeks. But I was desperate to get to my father.'

Justin looked grave. 'Victor was definitely not a man you should have trusted.'

'To be honest, he shouldn't have trusted me either. I told him the most terrible untruths. That my father was very wealthy, but lived abroad and I wanted to be with him.'

'That wasn't so untrue,' Justin said soothingly.

'The wealthy bit was. I made him believe I was a great heiress and that if he helped me travel to Spain, he'd be well rewarded.'

'As you never got to Spain, I take it he didn't help you.'

'No.' She shook her head miserably.

'So what happened?'

Lizzie shuffled herself to one side of the bench, abandoning his comforting warmth. Her voice sunk once more to a whisper. 'I find I don't wish to tell you after all. It was too terrible.'

Chapter Twenty-Four

Justin grasped her hands. 'Tell me, Lizzie! If nothing else, I'm your friend.'

There was a long silence before she spoke, her voice wavering. 'I told Victor I wanted to go to Spain, not back to the Seminary, and he said he'd take me. We stayed at an inn—he told me it was a very long journey to Dover and we'd need to rest. I expected him to ask for two rooms, but he said we'd have to share the same room. He didn't have sufficient funds for two. I couldn't argue with him. I'd no money myself and I was desperate to get to Dover. All I could think of was my father and Spain. It was the only chance I was going to have.'

Lizzie took a deep breath before she went on. 'Victor said I wasn't to worry, he'd be the perfect gentleman. There was a sofa in the room and he'd sleep on that. I was hugely tired from all the dancing I'd done, and from travelling to the inn, and I fell asleep almost instantly. But then—I don't know how long afterwards—all of a sudden I was awake and he was beside me in the bed.'

'My God, Lizzie. Didn't he know how old you were?'

She studied the hem of her nightgown intently. 'To be fair to Victor,' she said in the quietest of voices, 'he thought me eighteen.' And when her companion said nothing, she added unnecessarily, 'I lied to him.'

Even in the fragmentary light of a partial moon, she saw Justin's expression was severe. When he spoke, his voice was equally so. 'You need tell me no more. I've understood perfectly.'

'No, no!' she exclaimed, desperate for him not to think the very worst of her. 'You haven't understood. When I found him beside me, I screamed. He tried to hush me, then put his hand over my mouth to keep me quiet. But the more he tried to silence me, the more I struggled and the louder I screamed. It brought the landlady to the room. I remember that she stood in the doorway with a candle and just stared at us.'

Lizzie's eyes were wide with frightened memory, but she forced herself to go on. 'I thought I was saved, but then she turned to go—she'd assumed that we were newly weds and I was simply a scared bride. But when I called after her that I was fifteen and a schoolgirl, she stormed back into the room and wanted to throw us both out of the inn. It was only the fact that her husband interceded that I was allowed to stay the night.'

'And Victor? What happened to him?'

'He *was* thrown out and, as he'd spent all his money on the coach and his shot at the inn, he had to walk back to Bath.'

'I'm gratified to hear it. And did you have to walk back

to Bath, too?'

'No, indeed. The landlord sent a message to Miss Bates and she travelled to fetch me. I was in the most terrible disgrace. She said she didn't know what she was to do with a girl who had no morals and was bold beyond belief. She was so disturbed that she sent a message to my father and demanded that he come home immediately and chastise me.'

'I imagine he did just that.'

'Yes,' Lizzie said unhappily. 'He was furious. He never stopped berating me—though I think it was more because he'd been summoned from his regiment than because I'd run away. He never knew exactly what had happened since Miss Bates couldn't bring herself to speak of Victor. But what I'd done was wicked enough for him to say he was near to washing his hands of me for good. All the girls in school were told to ignore me, and nobody spoke to me for months. I was a pariah.'

'That seems very harsh.'

'Perhaps, but I think my punishment was just. It was a very bad thing I did.'

Justin looked into her eyes and she could see sympathy. 'And your father? Did you manage to part friends when he returned to Spain?'

Her eyes shadowed at the remembrance of their leave-taking. 'He bought me a dress,' she said sadly.

'And that was it?'

'He said that he must never again be called back to England in such a fashion and that I must obey Miss Bates in all things, even after I finished my schooling.'

'And that's why you came to Rye—Miss Bates decreed it?'

'To be fair,' Lizzie said judiciously, 'she gave me a choice, although not much of one.' She sucked in her cheeks. 'Piers, Piers Silchester was the alternative. He's the beau Miss Bates would like me to marry.'

'You had the chance of marriage and yet you preferred to be companion to an eighty year old?'

'Why should I jump at being wed?' Lizzie demanded. 'A husband like Piers would be the dullest thing.'

'You judge men severely.'

'*You* haven't met Piers.'

'I now have a lively interest in meeting him. Is he so bad?'

'No,' she wailed, 'he's so good. That's the trouble. He is most soulful. He teaches music at the school and has unimpeachable morals.'

Justin burst out laughing, and she slipped from his side and rounded on him. 'It's all very well for you to laugh, but can you imagine being married to someone who never says a bad thing about anyone, ever? Someone who is always fussing around you, someone who thinks you a goddess.'

'I doubt I'd marry anyone who thought me a goddess.' Justin grinned. 'Or even a god. But wouldn't you want to be worshipped, Lizzie?'

Her response was fierce. 'Only if I can worship equally!'

She was shivering and his arms were back again where she liked them most. She felt their strong clasp through the thin nightgown and shivered again, not from the cold this time, but from the delight of feeling him so close to her.

'And is the Victor story the only reason you refused to accept my invitation to Chelwood?'

'It was a very bad scandal. Miss Bates said I'd ruined myself and the best I could hope was to meet a man who lived retired from the world and knew nothing of such doings. That's why she champions Piers so strongly.' There was a pause before Lizzie continued in a voice that wobbled very slightly, 'I think she spoke truly. I didn't think—I don't think—that your friends, your neighbours, would judge me a suitable person for you to know.'

'Yet somehow I've got to know you. You were little more than a child when this happened and you were blameless.'

She shook her head vigorously. 'Not blameless, Justin. I behaved abominably. I used Victor and deceived him. He spent all his money on me and I left him penniless.'

'It was only what he deserved. Indeed, he got off lightly. He could have been dismissed from the army and put in gaol for abducting a girl of your age. He should think himself lucky that his only punishment was to walk back to Bath with his pockets to let.'

She nestled up to him. 'Doesn't it bother you that I was so wicked?'

'Dear Lizzie, you have no notion of real wickedness. What you have is a very small skeleton in a very young cupboard.' His lips brushed against her hair and came to rest on her cheek.

'I thought if I told you, you'd never wish to speak to me again.'

'How could you misjudge me so badly?'

'For a long time I didn't think you even liked me,' she said shyly. 'Not until that evening at Chelwood. Before then, you seemed cold and indifferent.'

'I was a fool. I liked you too much. And couldn't cope with the way you disturbed my peace of mind—and much else besides! You're not the only one to have skeletons.'

Lizzie had an inkling where those skeletons might lie, but her question was tentative. 'Was it perhaps your mother's friends who caused you distress?'

'One of her friends, certainly. I hated her crowd, Lizzie. Hated them with a passion. I loathed the way they descended on Chelwood, even after my parents' marriage had ended, polluting everything they touched, everything that was dear to me.'

'I can see you feel very strongly,' she said.

'I have good reason. I was little more than a stripling the last time she visited the estate. She brought with her a group of so-called society women and their husbands. One woman—she shall remain nameless—arrived with her cuckold of a husband and decided that I'd make pleasing entertainment for her. She came to my bedroom and... I imagine I need say no more. It was a shameful incident.

But bear in mind that I wasn't yet eighteen and that her husband was snoring in the next room. Some young men, no doubt, would be gratified by the attention. But I wasn't one of them. I was an innocent and deeply shocked. I would know how to deal with her now, but not then. I agonised for days over whether it had been my fault, whether I'd inadvertently suggested to her that I was attracted. At one point I was even going to confess to her husband! Instead, I went to my mother.'

'And what did she say?' The wretchedness in his face drove Lizzie to ask.

'She told me I should be grateful for what I could get.'

Lizzie felt sick.

'Now do you see why I don't want her here? She and her cronies are manipulative and immoral. That woman was happy—delighted—to pick on a vulnerable boy for her own base ends. She enjoyed the seduction. So did her husband. So did the whole company whom she lost no time in telling.'

'How very, very dreadful,' she said in a half whisper, and meant it with all her heart.

For a long time Justin was silent and, when he spoke, his voice was filled with regret. 'I'm sorry, Lizzie, I shouldn't have told you such a thing. It was selfish of me. I've kept it to myself all these years and that's where it should have stayed.'

She sank more deeply into his arms. 'Don't be sorry. I'm glad you told me. It means that you care for me enough to trust. I've been telling myself for days that I was an idiot to think you *could* care for me.'

'I care a great deal, and we've both been idiots, have we not? Maybe we can start again.'

'I hope so,' she murmured.

He tipped her face upwards and smiled down into her eyes. 'Shall we make a beginning? Right now?'

She tangled her arms around his neck and pulled him close. Her mouth softened, waiting for his kiss and, when it came, it was warm and inviting. Then more kisses—showering down on her, growing harder and hotter, gathering in intensity until her lips were bruised and swollen from his touch.

Finally, they pulled apart. 'One more kiss,' he whispered, looking longingly at her, 'and you must go. It's almost dawn.'

'One more kiss then,' she whispered back. 'But make sure it's a good one!'

Chapter Twenty-Five

Justin slept until noon, his valet having made no attempt to wake his master at the usual hour. Feeling well-rested for the first time in days, Justin was grateful. Not so grateful, though, when he learned that in his absence yesterday Chelwood had received an unexpected guest. His mother was this minute in the dining room, the valet told him, and partaking of a light nuncheon. The news caused Justin's heart to sink, but the thought of food jolted him fully awake, since he'd not eaten for hours and was extremely hungry. He had no relish for joining his mother at the table, but it clearly behoved him to welcome her to his house.

He might wish her miles away, but for the first time in years he needed to talk to her. Since he'd left Lizzie early that morning, Justin had been turning over in his mind an idea so shocking that it almost stopped his breath. It was impossible, he told himself, yet the idea wouldn't go away. And whatever plans Lady Lavinia entertained, might matter greatly for his own future.

Despite the pangs gnawing at his stomach, he took time

to dress carefully. A single-breasted blue tailcoat, a striped silk waistcoat and pantaloons of muted grey were set off by a dazzling snow-white cravat, arranged in precise and intricate folds. In half an hour, he walked into the dining room, complete to a shade. His mother had been making ready to leave and, as he walked through the door, tripped prettily towards him, trailing a heavy, sweet perfume behind her.

'Justin!' She threw up her hands in an exaggerated gesture. 'At last! How very good to see you.'

'Is it? It's been some years since you felt the need to see me, has it not?' His voice was bereft of emotion.

'Years indeed, but you appear to have changed little.' Lavinia couldn't quite conceal her sourness. 'Though it's true that you've grown—taller, broader. But that was inevitable, I imagine, given the soldier's life you've led.'

Justin had no intention of discussing soldiering with his mother, though right now his army career was uppermost in his mind. A mind fizzing with doubt and possibility. It was Lavinia's future he wanted to speak of, and its likely effects for him and the estate he loved. Food, he decided, would have to wait.

'Shall we repair to the library?' he asked. 'There's an excellent fire burning there and we can discuss your situation without fear of being interrupted.'

'And what situation is that?' she cooed, her tone at odds with the frown furrowing deep across her brow.

'Shall we go?'

He led the way out of the dining room and across the hall.

His words were not for the ears of even the most trusted of his servants, and he'd not speak until the library door was firmly shut. Lavinia's footsteps had dragged behind him. It was evident she was unhappy with this *tête-à-tête* and, once in the room, she eschewed the comfort of a fireside chair, and instead perched herself on the arm of the large, leather Chesterfield, as though ready to take flight at any moment.

'So, Mama,' he said abruptly, 'why are you here?'

'Why should I not be? Chelwood is your home and you are my son. There's no mystery to it.'

'That has always been the case, but you've not seen fit to visit before. At least not for many years.'

'There were reasons, as you well know,' she said pettishly.

'I could point out that you divorced your husband, not your son, but that would be stating the obvious. What I want to know is why you've returned now, having stayed away so long?'

Justin knew the answer, but he wanted to hear it from her lips.

'It's quite simple.' She attempted an airy tone. 'I believe sufficient time has passed since the unpleasant events you mention, and thought it time to see you again.'

Surely she could do better than that, he thought derisively. He wanted to laugh out loud, but schooled his face into blankness. 'So why didn't you write? Let me know you were coming? You arrive out of the blue and send my household into a flurry. I've little contact with polite society, but isn't it still usual to announce one's arrival? Even, dare I say, wait for a definite invitation?'

'Pooh!' Lavinia brushed aside his criticism. 'Chivers dealt with my arrival admirably. Really, he's grown into an excellent butler. You would never have thought it, since he was such an awkward young man when Lucien first employed him.'

She daintily re-arranged the folds of her dress, before continuing, 'May I ask *you* a question now, Justin? Where were you last night? I would not have thought country delights could keep you out so long and so late.'

He had no intention of explaining his absence, and neither was he going to allow his mother to change the subject. Ignoring her remark, he asked again, 'So why didn't you write to tell me of your visit?'

'I did write.'

'Only to say that your esteemed husband had found himself more entertaining company.'

'Surely that was enough. It was hard to write even that.'

For the first time, Lavinia's voice had lost its false animation and, for the first time, Justin felt the stirrings of pity. She bowed her head and he noticed how frail were her shoulders, how limply the rich satin of her dress hung on the thin frame.

'I'm sorry that things have come to this pass,' he said awkwardly. 'But I can't think that Chelwood is the answer to your problems.'

'What other solution can you offer me? I have nowhere else to go.'

And now he was staring into eyes that were wide and scared. Her face, so smooth and lovely when he'd last looked on it, had crumpled into lines of terror at the future she faced.

'Nowhere to go? You have friends surely?'

'Friends!' she almost spat the word. 'I have no friends. They are hangers-on, fair weather people who trim their sails according to the wind. And the wind is definitely blowing the wrong way for me. When I married the duke, my every move was dogged by a trail of admirers. Flattering, effusive. They were always in the house, always by my side. Of course, Dorian is so rich he could afford to support any number of fawning courtiers. But that's over now. I'm an abandoned woman, a poor prospect for a social climber.'

Justin knew his mother's world sufficiently to realise that this latest scandal must have rung out across London. There had already been too many in Lavinia's life, he thought, and this time she would not come through. None of her so-called friends would offer her sanctuary, for fear of being tainted by association.

'I presume the duke has closed up the London house?'

'Naturally. His latest *innamorata* is an Italian princess and it's to Italy that he's gone. He intends to buy a large estate there, I believe. Bianca will require the very finest, you can be sure.'

'And he's left you with nothing? Can that really be the case?'

'It may be hard for you to believe, Justin, but it's the truth. When I wed the duke, I had no voice in drafting the marriage settlement. I was without family to oversee the negotiations and I'd no money to afford a lawyer to protect my interests. And, after all, I was bringing little to the marriage except myself. By the time I met Dorian, I'd run through what small capital I possessed. It follows then, that as soon as I became worthless to the duke, I was forced to leave with as little as I'd come.'

Was Lavinia suggesting that his father had left the wife he adored without means? That couldn't be so.

'I imagine you received a settlement at the time of the divorce,' he said, in a colourless voice. He hated to talk about this most wretched time in his life.

'A small settlement, Justin. Your father was not ungenerous, but neither was he very generous. And I'm an expensive woman.' She gave a small, hesitant laugh. 'The money I received from Lucien ran out very quickly and a condition of the divorce was that I must never petition for more.'

It gave Justin a jolt to realise that his father could lack sentiment, even feeling, towards the woman he'd loved to distraction. There were reasons of course, but still it didn't quite accord with the image of Lucien Delacourt that he held in his heart.

In some agitation, he strode to the window, drumming his fingers on the wood of the broad sill. He looked out at the grassy expanse, still wet from the autumn mist and, in the distance, the soft lines of trees, a faded blur on the horizon. This was a landscape he loved, a landscape he would defend with his life. His mother did not belong here and he felt a vague, anonymous threat gathering pace and stiffened himself to meet it.

'I suppose there's no question of a reconciliation between yourself and the duke?' The question was crass, but he felt trapped, defensive.

Lavinia jumped up from her perch, twisting her mouth into a small, bitter shape. 'The *principessa* is twenty-five. Do you think he's likely to return to me?' She fixed her son with an unflinching gaze and, when he didn't respond, exclaimed in a voice that shook, 'Look at me!'

There was a long silence while they faced each other across the room. At length, Lavinia took a deep breath and said quietly, 'Would you really have me return to a man who has brought public shame on me? I've not been a good person, Justin, I think we're both agreed on that, but for the last seven years I've tried to be a dutiful wife. I believe I succeeded—perhaps too well. Those years have taught me there can be no greater comfort than an unspoiled conscience, and I would never willingly go back to a man who has sullied the new life I've tried to lead.'

'I understand your repugnance, but I can't believe you will be happy living miles from the slightest gaiety or distraction.' Justin paused for a moment, unwilling even now to capitulate, but then forced himself to continue. 'However, for as long as you wish to stay at Chelwood, you are welcome to do so.'

His mother smiled faintly. 'Thank you. I'll endeavour to be a conformable house guest. But there seems to be far more distraction in the neighbourhood than you're willing to admit. Do tell me, where were you last night?'

'I had business to attend to, and it took rather longer

than I expected,' he said shortly. 'If you'll excuse me, I must leave you to your own devices for the moment. When you walk out, you will see the estate has fallen into some disrepair and there's much to do. I've not met Mellors for several days—he is the new bailiff— and I'm aware that he has a long list of things he wishes to discuss.'

Justin nodded a brief farewell and made for the door, but then something prompted him to turn and say, 'I intend to invite one or two of my neighbours to Chelwood in the next day or so and you will most likely meet them.'

Lavinia raised her beautifully shaped eyebrows. 'They must be special people if you've invited them here. The place has always been so well guarded against intruders, or at least it was under Lucien's rule.'

He was tempted to retort that she and her friends had frequently breeched Chelwood's walls, but said, 'I'll leave you to decide whether or not they are special. You may remember Henrietta Croft—she was a good friend to my father. She has a young companion, Elizabeth Ingram, who will accompany her.'

'And I imagine it's Elizabeth Ingram who is the attraction,' his mother said shrewdly.

Justin brushed the comment aside. 'If you're to remain at Chelwood, I'd like you to meet them both.'

'Miss Elizabeth is evidently important to you. But why must I wait until she comes to Chelwood to meet her? Chivers tells me that today is Rye's annual fair and that it's magnificent. Why don't you send a note to Brede House—

have I that right—and ask them both to meet us there?'

'Mrs Croft is too infirm to attend any fair.' Justin was impatient to be gone, and annoyed that his mother was taking too much interest in his personal life.

'But the young woman would like it greatly, I'm sure,' Lavinia pursued. 'And I would love to go, Justin. It's a very long time since I attended such an event.'

'I doubt you'd enjoy it.'

'You'd be surprised. I've changed a great deal since we last met. For one thing, I've learned to find pleasure in simple things.'

He *would* be surprised, he thought. Simple pleasures and his mother were hardly bedfellows. It was far more likely that she was already planning to summon to her side the detestable people she'd earlier denounced.

'So you'll not be expecting London society to keep you company at Chelwood?'

'Have you listened to nothing I've said?' Her voice was tinged with anger. 'Or is it that you mistrust me so completely? You're too suspicious for your own good, my angel. You always were. I imagine that comes from Lucien. But you mustn't think so badly of me. There are always two sides to every question.'

She must have seen his sceptical expression because she went on, 'I understand more than you think. I'm aware of what you suffered in your youth. You're a grown man and yet you still flush when I talk of it. It pains you, I can see. The deed itself was nothing—a mere rite of passage—but the gossip, the innuendo, the husband who pretended he wished to call you out—my poor dear, that was a shameful humiliation to visit on you.'

Justin was shocked to realise his mother had divined his feelings so accurately. He'd always imagined her indifferent, or worse, laughing with her friends at his discomfiture. It seemed that wasn't so. She had not laughed after all, but been powerless to prevent his humbling. Powerless to prevent the scandal that had dogged his younger years and sent him hurtling into the army, desperate to escape the clutch of any woman.

Lavinia watched him measuringly. 'So will you escort me this afternoon and introduce me to this young lady? I'm most anxious to meet her.'

Justin thought for a moment. It was important that he very soon introduce Lizzie to his mother, bearing in mind what he intended, and an informal setting such as the fair might render a first meeting easier for them both.

He made a swift decision. 'I'll send Alfred with a note to Brede House.'

'Excellent. Meanwhile my maid can unpack my portmanteaux. The dresses will be horribly creased, but she can press a plain silk and this afternoon we will sally forth to Rye. Together.' Her tone was almost carefree.

He gave a small bow and walked back into the hall, but had gone only a few steps when Chivers approached him bearing a silver salver. 'A letter, sir, just arrived. I had no sight of the messenger.'

Justin glanced at the hand without recognition. The letter had to be from Lizzie, he thought, though the writing seemed clumsy. Eagerly, he tore open the envelope and found himself disappointed, but intrigued. It appeared that someone else wanted to meet him at the fair.

Chapter Twenty-Six

Lizzie woke from a deep sleep. Hester was moving around the room, gathering the clothes Lizzie had thrown off when she fell into bed at dawn. Somehow she would have to explain the crumpled and soiled nightgown, but not now. She lay still and soundless until the maid left to go downstairs. A thread of excitement fizzed through her, from the tip of her head to her smallest toes. Justin cared for her. Had cared for her from their very first meeting. She'd always dreamed of finding love and with a man she could love equally. Now she had. It was true he'd not actually said the words, *I love you*, but in every other way he'd shown the depth of his feelings. Last night she'd been left tingling with happiness, a bleak future suddenly turned rose-coloured.

Hearing Hester's retreating footsteps on the stairs, she felt it safe to open her eyes. The dawn had promised a beautiful day ahead and now, glancing through the bedroom window, Lizzie could see the promise had been fulfilled, a hazy circle of gold shining from a cloudless sky. It would be a more than beautiful day, if Justin were to call. She scrambled out of bed, washing quickly, and pulling from the wardrobe the dress of primrose floret sarsnet she'd not worn since its return from Chelwood, cleaned and pressed. Perhaps, today, she would be visiting the house again, wearing this selfsame dress, but not this time as a trespasser. Just in case, she'd make sure there were new slippers on her feet and a newly refurbished reticule in her hand.

Anxiously, she checked the mirror. Her complexion was smooth and clear and glowing with happiness, her hair shining but hopelessly tangled. She should go to Mrs Croft, but first she must set her hair to rights. Standing before the glass, she arranged her long curls to tumble from a chignon at the top of her head, then softly cluster about her neck and cheeks. It was a style that would have suited the ballroom, but Lizzie didn't care. Today, she wanted to look as special as she felt.

Satisfied with what she saw, she tripped down the stairs into the small, square hall. A thick white envelope lay on the console table, her name clearly inscribed on the front. It was from Justin—she recognised the writing. An invitation. As long as Mrs Croft was willing, she *would* be going to Chelwood this very day!

Hester appeared from the basement kitchen and hurried up to her. There was a doubtful expression on her face and her voice was just this side of querulous. 'What exactly's going on, miss?'

Lizzie tried to look blank. 'What do you mean, Hester?'

'There's a nightgown of yours I've put in the laundry

that looks as though it fell into the marsh,' the maid said accusingly. 'And you with it. But you're looking as fine as fivepence this morning.'

Lizzie laughed as naturally as she could. 'Now, what would I be doing in the marsh? As for looking fine, I've simply dressed for the day. The sun is shining and there's not a cloud in the sky.'

The maid sniffed a little too loudly. 'That's as may be, but what's happening within the house is more important. Mrs Croft has been asking for you. The poor dear is feeling weary this morning and still abed.'

'I'm so sorry,' Lizzie said quickly. 'I'll go to her this minute.'

Hester sniffed once more and, leaving the maid looking dubious, Lizzie ran back up the stairs to Henrietta's bedroom, clasping the envelope tightly in her hand. Mrs Croft's voice was slight and fading as she bade her enter. The old lady was sitting upright in bed, a mound of pillows behind her, and an empty tea cup nearby. Her face was tired and pale.

'Forgive me for being late, Mrs Croft. I suffered a bad night and no-one woke me.'

'I told Hester not to disturb you. You've been looking a little wan of late, my dear, and I don't want you to fall ill. One invalid in the house is sufficient.' The old lady gave her a penetrating look. 'But you seem much recovered this morning. Perhaps it was only sleep you lacked.'

'It must have been,' Lizzie agreed, grateful she need offer no further explanation. 'And now that I'm here, what tasks have you for me? The newspaper has arrived if you'd care to have it read. Or I could finish sorting your workbox while you watch—so far I've only tidied one layer.'

Mrs Croft shrunk back onto her pillows. 'I think not, my dear. I shall spend the day very quietly. But you have a letter.' She pointed to the crisp, white object in her companion's hand.

If she opened it here, Lizzie thought, she might get the permission she needed.

She slit open the envelope. 'It's from Sir Justin Delacourt. An invitation, Mrs Croft. He wants me to... to meet him at the fair. Wants both of us are to meet him—by the door of St Mary's.'

It was a surprise. Lizzie had expected a visit to Chelwood and here was Justin wanting to meet in a public place and amid a crowd of people.

'That will be the annual Rye fair. Hester mentioned it this morning and I told her she may go.'

'Then I'd better not.' She felt cloaked in despondency.

'Naturally, you must go. It's a marvellous occasion and not to be missed. Hester will be gone a few hours only and I've no need of constant attention—at least not yet.' The jest was weak, but the pressure of her hand on Lizzie's arm was determined.

'You must write to Justin, though, and tell him that I'm not fit enough to join you both. But give him my very best wishes and tell him there will always be a welcome for him here.'

Lizzie could see the old lady getting tireder by the

minute, waiting for her companion to leave so that she could once more fall into a doze. If so, it was fortunate. There was only an hour before she was supposed to meet Justin and it was a long walk into town.

'If you're sure you'll be safe on your own...'

'Go, my dear, go!' Henrietta shushed her out of the room. 'Walk there with Hester and make sure you both enjoy yourselves.'

~

Lizzie had expected a modest affair—Rye was only a small town—and she was taken aback when she and Hester walked through the Strand Gate. A veritable cacophony of smells and noises greeted them as they reached the bottom of Mermaid Street, today as innocent and unthreatening as any other in the town. Hester linked arms with her and together they marched determinedly up the infamous road to the square of streets above.

Each was filled with noise and bustle and everywhere booths and standings spilled out over the thoroughfare, many of them crammed high with food. There were stalls for oysters, stalls for hot pies and sausages—disappearing at a rapid rate—and tables filled with rows and rows of gilt gingerbread. Benches were set out here and there for people to sit and eat their fill.

There were stalls selling clothes, and toy stalls for the children, gay with decorative paint and coloured lamps. But the predominant interest of the fair was entertainment.

Lizzie saw in the distance the Rector of St Mary's looking somewhat aghast, and she wondered whether he'd given his approval to such wholesale abandonment: horse riders doing tricks were everywhere, tumblers, illusionists, even a knife swallower. In the background, a band of itinerant musicians consisting of a double drum, a Dutch organ, a tambourine, violin and pipes was playing a selection of military tunes.

Lizzie strolled past food and toy stalls, past the fire eater who was drawing gasps from his captive crowd and past the puppet show. By now she'd lost sight of Hester, who had lingered at several of the stalls. She would leave the maid to choose new trimmings for her hat, Lizzie decided, while she made for the church. It was almost two and Justin would be waiting.

Ever since she'd opened his message, she'd been puzzling over why he'd chosen to meet her in such a public place. When they'd parted early this morning, his invitation had been to Chelwood, and she'd been cherishing the thought that this time she would visit the home he loved, as his sweetheart. She'd imagined them walking in the gardens together, talking—just the two of them—exchanging confidences, exploring feelings. A tryst at Chelwood would have been so much more romantic than the hubbub surrounding them here in Rye.

Out of the blue, Lizzie was hit by an uncomfortable thought. Had Justin changed their meeting place because, when he'd woken this morning, he'd felt Chelwood too intimate? Had last night been too good to be true and he was already regretting his words? If so, he'd want to let her down gently. He'd meet her as promised, but choose a place where they were not alone. A place in which he could melt into the crowd, escape an intimacy he wished to be free of.

The chimes of St Mary's great blue and cream clock rang out the hour. Lizzie looked up as she passed beneath its tower, and the slightest of shivers nipped at her spine. The clock's stern message, *For our time is a very shadow that passeth away*, seemed even sterner today. There was no sign of Justin at the front entrance and she walked quickly past the wide oak door, impatient to find him. To shake off the doubts that had suddenly descended on her.

Rounding a corner buttress, she was relieved to see his figure in the distance, his bright halo of hair glistening beneath the strong sunlight. Dressed in the palest of grey, he could have been a classical statue dropped amid the dark lichen of the gravestones. But he was not alone!

Lizzie stopped in her tracks. A garrulous neighbour, perhaps, waylaying Justin and preventing him from meeting her at the church door? Lizzie looked again. He had a woman with him, a young and shapely woman: a voluptuous figure emerging from the clinging folds of a bright green dress, and an abundant tangle of long, dark hair hanging down her back.

It was Rosanna!

Chapter Twenty-Seven

Lizzie watched, half-hidden by the ancient stone buttress, her mind churning. The two of them had their heads together, as though in intimate conversation. Whatever they were saying, it seemed to engage them to the exclusion of all else. What was Justin doing with a woman he knew to be his enemy? He'd said that Rosanna had nothing more to tell him, and sworn that he'd have no further dealings with the smugglers. So why was he talking to her? Rosanna had sufficient charm to deceive any man, even Justin, but surely he'd not trust her a second time—unless he was so fascinated that he couldn't help himself. The thought that Justin might be no more steadfast than any other soldier she'd known made Lizzie's heart contract.

At last, the conversation came to an end and they were saying goodbye. Justin was walking in her direction now, and Lizzie moved out of the shadow of the church into his path. She thought she saw an expression of guilt flit across his face.

'Why were you meeting that woman?' she demanded.

He looked shocked at her curt greeting, but answered readily enough. 'She asked to meet me, Lizzie.'

'But why? You said you'd have nothing more to do with her or with the Chapman gang.'

'She sent me a note saying she had information and, as I'm still looking for Gil, I agreed to meet her. I thought it my last chance.'

His voice was quiet, but Lizzie sensed his growing displeasure. It made no difference. Inside her, a fiery ball was unfurling—a ball of misgiving and anger.

'Rosanna will tell you nothing. You said so yourself. She wants only to dupe you again.' And lead you into danger and misery, she thought.

'Things may have changed,' Justin said evenly, trying it seemed to defuse the tension. 'When Rosanna learnt that I'd joined the gang, she remembered our earlier conversation and believed she knew why. Not that I was a disgruntled ex-soldier as I told Chapman, but that I hoped to discover Gil's whereabouts. She reasoned that if I was prepared to go to such lengths, the matter must be far more important than she'd thought. The gang boasts some evil men and I was prepared to put myself in danger. She is fearful of them herself.'

Lizzie's laugh was short and scornful. 'Fearful? Rosanna? She is Thomas Chapman's lover and hangs on his every word.'

'She *was* his lover,' Justin corrected, 'but she is disenchanted with Chapman and regrets keeping company with his gang. Above all, she is desperate to be free—of them and all their doings—and has promised to aid me in return for helping her to settle elsewhere.'

Lizzie wanted to hit him and hit him hard. She couldn't believe that such a clear-sighted man could be so badly taken in.

'And how precisely does she propose to aid you?'

'She knew Gil a great deal better than she admitted when I last spoke to her.'

'Of course she did. That's always been evident—at least to me. But she's not previously been forthcoming, so why is she talking now?'

'I told you. She came to the conclusion that I'd only joined the gang to find Gil. And that gave her the chance to break free—if she helped me, I would help her.'

'And you believe that?'

'Why are you so suspicious, Lizzie? You sound angry and jealous. I'd not thought it of you.'

His remark served only to stoke the fires. 'Jealous of Rosanna? No, indeed! But I am a woman and not so easily deceived.'

Justin glowered, but she went on, 'You didn't see her with Thomas Chapman. If you had, you would not believe she'd ever leave him, let alone work against him.'

'It's possible for people to change,' he said slowly. 'Rosanna may have been infatuated, but she's come now to see the man's true nature and doesn't like what she's discovered. I believe her—and my judgment must prevail.'

Lizzie raised her eyebrows. 'Your judgment has proved faulty in the past. Why can't you believe me when I tell you that she is still deceiving you?'

'I believe your woman's heart is leading you astray. What, after all, has she to gain by deceit?'

'*You*. She has you to gain. Rosanna is the kind of woman who gets her man, and you are now the man in her sights. She is aiming for you, Justin, even if you don't or won't see it.'

'That is utter nonsense.'

'Is it? Then consider. Why did the gang decide to recruit you? You were a most unlikely candidate. The story you spun would not have stood up to any close inspection— unless, of course, Rosanna was urging Chapman to employ you and, to please her, he agreed.

'What!'

'And you agreed, didn't you? When they approached you, you accepted their proposition without hesitation. I wonder, was it in order to get closer to her? Did you become a smuggler because of her?'

'Lizzie.' He grabbed her by the arms. 'I cannot believe we are talking like this. You know very well why I joined the gang. I've no reason to believe Rosanna had anything to do with it. I can't know, of course, if she suggested the idea to Thomas Chapman, but my motivation was clear. Just as it is now. Gil's story is unfinished— I want to complete it, and not just for my sake. Remember that his parents are living a nightmare. I want to be able to tell them the truth of what happened to their son. And if Rosanna can help, then I'll take that help.'

Lizzie struggled free of his hands and planted herself

firmly in front of him. 'If she is so keen to help, what information did she give you? You were speaking for long enough.'

'We spoke for a few minutes only—she dared not be seen talking to me. Whether she's still with Chapman or not, she's frightened of him. He's a very dangerous man and I wasn't willing to expose her to risk by keeping her talking too long.'

Lizzie turned from him, exasperated, and began to pace up and down between the gravestones, only stopping when her shoes were dark from the damp of long grass. Justin was wrong, utterly wrong, and she feared his refusal to believe her would one day return to haunt him. But it was the knowledge that he'd rather trust Rosanna's words than her own that filled her with despair.

When she spoke, though, she tried to keep her voice level, almost indifferent. 'So what now?'

'She has promised to arrange another meeting at a time and place where she'll not be seen.'

'A lovers' assignation?'

She could almost hear his teeth grind. 'I'd like to shake some sense into you, Lizzie. You must know how I feel about you.'

Did she? Did she really know how he felt? When it came down to it, all she knew was that he thought her a charming companion to walk beside, a lovely face to look at, an enticing body to embrace. He'd made no vow of enduring love, no vow they had a future together. She had come to meet him today, hoping to hear those words.

Instead, she'd seen him talking secretly to another woman. And what a woman! Made desperate by the idea, Lizzie was stung into unrestrained speech.

'I know how you feel? It's my misfortune that I'm beginning to understand. Last night—' she broke off, struggling to keep her voice steady,'—last night you kissed me as a lover, but not one mention of love passed your lips. You want no ties, it seems. A wandering soldier— just like Victor. Before you leave for Spain, were you hoping to complete what he left unfinished?'

Her sentiments were bitter, but she wanted to hurt him. Perhaps she had. She'd certainly enraged him, since she had never seen him so angry. His hands clenched into fists, his eyes blazed dark and, beneath the tan, his face was deeply flushed. Even the golden halo of his hair seemed on fire.

'How dare you say such a thing! And to liken me to that man!'

'Why not?' She was in the thick of it now, so why hold back? She was hurt, bleeding, and she lashed out indiscriminately. 'Women are incidental to military life— I've always known that. My own father cannot be bothered with me. The focus of his world is elsewhere. Yours, too. I've been an entertaining interlude for you, that is all.'

'I can't believe you would say such a thing.'

'But why not? A few hours ago I almost gave myself to you, and yet I find you conversing intimately with a woman who has known half the men of this town. And not content with that, you intend to meet her again. And your reason? That she might just help you. Another meeting, another delightful *tête-a-tête*,' Lizzie mocked. 'What else am I to think?'

'If you value me so poorly, think it then.'

'Is this the young lady, Justin?'

Startled, they turned to stare at the newcomer. Lady Lavinia rustled delicately along the path towards them. As she drew near, she looked interestedly from one inflamed face to the other.

Justin compressed his lips and said in a voice tinged with an arctic cold, 'Mama, this is Miss Elizabeth Ingram. As I told you, she is companion to Mrs Croft. Miss Ingram, allow me to introduce my mother, the Duchess of Alton.'

Lizzie curtseyed briefly and received a nod in recognition. There was an uncomfortable silence while the duchess, a bland expression on her face, waited for one of them to speak. It fell to Justin.

'If there is nothing further Miss Ingram, Mama, I hope you'll excuse me. A great deal of work awaits me at Chelwood and I should be returning there.'

And with that, he strode off, his feet beating a tattoo on the uneven pathway. His mother looked thoughtfully after him, and then turned to Lizzie.

'Well, my dear, hats off to you. In all my misdemeanours, I have never managed to make Justin quite so furious. Cold and unforgiving certainly, shocked and determined, too. But never quite so angry.'

Lizzie, shocked into speechlessness by the disasters of the afternoon, had grown pale, but the duchess's speech caused her to flush with embarrassment. 'I don't take that as a compliment, Your Grace. The conversation... I'd not meant, you see... '

'I do see. No-one better. In the heat of the moment, words have a habit of running away with one, do they not?'

For the first time, Lizzie looked properly at the woman who'd interrupted their bad-tempered tirade. The richness of her clothes was overwhelming, the perfume she wore heavily expensive, and the jewellery that clasped her neck and her arms surely worth a queen's, if not a king's, ransom. But though she exuded wealth and ease, behind the façade Lizzie sensed that she was looking at a lost and lonely woman. It made her more candid than she would otherwise have been.

'I can't help but feel as I do,' she responded, 'but I should not have said some of the things I did.'

Lavinia's gaze was shrewd. 'I'm sure you'll not relish my advice, but I'll give it anyway. A simple adage only—don't let the grass grow beneath your feet.'

'What do you mean, ma'am?'

'I have a difficult relationship with my son, Miss Ingram, but I'm quite aware that he is a man worth winning and keeping. The winning I think has been easy for you, but the keeping...ah, that's a different matter entirely. And as a woman who has managed in her time to win the most appalling of men, and lose one of the best, I know what I'm talking of. Don't allow the wounds to fester. Go to him as soon as you can!'

Chapter Twenty-Eight

For at least an hour, Justin sat at his desk without moving. He'd returned from the fair to work, but been too disturbed to make a start. The encounter with Lizzie had been short, sharp and devastating. It had never for one moment occurred to him that she'd challenge his decision to talk again to Rosanna, or misinterpret the woman's presence in the churchyard. When he'd received Rosanna's note, it had seemed sensible they met in the churchyard, where he'd already arranged to be waiting for Lizzie.

The meeting had gone well, but then... Lizzie had accused him of poor judgement and, even worse, the grossest conduct. She'd refused to believe his denials, no matter how vehement. Rather, she'd chosen to believe her own fabrication, accusing him of playing with her affections. It sickened him to think she believed he cared nothing for her, that he was using her as a plaything.

Yet when she'd accused him of not speaking one word of love, he knew himself guilty. Last night, as she'd said, he had kissed her as a lover, but not vowed his love. He'd grappled to say the right words and failed. And he'd been right to fail. Right to keep silent. If he spoke words of love, Lizzie was entitled to expect more. And though he might kick against it, he knew now that he couldn't give more.

For a while, the dream of a different future had hovered before him, but he'd come to realise it was impossible. Chelwood might survive without him, but a wife would not, especially not a wife such as Lizzie Ingram. He couldn't marry and then abandon her to go to war. She was unlikely to sit quietly and wait for his return from Spain, and he couldn't expect that of her. He was trapped by the allegiance he owed elsewhere. To the army, to his father. Trapped in a life without love.

And what if he were to lose all sense of duty, as he'd been so tempted to do in the hours since he'd last seen her? Would that result in happiness? For him, for her? How happy would he be retired from the army? How happy would he make her? The marriage could be a disaster for them both. She was a restless spirit, constantly seeking distraction. She'd poured scorn on marriage and no wonder. She would find it a straitjacket.

The thought made him grasp his pencil so fiercely that it snapped clean in two. She would find marriage a straitjacket! She'd told him that. Did Lizzie, in fact, have no serious thoughts of a future with him? Was that the real truth? Then why was he allowing himself to be torn apart by opposing loyalties, when she could be the one who was guilty—guilty of playing with *his* affections? He was stunned by the notion, but the more he thought of it, the more he realised it could be true.

Their quarrel had come out of the blue. It seemed to him now that Lizzie had acted deliberately in setting her opinion against his, insisting that Rosanna was deceiving him. Yet she'd offered no sensible reason why that should be. Her accusation that Rosanna was out to attach him was ridiculous. Lizzie couldn't seriously believe it. So had it simply been a ploy to walk away? A convenient ploy if she was regretting those kisses.

His life in the military must have made him attractive to a girl who craved adventure, but what if he were no longer a soldier? If, today, he'd given in to temptation and abandoned his military career? He would end up boring her as thoroughly as the hapless Silchester. If he should ever doubt Lizzie's need for excitement, he had only to remember her past. A child's wish to find her father was forgivable, but did her uneasy relationship with Colonel Ingram make any soldier she met fair game? The incident with the wretched Victor—how forgivable was that?

In Lizzie's account, she appeared the wronged innocent, but she'd also admitted to making up stories to deceive her abductor, or to put it plainly, had admitted to telling lies. Of course, the man was an unscrupulous philanderer and deserved all he got. But how dared she utter his and Victor's name in the same breath!

It would seem that he'd misjudged her badly. He had thought Lizzie different from the society women he disdained—innocent and free-spirited—but today's bruising encounter had left him wondering how different. Was she just as manipulative, just as unfeeling, simply able to disguise it better? To think that he'd opened his heart to her, confessed a vulnerability that he'd buried so surely years ago. How could he have done that?

There was a knock at the door and he lifted his head impatiently. He knew Mellors to be riding to a far distant tenant, and had hoped that he'd not see his bailiff for many hours.

'May I come in?'

His mother stood on the threshold, the newly donned gown of aubergine satin incongruous amid the rough furnishings of the estate office. Justin stood up as she walked into the room, but made no attempt to offer a seat.

'I'll not stay long,' she said, having evidently understood his mood. 'I've come to speak to you of your young friend.'

He stiffened. 'What of her?'

'She is a lively young lady, is she not? Intelligent, sharp. Beautiful, too. You could do far worse if you should be hanging out for a wife.'

'I'm not,' he said shortly.

'That's a pity. I think she would suit you well.'

He shifted irritably onto one foot. 'Cut to the chase, Mama, what is it you want?'

'For once dearest, Justin, I want nothing. But you do, I think.'

He didn't pretend to misunderstand her. 'Forgive me for being blunt, but your knowledge is imperfect and I'd ask you not to interfere.'

'I've no intention of doing so. I've come merely to

remind you that intransigence is likely to lose you what you want most.'

'I thank you for your concern, Mama. However, you have no need to bother yourself further.'

'In other words, mind my own business. I will, I promise, but it seems to me that the pair of you are behaving somewhat stupidly. Like star-crossed lovers. But you're not in a play, my dears. This is real life and, as an old hand at it, you should take my advice and not play too long.'

'Is that all?' He was wishing his mother at the other end of the world.

'It is—a simple message. You love her. I can see it in your eyes, hear it in your voice, but you wish to deny it to yourself.'

Justin refused to look at her, fixing his gaze some distance away at a broken floorboard.

'You love her,' his mother continued inexorably, 'and love does not come easily, or often. Don't let it slip through your fingers.'

Her skirts swished through the doorway and she was gone. Justin closed the door loudly behind her and grabbed a cluster of files that had been gathering dust on a nearby cabinet. He would work on these, he decided. Anything to keep his mother's voice at bay. If *he* knew Lizzie so little, how could Lavinia be an expert? Whatever she might claim, his mother was simply interfering, and no doubt enjoying it. She must already be bored at Chelwood and looking for something to enliven her day. He opened the first file.

But what if she were right and they were both behaving

as stupidly as she claimed? What if the fears tormenting him for the past hour were mere will o' the wisps? A heaviness sapped his spirits. But even if they were, he thought, it would change nothing. His future could be no different. He owed too much—to Lucien Delacourt who had been mother and father to him, to his army comrades who'd supported him through thick and thin. He must keep to the path he had chosen.

His mother had advised him to marry, but she took no note of loyalties, of duties that must be met. To Lavinia, the military was what men played at until they found something better. She had nagged his poor father to distraction until he'd given up the world he loved, and for what? Now she was doing the same to him. He closed the file and returned it to the pile with a loud smack, sending clouds of dust rising thickly into the air. But in one thing she *was* right, damn her. He'd never felt so deeply for any person on earth as he did for Lizzie Ingram, and he knew that he never would.

He must forget such feelings, he thought grimly, put behind him the role of lovesick swain, and return to the life he knew. Chelwood was in better shape than it had been for years and he need tarry no longer. In the next few days, he would hand the reins to Mellors and say goodbye to his neighbours. They would feel little surprise since he'd already hinted at his departure. A few more days and he'd be packed and ready to leave—back to a man's world. That's where he belonged and where he'd stay.

A sudden squall of rain beat at the window. The weather

had turned and a storm was setting in. He sat for long minutes staring through the glass, then irritated by his lack of action, picked up the piece of paper lying crumpled at the side of the desk, and smoothed it out to read again. Rosanna had been swift to keep her promise, and their meeting was already arranged for this very night. He must put aside his warring emotions and hold to the fact that he might at last discover Gil's fate. And tomorrow, he would brave one last encounter with the woman he loved.

Once again, he sat down at the battered desk and this time took up his quill. His note to Brede House took some time to compose and several wasted sheets lay in the paper basket before he was satisfied with the result. He kept the note crisp and neutral, merely informing Lizzie that he had heard from Rosanna and that their meeting was tonight. If it was convenient to Miss Ingram, he'd be at Brede House at midday on the morrow, when he would convey whatever information he'd garnered.

Chapter Twenty-Nine

Lizzie turned the note over again, and for the hundredth time read its cold, unfeeling message. It was clear that when Justin called tomorrow, it would be their last meeting. In a short while she would be sure to hear that he had left Chelwood Place to return to Spain, and that would be the end of everything. How had it come to this?

Twenty-four hours ago she'd been deliriously happy, yet now... She let the note drift to the floor and wandered to the window. The rain had stopped, but mists were already stealing out of the twilight and an ice-cold moon had risen in the sky. Winter was beckoning, and all she had to look forward to was this quiet house and the narrow, loveless life that went with it.

A sheaf of drawings was laid on the window seat and she flicked idly through the pages, stopping at one that she'd hidden from sight. The sketch had been done only that morning, just before she'd set off for the fair—it was one of Justin and herself, entwined in each other's arms. For long minutes, she couldn't tear her eyes from it. Slowly, overwhelmingly, waves of sorrow built and toppled within her. But then Hester's voice was sounding from below, calling on her to attend Mrs Croft, and she hastily stifled the tears that threatened.

Henrietta was propped upright in her favourite fireside chair, her feet resting on an old brown velvet stool. A bright fire burned in the grate and, despite the gloomy furnishings, the room looked warm and welcoming.

'You called for me, Mrs Croft. Are you ready to retire?' Lizzie asked.

'Not quite ready, my dear. I shall read a little while longer I think, but I have news for you. Good news.'

Lizzie's heart quickened. Had Justin regretted the cold note and sent another message, one that sought to make amends? A ripple of joy spread itself outwards, radiating through her whole body.

'A message has arrived,' Mrs Croft continued. The rippling grew intense, and Lizzie looked eagerly across at the old lady. 'Two messages, in fact. They came this morning, but in some strange fashion became entangled in my books from the circulating library. Hester has only just this minute found them.'

If they'd come this morning, neither could be a message from Justin. Lizzie's joy died as instantly as it had flamed.

'Who are they from?' She tried to infuse her voice with interest.

'From my cousin, my dear. From Clementine. She promised to pass on any news she had of your father, and she has done exactly that.'

For a moment, Lizzie was stunned. 'How is he?' she stuttered. 'He's not—'

'Don't be alarmed, Elizabeth, he's suffered no harm. On the contrary, he's been given leave. And from what you say, it's not before time—the poor man has enjoyed little respite from the fighting.'

'My father is returning from Spain?' Lizzie was still trying to grasp the news.

'He is. Isn't that wonderful, my dear? And Clementine writes that she has given him our direction and that he will be with us as soon as he can make passage across the Channel. I must get Hester to clean and tidy the large room next to yours,' she murmured, a little flustered at the thought of this new housekeeping. 'At the moment it's full of odds and ends, and we must make sure it looks a good deal more inviting when Colonel Ingram arrives.'

Lizzie couldn't bring herself to speak. For years, she'd been longing for this moment and, now it had come, somehow the Colonel's homecoming was not as welcome as it should be. She felt a traitorous guilt. She should be ecstatic and she wasn't. She knew why. Her heart was broken and she wanted no-one to know, least of all her father. He would be unsympathetic. He might even be angry that she'd become involved with a fellow officer. He'd think she was up to her old tricks again and couldn't be trusted still. She would have to put on a smiling face for him, maintain a façade. Pretend to herself that she felt whole, and that whatever she'd enjoyed with Justin Delacourt had been a silly diversion.

Henrietta was looking at her thoughtfully. 'It is good news, I hope, Elizabeth?'

'Yes, of course. It's taken me by surprise, that's all.'

'Naturally, it has my dear. But I imagine it will be a few weeks before the Colonel arrives. A few weeks to plan how you will spend your time with him. While he's with us, I want you to have a holiday.'

'I can't do that, Mrs Croft. You will need my help.' And feeling the way she did, Lizzie thought, she'd no wish to be always with the Colonel. It would be torture.

'You *can* have a holiday, and you will. I shall insist. Hester can do anything I need.'

'You're most kind,' was all Lizzie could murmur.

'Now tell me about your afternoon.'

It was the last thing she wanted to do, but she'd already allowed her feelings to show too clearly. She sensed the old lady's sharp eyes on her and wondered if Hester had been telling tales. The maid had returned early from the fair and, when Lizzie had come through the door, had stared in surprise at the young woman's flushed face.

'It was a very large event,' Lizzie began, 'but then I imagine you know that. I was surprised at its size...' Her voice trailed off. Really, she could not bear to think of the afternoon.

'And Justin? He was there to escort you? He was to escort both of us, if I remember rightly. I trust he proved a helpful guide.'

'Yes, we met each other at the church.' It was inadequate, but even so Lizzie couldn't keep the quaver from her voice.

'I've always found Justin an excellent host, and today would be his last chance to play the role. At least, for some time,' Mrs Croft added gently. 'James Martin called while you were out. His wife is still deeply distressed. There has been no news of their son, and now James thinks there never will be. He mentioned that Justin is preparing to return to the war very shortly and, when he goes, Caroline's last hope will go with him.'

'Sir Justin is to leave Chelwood so soon?' The lump in her throat was so large that Lizzie felt sure she would never again be able to swallow.

'Why, yes, my dear. He was always set on returning to Spain once the estate was on its feet. I fear we must get ready to say goodbye to him.'

Her voice was kindly but firm. She is telling me to abandon any foolish hopes I may have cherished, Lizzie thought.

Mrs Croft settled herself more comfortably. 'Could you pass me the newspaper, Elizabeth? I intend to read the political columns. They're bound to make me sleepy, but you need not see me to bed this evening—Hester is on hand to help.'

Lizzie could only nod and walk miserably to the door, but her hand had barely turned the handle when Mrs Croft said abruptly, 'Stop! I'd almost forgotten,' and began to rummage in the folds of her gown.

'Here, my dear, here it is. The other message.' Lizzie walked over to the chair and took the proffered envelope. 'Clementine enclosed it with her letter. It must be important since she paid extra for it to be delivered. You must read it straight away.'

~

Once in her room, Lizzie tore open the envelope and drew out three closely written sheets. The handwriting was vaguely familiar and, when she flicked the pages to find a signature, she knew why. Piers, Piers Silchester! She skimmed sentence after sentence: he hoped she was happy, felt sure the sea air must be bracing, imagined her employer to be a woman of generous spirit. Lizzie frowned, trying to find a purpose to the missive. And there it was—on the final page.

> *... But even the most benevolent employer, Miss Ingram, must leave you wishing for your own establishment, and it is for that reason that I have dared once more to approach you. Miss Bates has given me kind permission to write and ask if you might now be willing to consider my offer of marriage...*

She dropped the letter onto the bed, too agitated to read more. At this lowest ebb of her life, nothing could be less welcome than the renewed attentions of a man for whom she felt so little. If she had ever dallied with the notion that one day she might agree to marry Piers, it was now an impossibility. Lizzie was aware now of how deep her emotions ran, and she knew that she would never settle for anything less.

She would rather stay a companion until she was eighty than agree to Piers' proposal. He was offering her an establishment, he wrote, and surely she would be pleased. Lizzie didn't want an establishment, she wanted a home. He was offering her his deepest affection, but it wasn't this cautious, tepid love that she needed. She walked back to the bed, picking up the letter and tearing it in two. Its limp sentiments, its mediocre emotions, were furiously rejected. What she wanted was fierce words of love, words that scorched the very paper they were written on. She wanted Justin's words, only Justin's.

But she'd not get them. Ever. Listlessly, she sank down onto the window seat, a shawl draped around her shoulders to keep her warm. There was no point in going to bed since sleep would elude her. All she could do was sit and think. The letter from Piers was soon forgotten, her mind too busy replaying her angry encounter with the man she loved, too busy questioning why they'd quarrelled so badly.

But why question? It had been inevitable. Her father had abandoned her, Victor had taken gross advantage of her youth, and now Justin. Perhaps, she thought mournfully, she didn't deserve a man who was true, who would take her heart and keep it safe. She might be pretty and lively and spirited, but that hadn't been sufficient to keep her father by her side. So why should it be any different now she was a grown woman?

If she were honest, she had never quite believed in Justin's love, and she'd been right to be doubtful. For days, he must have been planning to leave Rye, yet he'd not seen fit to tell her. Lizzie had had to learn the news from her employer. Justin was moving on, and their quarrel today gave him the perfect excuse to walk away without a backward glance.

She heard the clock in the hall strike eleven. Two hours had gone by, yet she'd hardly noticed their passing. The house was deathly quiet, and she wandered over to the bed and laid down on the coverlet. There was no possibility of sleep, but she must rest. She would need to have herself under control when Justin came calling in the morning. Something scratched at her neck and she extracted his abandoned note and held it up to the flickering candlelight. Three letters in one day, and not one of them had brought joy.

His words seemed even colder than before. What would he have to tell her when he called tomorrow? Was there any chance at all that Rosanna would impart new information? And why had the woman chosen to meet at night? Because she was as scared of Chapman as she'd said—or because she hoped to make Justin her lover? This afternoon, in the heat of the moment, Lizzie had jumped to that conclusion. It was possible, she supposed, she could have been wrong, but was it likely that Rosanna was scared? One thing was certain: the tow- headed man was villainous, and if he knew his lover was confiding a dangerous secret to Justin, he'd not hesitate. And what? Would he kill her?

The nape of Lizzie's neck prickled. The man was capable of murder, of murdering anyone. She had always hoped that somewhere Gil was a prisoner, kidnapped and kept out of sight until the gang had finished their smuggling operations along this stretch of the coast. But what if Chapman had not kidnapped Gil, what if he'd killed him?

She realised the idea had been lurking at the back of her mind for weeks, and she suspected similar thoughts had plagued Justin. Neither of them had ever spoken of it, unwilling to give life to such a dreadful outcome, but they both knew that if the gang had killed the excise man, they wouldn't hesitate to kill another, if it was necessary. Gil would be costly to guard all these months and any ransom money was uncertain. Why, in fact, would they hesitate to kill anyone who knew too much? Including Justin.

As a member of Chapman's gang, Justin had made himself vulnerable. It was all very well for him to say that he was a pillar of the community and safe from retribution, but hadn't Gil been such a pillar? Lizzie's thoughts were now roaming the darkest of alleys. Suddenly, it seemed more than possible that Justin was in danger.

If Chapman had decided that his erstwhile gang member was too much of a threat, how would he kill him? He could hardly storm Chelwood Place or accost his victim in full view of the town. No, he'd lure him to a lonely spot where his cries would go unheard and his body never found. Might that actually happen? Of course not, she scolded herself. Justin was far too good a soldier to fall into such a trap.

Unless...Rosanna. Chapman would get Rosanna to lure him, either with her beauty or by dangling the hope of more information. Lizzie's stomach lurched as the thought scissored its way through her. The meeting tonight, the meeting that Rosanna had arranged. In an instant, she knew that Justin would learn nothing, only that he'd been betrayed.

Chapter Thirty

L izzie scrunched the note into a fierce little ball. Justin was facing death! She was sure of it, but could do nothing to help him. She had no idea where he'd arranged to meet Rosanna, or when—it was pitch black now and they could be anywhere. Perhaps on the marshes? Trying to find them there would be hopeless, she knew from experience. But after last night's adventure, would Justin return to the marshes? Surely he'd be suspicious of any suggestion by Rosanna that they meet there. No, it couldn't be the marshes, but where? Lizzie stared through the uncurtained window, her gaze intense, as though she could break through the glass and fly on wings to his side.

The cove! The thought burst into her mind. The cove beneath the garden of Brede House! It had to be. She knew it to be the haunt of smugglers and knew that no-one else visited. Mrs Croft and Hester hardly ever ventured into the garden, certainly not once darkness had fallen—it held such bad memories for them. So what better place to commit foul murder than a quiet cove below a deserted garden, with a convenient river running by?

In seconds, Lizzie was off the bed and grabbing her cloak from the wardrobe. Whatever stupid mess she'd made of her friendship with Justin Delacourt, she would move worlds to keep him from harm. Silently, she stole downstairs in her stockinged feet. Her employer would be long asleep, but she was wary of meeting Hester. The maid might still be up and about, clearing dishes or setting the table for breakfast. Lizzie craned her head around the kitchen door and saw with relief that it was empty. Light from a half moon was shining through the window, and in its hazy sheen she found her boots tucked neatly behind the large black cooking range. Then, slowly and carefully, she unlatched the door that led into the garden.

Moonlight glistened off the winding path, guiding her onwards, past the folly to the wicket gate. The wind had fallen away and, above her, an enormous sky shone a dark blue enamel. She flitted along, her black cloak melding her into the darkness. The garden lay quiet and unmolested. No sounds reached her, no sights disturbed her. But her heart began to thump louder when she passed through the wicket and started down the stairs to the shore.

The beach lay still and empty in the moonlight. The whole world was still, it seemed, the mirror surface of the river blurred only by lowering mists. Not a movement. She looked upwards along the path that led to the cliff top, the path she'd taken only last night in pursuit of the smugglers. But again, there was no-one. If the gang had ever been here, they'd dissolved into thin air; wherever they planned to attack Justin, it was not on this beach.

Lizzie turned to go, feeling a leaden disappointment. She had been so sure that she'd find them here, but she'd been mistaken. And what a mistake! Even now, in some unknown place, Justin could be suffering pain, torture. The thought was anguish, but she could do nothing. All that was left to her was to return to the house and pray.

She'd reached the second step of the wooden staircase when the slightest sound caught her ear, and she stopped to listen. In a second, a whirlwind had descended. A large hand covered her mouth and another thrust an ill-smelling gag between her lips. With her arms pulled painfully behind her, she was pushed roughly down the stairs and on to the strand.

'What 'ave we 'ere then?' A man emerged from the shadows and it was Chapman. The bleached hair and colourless eyes were almost invisible in the moonlight, but Lizzie could read his expression clearly.

His smile was jeering. 'Were yer lookin' for someone? I wouldn't want to disappoint yer, not when yer such a pretty little miss.'

The man was truly evil and foolishly she'd fallen into his hands. He came closer and thrust her chin upwards. She felt his sour breath hot on her cheeks and told herself that at all costs, she mustn't faint.

A circle of men surrounded her, dark looking cut-throats, salacious smirks on their faces. 'What d'yer want us to do with 'er?' one of them dared to ask.

Chapman spat. 'All in good time. I might just have a little bit o' fun first.'

The man who had spoken jerked his head towards the cliff top and Lizzie could see the faint outline of a woman. Rosanna! So Justin wasn't with her, and she'd been mistaken again. Whatever had made her think she was cut out for adventure? If she escaped this terror, her life must change. Her longing for excitement had done nothing but lead her into danger, and upset those she loved. It was time to stop—if only she'd not left it too late.

Chapman glanced up at Rosanna and shrugged his shoulders, as though relinquishing whatever 'fun' he'd planned. 'Tie 'er up proper. Get rid of 'er,' he said, walking away.

The words were barely out of his mouth when two of his comrades lunged forward and grabbed Lizzie, tying a rope around her wrists so tightly that she felt her skin break and bleed beneath its force. Struggling fiercely, she was forced to the ground. Don't give up, she told herself, don't give up. She kicked out at them, managing to land the occasional blow, until a third member of the gang arrived at their calling and sat down heavily on her legs.

'Yer shouldn't do that, missy. We can git narsty,' he said, pantingly.

Another length of rope was bound tightly around her ankles, and she was lifted horizontally into the air.

A fourth man, who had stood looking on, silent and motionless, let out a hoarse guffaw. 'Nicely trussed, lads. We're gettin' good, ain't we?'

''old the lantern, Nat. 'Tis black as pitch.'

For the moment, the moon had disappeared into a

basket of cloud and, in near obscurity, Lizzie was carried across the shingle towards a dark wound in the cliff. The light from the lantern swung back and forth in an erratic arc but, when they drew nearer, she could see that it was the opening to a cave. They were going to leave her in a cave. For a moment, she felt a wash of relief. They were not going to murder her after all—or worse. But why leave her here? The answer was swift and stomach-turning.

'Take her gag orf, Jack. She can yell all she wants, but no one will 'ear 'er.'

'You sure?'

'Yeah, that way she'll drown quicker. We're compassionate, ain't we?' Again that rough guffaw.

Lizzie lay rigid as they carried her deeper into the cave. A terror had overtaken her and she was numb with despair. This was the end after all. She would die alone in this wretched place and no-one would ever find her. Mrs Croft would think she'd left without notice. Her father, when he arrived, would decide his daughter had gone off on one of her mad adventures and wash his hands of her for good. And Justin, what would he think? Certainly not that she'd tried to save him from a fate he didn't even face. More likely, he'd imagine that she had left Rye as swiftly as she'd arrived, and then dismiss her from his mind.

She was dumped unceremoniously on the shingle floor of the cave amid a huddle of large rocks. There was the sound of retreating footsteps, and then she was alone. Gradually, her eyes adjusted to the dark, and in the distance she made out a shard of light. The moon must have broken free of its prison of cloud and she was looking back at the cave's entrance. She wondered if it were possible to roll herself towards it, but rocks and stones littered the path—and what if she succeeded? The tide was already rising and, shackled as she was, instead of dying here, she'd simply die on the beach.

She shuffled her body around, trying to get more comfortable. What a ridiculous notion! How comfortable could you get with hands and feet tightly bound, waiting for certain death? As she squirmed this way and that, her hands fluttered slightly, and a trickle of light flashed across the opal in her ring. Her mother's ring. How different might her life have been, if her mother had lived? But she hadn't, and now her daughter must prepare to follow her.

Lizzie's thoughts were brought to an abrupt halt. A voice came out of the dark, punching the breath from her.

'Lizzie? Is that you? Is that really you?'

Chapter Thirty-One

'Justin?!'

'I saw your opal ring, shimmering in the dark. But what are you doing here?'

In the circumstances, it seemed the strangest of questions, yet the entire day had felt surreal to Lizzie, unfolding in fits and starts like the worst possible nightmare.

'I came to look for you,' she stammered.

'But why? I thought...'

He didn't finish, but she knew he was remembering their dreadful quarrel. Didn't he realise it made not a scrap of difference? When you loved truly, you had no choice but to continue. You loved forever.

Aloud, she said, 'I was sure you were in danger.'

He seemed to be pondering her words, and for a while they sat in silence, the only sound the slow wash of river water. 'Have they bound you?' he asked.

'They have—my hands and feet.'

She felt an uneven movement to her right and sensed the warmth of his body coming closer.

'What happened to you?' she asked, though she didn't

253

need to. She knew exactly what had happened, since hadn't she foretold it in her darkest imaginings?

'Chapman used Rosanna to get me here,' he said bitterly. 'She betrayed me. She never intended to tell me a thing.'

Lizzie said nothing. It was cold comfort to have been proved right.

'We must get out of here,' Justin continued. 'The tide has turned, and it won't be long before the river reaches us.'

'I don't see how we can. These bonds are so tight, it's impossible to wriggle free.'

'It has to be possible,' he said, with a fierce determination.

Lizzie felt him striving to stand upright, but the rope binding his ankles must have caused him to lose balance, and he crumpled painfully down onto the uneven floor. In the distance, she heard the sound of water. It was growing nearer, its thunder filling the rocky bay and echoing eerily around the hollow space of the cavern. She had to fight hard against panic. The water was still some way off, she told herself, and closer to hand she heard Justin moving again, then a few suppressed curses and, somehow, he'd managed to slide himself into a sitting position beside her. There was something immensely comforting at having him close. If there was no escape, they would at least die together.

'We're not going to die.' He'd read her thoughts with uncanny accuracy. 'I'm going to rub my wrists against the rock behind me and try to fray the rope. The surface feels sharp enough. It will take time, but it's the only thing I can think to do.'

'But you'll damage yourself badly.'

'I'll be a lot more damaged if I don't get free,' he said, with an attempt at humour. 'And so will you.'

A moment later, she heard the sound of chafing rope. She couldn't bear to think of the rock cutting into his wrists and hands, as surely it must be. Feeling his body tense beside her, she knew he was in pain.

'What made you come to the cove of all places?' he jerked out, trying she thought to distract himself. 'You should be safe in your bed.'

'I wanted to warn you. I was sure the meeting with Rosanna was a trap, and that you were in danger. The cove seemed the most likely place for the smugglers to lure you.'

There was another moment's silence. 'You shouldn't have come, Lizzie.' Then, when she said nothing, he went on, 'But how? How did you know I was in danger?' He stumbled on the words, the rock evidently cutting deep into his skin.

'I didn't trust Rosanna. I never have. She could easily have told you what you wanted to know in the churchyard. Instead, she arranged to meet you at this late hour.'

'She is still with Chapman,' he said bitingly. 'You were right and I was wrong. Very badly wrong.'

'You didn't see them together, Justin. If you had, you would have known she'd never betray him.'

'So even women like Rosanna have their principles?'

'She loves him,' Lizzie said simply.

There was a loud exclamation as Justin's wrists once again hit rock. 'Stop!' she cried out. 'I can't bear that you hurt yourself any more.'

'Would you rather we drown?'

She wanted to say that yes, she would rather, for at least in death they wouldn't be separated.

'You're not going to end like this, Lizzie,' he said urgently. 'You're far too precious.' He set to rubbing again with even greater energy.

The hissing of water over shingle was growing ever louder, but it was the sound of sawing that filled Lizzie's ears as the rope gradually began to fray under Justin's pressure. The rhythmic echo sent her eyelids closing and, despite her discomfort, she'd begun to doze when she felt the first trickle of water nip tentatively at her toes.

'The river is rising fast,' he said grimly.

'Does it fill the cave as those men suggested?'

'At high tide it does and we're not so far from that.'

'Should we try to move further back?'

'With boulders in our path, it will be difficult, if not impossible. And it would gain us only a little time. I need to stay here—I think the rope is loosening.'

'Then we'll stay here together.' She felt his thigh nudge warmly against her.

'Did you really think I was Rosanna's lover?' he asked out of the blue.

'Yes, no,' she said confusedly.

'How could you think that?'

'I didn't—not really. But when I tried to warn you, you wouldn't listen. You preferred to put your trust in an untrustworthy woman.'

'If only we'd not quarrelled—' he began, and then let out a loud groan. There was a thud as a length of rope was hurled into the distance. 'I've done it, Lizzie, I've done it!'

His legs freed, Justin moved quickly towards her. She felt his hands on the rope securing her feet and at the same time a splash of liquid on her hands.

'The river, it's coming in more quickly than ever,' she said urgently.

'Not too quickly, I hope. The water is still only ankle deep.'

'But—' she began, then realised that what she was feeling wasn't water, but blood. Justin was bleeding profusely.

Her limbs shaking, Lizzie reached down to her skirts and tore a strip of material from her petticoat. 'We must bind your poor wrists, or you'll lose too much blood.'

'They are sore,' he admitted.

That was an understatement, since blood was now gushing from his wounds. In a darkness that was near impenetrable, she bound his wrists as tightly as she could, hoping against hope that the makeshift bandages would be sufficient. If he continued to bleed... she blinked back the tears.

'You're crying!'

'I'm not,' she sniffled.

'You are crying, Lizzie. Please don't.'

And his arms were around her and he was kissing her full on the lips. It was madness. If they had any sense, they would be scrambling to their feet and running for their lives. Instead, they clung to each other, locked fast in an embrace, unable to let go. The cave, the rocks, the sound of the approaching river, retreated into nothingness. All Lizzie knew was that she was in his arms again, and he was kissing her over and over. Deeply and tenderly.

A sudden rush of water soaked them to the skin. 'You were right, the river *is* rising quickly.' Justin's voice assumed a deliberate calm. 'Our way out is through the entrance to the cave, but the water is deep now. We would have to swim and I fear it's dangerous—the currents are very strong.'

'I can't swim.' Lizzie's words were barely audible.

'Then we must think again.'

'There's nothing to think about. *You* have to escape, Justin. You can swim out into the river—I'm sure you're strong enough to manage the currents—and bring help back with you.'

She sensed rather than saw him shake his head. 'By the time I could do that, you'd be swimming with the fishes. There has to be another way.'

Lizzie couldn't see how. It wasn't that she wanted to die—Justin's kisses, the realisation that he truly loved her, had filled her with a new energy, a desire to hold on to life. But if *she* weren't destined to survive this terrible night, Justin must. He must save himself.

'You have to go!'

'*We* have to go,' he corrected her. 'We must climb to the back of the cave. There are passages linking one cave to another. When Gil and I were boys we'd dare each other to travel as far along them as we could, before we reached the sea. And if there are passages running parallel to the river, there should be at least one leading inland.'

Another great rush of water had them scrambling to their feet. From behind came the sound of the river filling the space they'd occupied just minutes before.

'Come, we must move quickly.'

He clasped her hand in his and, in the dense gloom, began a perilous climb over rocks and rough stones towards the rear of the cave. The further they moved from the entrance, the darker it grew. Lizzie was fearful, not sharing her lover's optimism that they would find another way out.

As foot by foot, they moved further into the cave, Justin's cheer seemed to be waning, too.

'It looks as though we might have to swim after all.' They had come to a full stop at the very rear of the cavern, and before them stretched an enormous lake of water, left by the retreating tide.

'I can't,' she protested, aghast.

He squeezed her hand tightly. 'We'll go together, Lizzie. It may not be as deep as we think.'

She stood on the brink of the pool, unable to take the first step. Behind them, the roar of river water grew louder, tumbling itself through the narrow entrance and crashing over the barrier of rocks.

'We must at least try,' he said into her ear. 'It's our only hope. Hold very tight to me and all will be well.'

Lizzie did as he told her and walked forward. Almost immediately, she was plunged waist deep in water and had to smother a terrified cry. She had wanted adventure to knock at her door, hadn't she? Well, here it was, and knocking loudly. Frantically, she clutched hold of Justin's hand and, though the water rose breast high, she continued to walk beside him. Something knocked against her, and she put out her hand to fend it off. It seemed like clothes, but what were clothes doing floating in this horrible, murky pool?

'Justin,' she curled her fingers into the palm of his hand. 'There's something odd.'

'Odder than trying to wade through how much water we've no idea, fifty feet into the cliff?'

Her voice grew strained. 'There's definitely something wrong—I can feel it. If only we had a light.'

'We just might have. Only to be used in emergency, but this could be it.' She felt him fumble in his breast pocket, then the sharp crack of glass being broken and a strip of paper burst into flame. He held the flickering light aloft. 'I may have forgotten to bring a knife—a bad mistake—but I did manage a light.'

'What on earth...?'

'It's a new invention—a phosphoric candle. We had them in Spain, but they're not ideal. Expensive and dangerous. We must protect the flame as best we can.'

Lizzie looked up, temporarily distracted. Candlelight revealed for the first time the enormity of the cavern. A huge domed ceiling swept down to jagged walls of white chalk, discoloured at intervals by great patches of green seepage. At floor level, chalk teeth guarded an abundance of small crevices, any of which might lead somewhere or nowhere.

Candle in hand, Justin waded to the far side of her. In the thin beam of light, she caught a glimpse of blue, then a flash of white. They *were* clothes, she thought. How extraordinary.

'Oh, my God!' Justin was bending close to the water and peering intently.

'Whatever is it?'

'I can't tell you. Look away, Lizzie.'

Chapter Thirty-Two

Lizzie could feel him trembling and grasped hold of him. 'Whatever it is, tell me. What have you seen?'

But somehow she knew. Knew that at last the mystery of Gil's disappearance was solved and in the most dreadful way.

Justin took hold of her hand again and, with the candle to light their way, they waded together through the deep water to dry rock beyond. Once there, they collapsed on the floor, both of them shaking and sick to the stomach.

'I'm so sorry.' It was inadequate, but what could she say? No words of comfort could make this better.

Justin put his arms around her. 'I suppose deep down I always knew I'd never find him alive.

'But this...'

'It's too terrible to think of. And we shouldn't think of it—not now. We must focus on saving ourselves. Getting help. Gil must have a Christian burial, a grave for his parents to visit. And we must make sure they do.'

He jumped to his feet, newly determined. 'We have to find a way out. While we still have the candle, we must search every inch of these walls for a passage through.'

He began to wave the light, first up and down, then from left to right, his eyes anxiously scanning the rough surfaces of the cave. A large passage swam out at them from the darkness, but Justin remained motionless.

'That's the route Gil and I travelled,' he said, gesturing towards it, 'but it leads only to the sea. There must be another one. A passage that runs upwards to the surface of the cliff. I wonder if fingers rather than eyes might find what we're seeking.' He spread his hands and began slowly to feel along the walls.

Lizzie was standing a few feet back from him, and gradually became aware of a darker smudge against the white chalk.

'It's there! I'm sure it's there.' She pointed to a hole in the rock no bigger than two feet high. 'But it's so small.'

'And it may lead nowhere,' he warned. 'Hold the candle and I'll crawl through. First, though, I need to rid myself of these wet clothes or they'll stick to the sides of the tunnel.'

Without a moment's hesitation, Justin tore off his shirt, shoes and breeches and threw them to the ground, his strong male body glowing in the candle's faint light. The thought of his poor, dead friend rose unbidden to Lizzie's mind—staying alive had never seemed more important.

'I'll travel as far along the passage as I can, and try to make sure it's going in the right direction. If I think it is, I'll call you. Listen out for my voice.'

He crouched down at the small aperture, but suddenly straightened up and walked back to her.

'Gil is no more, Lizzie, but we must try to live. For him and for each other. But if anything should happen to me, if anything should happen to either of us, know that I love you.'

He had said the words—words she'd so wanted to hear—and joy, pure in its intensity, sang through her. She wanted to clasp him close, tell him not to risk his life alone. They would stay here together and face whatever fate had determined for them. But he had already left her side, and was bent double on hands and knees at the tunnel's cramped entrance. In a few seconds, he had disappeared from view.

For anxious moments, Lizzie held the candle aloft, its light seeming ever dimmer in the encroaching darkness. She could hear Justin scrabbling along the rocky surface, but gradually the noise faded until there was nothing. Though her pulse was beating fast, she tried to think calmly. If the passage proved a dead end, Justin would return, but if it climbed upwards as he supposed, she hoped he would find his way out and bring help. It would be quicker than returning for her, and surely the river water never came this far inland. She would be safe here until rescue arrived. She tried not think of how long she must wait in this dark, echoing hole, with a dead man floating close by.

A faint noise came from the opposite wall. Justin's voice! Quickly, she navigated a path through rocks and stones to the tunnel entrance, and bent down to hear. But as she did so, the candle fell from her hands, and the light was extinguished. Immediately, she was engulfed in a darkness so dense that not even a sliver of moonlight found its way this deep into the cliff. Lizzie felt the beginnings of a new panic take her in its grip.

But Justin's voice sounded again and, this time, she could make out several words. 'Come... long passage... more light.'

There would need to be, she thought fearfully, since all around was black. But, following his example, she stripped off her sodden gown and petticoat, and crouched near to where she thought the entrance to the passageway must be.

Feeling along the wall with her hands, it took her some minutes to find it, but then she was on her knees and crawling forward, trying not to think what she was doing. She could see nothing, only feel the thick, hot darkness. Slowly, she moved along the passage, shuffling forward in an endless and unforgiving journey. The sharp flints bit into her soft flesh, and the tunnel walls seemed to close in on either side, intent on crushing her between them.

She mustn't think, must keep her mind a blank, until she came out at the other side. She sensed she was travelling upwards and could only hope it was true. Now Justin was speaking again, his voice growing louder. A glimmer of light and, at last, the hazy outline of his form. She was through! Prostrate, she collapsed on the floor, her breath coming in sharp gasps. Justin scooped her up in his arms and set her on her feet.

'Are you hurt?' he asked anxiously.

'Not hurt—terrified. I can't bear enclosed spaces.'

He smoothed her hair from her face and kissed each

eyelid. 'My poor darling. What have I brought you to?'

'I brought myself,' she reminded him. 'But it seems that I'm a coward after all.'

'Dearest Lizzie, a coward is something you're not! But see—your courage is rewarded. There's space to stand here and more light. Only a small amount, but it's coming from somewhere. We must be near the surface.'

He took her hand again, and together they began to work their way around the huge boulders of chalk that over the years had detached themselves from the walls. With bare feet, the terrain was rough and painful, but they managed to make good progress and, within a quarter of an hour, stood facing what appeared to be the end of the massive chamber. Justin moistened his finger and held it high.

'I thought so. There's a current of air that's quite strong. I wonder... it seems to be coming from that far corner.'

Lizzie looked across to the spot he was pointing to, and hoped he was wrong. A thick darkness hung there. 'It doesn't look too promising,' she said.

'Yet I would bet my regimentals we'll find that's the way out.'

And so it proved. Hidden in the darkness was the first of many steps that had been hewn from the rock by some unknown hand. One step at a time, they mounted the spiral staircase, winding round and round up the cavern face, until Lizzie became thoroughly dazed. Lack of sleep, the terror of being trapped and the dreadful moment when they'd discovered Gil's body, had combined to make her feel she was walking through an unreal world.

Justin wrapped his arms around her waist, helping her climb each step, and at the top, lifting her bodily onto the safety of a small stone platform. Confronting them, though, was a blank cliff face. Surely, Lizzie thought, they had not endured such a fearful journey, to be thwarted at its very end?

But the faintest pencil of light gradually became visible, light that traced the shape of a door. Justin put his shoulders to the wood and there was a loud cracking. A rush of fresh air hit them, and they were out. Standing in moonlight, standing in the middle of the folly.

'I always wondered where that door led to.' There was a surprised look on his face. 'Whenever I came to tea as a child, I'd play here and marvel at it—a door without a handle!'

Lizzie sank down on to the stone bench, body and mind exhausted, and when Justin followed her, they sat locked in grateful silence. Then, without warning, tears began to fill her eyes and spill down her cheeks.

He wiped them away as delicately as he could with the palm of his hand. 'No handkerchief, I fear.'

She looked at him in his half naked state and shook her head. It was too ridiculous and she couldn't prevent a small giggle. The bandages around his wrist were dark with dirt and dried blood. His underwear was green with the slime of seaweed, his wonderful golden hair sticky with chalk and his naked feet cut and bruised.

'Laugh away, Miss Ingram! But consider—how elegant do you look right now?'

Lizzie knew she must present the most frightful sight, but didn't care. They were safe, they were alive and, for the moment, they were together.

He put his arms around her and gave her a gentle kiss. He tasted warm and salty and she kissed him back, hugging her partly clothed body to his, until they broke from each other in sudden dismay. The image of Gil, so recently left behind, haunted them. Yet the drive to live and love was strong and, within a minute, they'd begun to kiss again, more fiercely this time, until she shivered from the penetrating cold.

'We shouldn't be dallying here,' she said, breathlessly. 'We need to get warm. And what about the Preventives? Shouldn't we alert them?'

'I warned them there'd be trouble tonight and their ship, *The Stag*, is waiting off the coast. I told them the gang was due to make a run for it to France. Presumably, Chapman planned to leave after disposing of me.'

'How did you know the gang intended to escape to France?'

He smiled. 'Wasn't I a smuggler, too? I didn't admit to it, of course. I was suitably vague when I sent a message to the new excise man but, with luck, he'll have alerted his colleagues and they'll catch the gang red-handed.'

'Then we are quite done with our adventuring.'

Lizzie felt suddenly empty. Justin loved her, she must hold on to that, and if this night were the beginning and the end of their love, then at least she would have the memory.

'I wouldn't say quite done with,' he said enigmatically. 'But right now, it's a hot bath and warm sheets that we need.'

Chapter Thirty-Three

Lizzie had never been so fussed over. Hester had heard her stumbling up the stairs an hour before dawn and taken the sight of a bedraggled, near naked girl, surprisingly well. Her first response was to boil cans of water and plunge Lizzie into a hot bath. Only when the young woman was wrapped in sheets, warmed by a hot brick and sipping milk straight from the stove, did she ask for an explanation. Lizzie told her story haltingly and even to her ears it sounded fantastical. The maid listened stolidly without passing comment and, when the last words had been murmured, said only, 'You should sleep now.'

Lizzie thought it highly unlikely. She had passed the most terrifying night of her life and her mind was still vivid with fearful images. But as soon as her eyelids closed, sheer exhaustion sent her into a deep sleep, where she stayed until well into the afternoon.

It was her employer tiptoeing into the room that finally woke her. In the beam of bright light stealing through the curtains, Lizzie glimpsed the outline of Mrs Croft's figure. She blinked as the old lady hovered at the foot of the bed.

'I hadn't meant to wake you, my dear, but we were growing anxious.'

Lizzie turned her head and glanced at the small timepiece sitting on the bedside table. Startled by the late hour, she struggled to sit up.

'I'm so sorry, Mrs Croft.' She was dry-mouthed and her head was spinning. 'I should have been up and dressed hours ago.'

'You will not be working today, Elizabeth,' Mrs Croft said firmly. 'Hester has told me a story I could hardly credit, but whatever the truth, it is evident you've been through a dreadful ordeal and you need to rest. By all accounts, you will be lucky to escape pneumonia. Hester said you were soaked to the skin when she found you.'

'I was, but thanks to her, I'm sure I'll suffer no lasting ill. You have both been very kind, but I must get up.'

'Only if you're quite certain. Hester is bringing you a cup of chocolate and once you've drunk it, you may dress if you feel well enough. But no working, mind you.'

'But—'

'And no 'buts'. I want you fit and well. A message has come from Chelwood. Sir Justin intends to visit and will be here within the hour. He is most concerned to know how you fare.'

She paused, waiting, it seemed, for Lizzie to speak, but when the girl made no response, continued, 'I must say that Justin did not feature excessively in Hester's account. She mentioned him only in passing, yet he appears most anxious to talk to you.' She looked hopefully at Lizzie, then gave a small sigh. 'I expect I will eventually learn what has been happening right beneath my nose. I'm sure it's quite a story.'

At that moment, Hester came in with a cup of steaming chocolate and the two older ladies went quietly downstairs together. What decadence, Lizzie thought wryly, as she sipped at her cup. Now if I were mistress of Chelwood, chocolate in bed would be commonplace. But at that point, her thoughts slammed to a halt. Justin had said he loved her and with that she must be content. True his declaration had come at a moment of the greatest danger, and it was well known that people in desperate situations were liable to say things they later regretted, but she would keep believing that his love was sincere.

The terrible events of the night came back to Lizzie with crushing force. Over the last few weeks, she'd had sufficient adventure to last her a lifetime, and imperceptibly she'd begun to value the settled existence she'd always rejected. But not just any settled life. A married life—with a strong and loving man who could make her giddy with just one look from those beautiful, changeful eyes. If only... but it was no good daydreaming. Whatever his feelings for her, Justin would never give up soldiering. From their very first meeting outside St Mary's, he'd made that clear.

She swung her legs out of bed and her limbs felt tired and sore. Indeed, her whole being felt drained. If she was hankering for the security of marriage, she thought unhappily, the choice was there to accept Piers Silchester. And that she couldn't do. He was far too good a man to deceive in such a miserable fashion.

No, she must remain a companion, perched on the edge of someone else's world, never quite belonging, never quite at ease. Right now, though, she couldn't think of the future. She must concentrate on looking her best for Justin's visit, since these would be the final precious moments she would have with him.

Mrs Croft had said he was coming to see how she did, but her employer didn't know the whole truth. He was coming for much more, Lizzie was certain: he was coming to say a lover's goodbye. He wouldn't want last night's confession to beguile her into thinking there was a future for them. There was nothing now to keep him in Rye: Chelwood had once more begun to flourish, and he knew at last the dreadful truth of his friend's disappearance.

She heard the murmur of voices below. He was here already! Hastily, she splashed water on her face and dragged a comb through untidy curls. In the stark winter light, her glass showed a pallid face with dark smudges beneath the eyes. She would wear her very best dress—a charming confection of deep peach sarsnet and creamy lace—and hope its vibrant colour would compensate for her pallor. Scrambling through the contents of her chest drawer, she unearthed a ribbon of the same deep peach which she threaded through her curls. Another swift glance in the mirror and she was satisfied.

～

Justin rose as she walked through the door, and his eyes rested on her trim figure just a moment too long.

'How are you feeling, Miss Ingram?'

'Ashamed that I've slept so long.'

'You shouldn't be. You look charmingly for it.'

Mrs Croft's face registered surprise at the compliment, but she said nothing, merely making space for Lizzie beside her on the brown velvet sofa.

'I was saying to Mrs Croft that I've this moment come from Five Oaks,' he said. 'I couldn't tell the Martins everything they wanted—how Gil became caught up in Rosanna's net must always remain guesswork—but I think I managed to piece together the final details of his story accurately enough. It was the telling that was difficult.'

Lizzie's face clouded with sympathy. 'I imagine your visit must have been unbearable for all of you.'

He nodded. 'Gil's death was always going to be a dreadful thing for them to accept, no matter how gently I sought to break the news. But it's done and at least they have certainty. I've organised a work party from Five Oaks to retrieve his body at low tide, and the Rector has agreed to a date for the funeral next week.'

And that is when you'll go, Lizzie told herself, but aloud she replied as cheerfully as she could, 'You *have* been busy and all I've done is sleep.'

'I would have slept, too, but I couldn't rest until I'd spoken to James and Caroline.'

There was a pained silence while each of them contemplated the terrible fate that Gil had suffered. Then Justin said a little more brightly, 'You'll be glad to know that the Preventives caught the gang half way to the French coast. They believe they've captured them all. And there's sufficient evidence to hang Thomas Chapman for the murder of the excise man, if not for Gil.'

'And Rosanna?' Even now, Lizzie couldn't keep the note of uncertainty from her voice.

'Apparently, she's turned King's evidence to save her skin. In return for a lighter sentence, she's agreed to incriminate Chapman. So much for love!'

The contempt in his voice made Lizzie's stomach clench. Justin's opinion of women had never been high and, once she'd heard the story of his youth, she'd understood he had good reason. But she'd hoped that his harsh judgment had been tempered by knowing and loving her. Not so, it seemed.

Mrs Croft rose unsteadily to her feet. 'I should not be glad to hear such a thing of a fellow human being, but I have to confess that I'm delighted Chapman will hang. The more I think of it, the more I'm convinced that it was one of his gang responsible for poor, dear Susanna's untimely death. I can feel no regret at his fate.'

Justin had risen, too. 'Nor should you. Chapman will be given justice, no more and no less.'

Then turning to Lizzie, he offered his arm. 'I wonder, Miss Ingram, if you'd be good enough to walk with me a while.'

Lizzie was about to demur when the old lady intervened. 'After last night, you will want to talk together, I'm sure. But be careful to wrap up warmly.'

Unwillingly, Lizzie followed him into the hall. She didn't want the encounter that was coming. She wanted to push it away, pack it tightly in a box and mark it *not to be opened*. But she had no choice. Better, then, to get it over with as swiftly as possible.

Reaching up for her cloak, she brushed against a small posy of white freesias that had been left lying on the rosewood console.

'They're for Gil,' Justin said, coming up beside her. 'They were his favourite flowers. Fortunately, the succession house had some still blooming.'

Lizzie put her nose to them and breathed in their sweet, fresh scent. 'They are quite beautiful.'

'Would you object if we were to walk to the cove? The flowers are by way of a wreath.'

'No, I suppose not,' she said, but there was a tremor in her voice.

'It might be good to exorcise the demons,' he said gently.

The cove, the flowers... he was saying a last farewell to Gil. And a last goodbye to her. The cove had loomed large in the short drama of their love affair. It was a fitting backdrop to a final scene.

Justin unlatched the kitchen door, and together they passed through into the garden, lying quiet and still in the late October afternoon. She walked beside him along the path towards the wicket gate, trying to feel confident but unable to stifle completely a returning fear. A group of rooks rose noisily into the air at their approach, and then swirled southwards making circles against the darkening sky. Their sudden flight startled Lizzie, pushing her into speech.

'How is your mother? Does she know all that's been happening?'

'I've told her some of it, but not all. I think it best I don't feed the gossip too voraciously.'

'Is she likely to spread the story to her friends?'

'Her "friends" are currently on her black list, so I'm hoping we can keep the dreadful news here in Rye. But she was definitely intrigued. She can't quite believe that a small town can be every bit as exciting as London. I fear she's in for disappointment, though, if she stays too long.'

'And is she staying?'

'In the district, yes. At Chelwood, no.'

A small frown flitted across Lizzie's face. Seeing it, he made haste to say, 'It would never do. We are chalk and cheese and her constant presence at Chelwood would suit neither of us.'

'So where will she go?'

'An acquaintance of hers is selling a manor house towards Hawkhurst.' Justin grinned, looking surprisingly boyish. 'We're not likely to upset each other, ten miles apart. At least, not often.'

Lizzie didn't respond. They were passing the folly, and the memory of the time they'd spent together there was threatening to unleash her tears.

Justin seemed not to notice the folly or her silence. 'I've undertaken to drive my mother over there tomorrow,' he continued, 'and, if she likes what she sees, the Delacourt lawyers will start proceedings to buy. At least the duke seems to have come to his senses and is now willing to meet his obligations by setting aside a considerable sum of money. Of course, if she takes the property, you can be sure she'll spend every penny on refurbishment.'

He swung the wicket gate to one side and, in single file, they made their way down the wooden steps to the deserted shore. In the grey-tinged light, the cove stretched before them, bland and innocent, the river flowing calmly by. They crunched their way across the shingle to the water's edge. The tide was on the turn, but it would be several hours before the cave once more filled with its deathly freight. She resolutely faced away from the dark, gaping hole.

'The adventure is over, Lizzie,' he said softly, noticing her stiff shoulders and determined back.

A spiteful gust of wind rose out of nowhere and, lifting the edges of the cloak she'd draped loosely over her shoulders, tossed it onto the pebbles below. Swiftly, Justin bent to retrieve the garment and gently replaced it. She could bear this no longer, Lizzie thought. She must get this parting over and then she could cry alone. She would make it easy for him.

'*This* adventure is over,' she agreed, 'but you'll be leaving for Spain very soon, and I'm sure there'll be plenty more waiting for you.'

'There's only one that's waiting,' he said carefully. 'One last adventure.'

'A final battle, I suppose? I hope the Duke of Wellington knows of it!'

'Not a battle, Lizzie. Not a war either.'

What was he talking about? Was Justin trying to confuse her?

'Marriage,' he said in response to her questioning look. The single word echoed and re-echoed across the beach, shattering its peace. 'I'm told that's quite an adventure.'

She felt the breath catch in her throat. 'Whose marriage?'

'Mine,' he said.

Chapter Thirty-Four

If hearts could stop beating, then Lizzie's did, right there, at a stroke. Why hadn't she guessed? Why hadn't she thought of it before? Despite his misgivings, Justin would have to marry—eventually. He owed it to the family name to produce an heir for Chelwood.

But she'd been so certain that he was set on re-joining the army. On returning to Spain. Perhaps he still intended to. Perhaps he had found a woman happy to lead a life alone, in exchange for a title and estate.

Or someone had found the woman for him. Had Justin been persuaded that he'd reached an age when it was his duty to take a wife? And had that been his mother? Had she used her contacts and arranged the marriage before he could leave? She would expect Justin's bride to be a member of the *ton*, certainly not a humble companion. Dabbling in her son's future must have given Lady Lavinia an interest when there little else for her at Chelwood. For a society woman, bored with country life, it would be the perfect antidote.

It wasn't just to say a simple farewell then that Justin

had brought her to this cove, but to tell her as gently as he could what his future was to be. Lizzie had known they must say goodbye, but this... She wanted to turn and flee, back up the stairs, back along the path, back to her room. And never, ever come out.

'And your marriage, too, of course,' he was saying, his voice sounding a little less confident. 'That is, if you feel you can trust a soldier after all that's befallen you. Can you, Lizzie? Can you entrust yourself to me?'

She felt the earth shift beneath her feet. There was no way he could mean it. No way at all. Her face was deathly white. 'I can only imagine that you're jesting, but if you are I should tell you that it's in very poor taste.'

'It would be in abominable taste, if I *were* jesting. How am I to convince you?'

Before she had time to answer, he knelt down on the pebbled beach and fixed her with a hesitant smile. 'Elizabeth Ingram, will you marry me?'

'But—'

'Just say, yes, Lizzie, if you mean yes. My knee is already cut to ribbons.'

'Yes,' she said, laughing and crying at the same time. 'Yes, yes, Justin. And do get up or you'll ruin another pair of breeches!'

In seconds, he was on his feet and his arms were around her. He tipped her chin upwards and brought his mouth down on hers. She'd not thought she would feel those lips again, and she clung to him as though she'd never let him go, kissing him over and over, until they broke from each other, breathless and laughing.

But almost immediately an anxious expression shadowed his face, and he held her at arms' length. 'Are you sure you'll not find life dull with me? I remember what you said about marriage.'

'I was talking nonsense. It was other men that I found dull, not marriage. I had to meet you before I came to see that.'

'And you think you could be happy at Chelwood?'

'More than happy. I've loved it from the day you sat me down in the library and scolded me for trespassing!'

'Tried to, you mean. I doubt anyone has managed to scold you successfully, unless it's your father.' Justin paused, and then said more seriously, 'By rights, I should have asked his permission before I asked you, but circumstances being what they are...'

'You'll soon have the chance. My father is coming home.'

Justin looked astonished. 'But when did you learn this? You said nothing.'

'I heard only yesterday and there's hardly been a chance to speak of it. I'm still finding it difficult to believe myself.'

Difficult but delighted, Lizzie thought, so very delighted. She could meet the Colonel with pleasure now, confide her love and know he'd approve her choice. He must always have wanted this, she found herself conceding. He'd acted in her best interests, even when it appeared otherwise. Through the long years, he'd protected her in the only way he knew, so that one day she could enjoy this happiness without fear and without regret.

'It's excellent news, Lizzie. While he's here, we can plan our wedding. I know that you'll want him beside you on the day.'

She didn't answer immediately, but walked a few steps along the beach and when she turned towards him, her smile was a little awry. 'Are you certain of this, Justin, certain that you wish to marry?' Some part of her was still saying this had to be a fantasy.

'Why do you ask, Lizzie? Surely you can see I'm in love, desperately so. Unless I'm to go through the rest of my life as blue as megrim, we'll have to marry.'

But had he thoroughly considered the problems ahead, she wondered? She walked back to his side and nestled her head against his shoulder. 'Will marriage mean you must sell out?'

'As I've no intention of dragging my wife from battlefield to battlefield, yes, I must sell out.' He tickled her chin lovingly. 'Lizzie, such a great sadness for you. Your ambition to follow the drum will never be realised now!'

'I've gained another ambition,' she said shyly. 'And one that's likely to prove far more satisfying. But the army, your regiment... have you considered?'

'How could I not? The army will go on without me—sad but true. Even my regiment will soon forget I was ever part of it.'

'You were so sure, though, that you'd never leave the military. You love the life dearly.'

'I've learned to love something else more dearly. Then seeing the trouble in her eyes, he continued forcefully, 'I've been a fool, Lizzie. I joined the army as much for my father's sake as for mine. I felt I owed it to him, after the wretched unhappiness my mother caused. He'd sacrificed himself and it was my job to make that sacrifice count. Or so I thought. That was a burden that Gil and I shared—a parent who loved us a little too much. But husbanding Chelwood will be an even better means by which to honour him, and lately I've been talking to Lavinia in a way I couldn't before. I don't like to admit it, but it seems that my father must share some of the blame for what happened between them.'

'Sir Lucien wasn't the only reason you became a soldier, I think. You will still find it very difficult to leave the army.'

'Not so difficult. It's true that for years my father's tales of soldiering stirred my blood, but I had other less praiseworthy reasons for joining up. I needed to escape—from gossip, from innuendo. I needed to be as far away from women and *ton* society as possible.'

'And now?'

'Now I've no need to escape. Not that I haven't tried. For weeks, I refused to accept that I loved you, that you were far more important to me than any army career, no matter how illustrious. If ever the truth began to break through the lies I told myself, I'd hound it from sight. But last night when we found Gil, when I thought that only death awaited us, too, I knew without a shadow of a doubt that I had to live. But it was for you that I had to live. Only you.'

He bent his head towards her and once more found her lips. 'How good it is to be alive, Lizzie,' he murmured.

Then reluctantly breaking away, he retraced his steps and collected the small bunch of freesias from the rock on which he'd laid them.

'I am sure that Gil would be happy for us,' he said slowly.

'I'm sure, too,' Lizzie replied. 'And we must stay happy for him. Always.'

Together, they took hold of the bouquet and threw the flowers into the river, watching as the posy bobbed on the water's surface, a small splash of colour amid an expanse of grey. Then, very gradually, the turning tide took the flowers in its clasp, and sent them sailing towards freedom and the open sea.

If you enjoyed reading *Lizzie Meets Her Match*, do please leave a review on your favourite site. Authors rely on good reviews – even just a few words – and readers depend on them to find interesting books to read.

Other books in the Allingham Regency Classic Series:
Duchess of Destiny (2017)
Dance of Deception (2017)
Masquerade (2018)
Romancing the Rake (2019)
Dangerous Disguise (2019)

Other books by Merryn Allingham:
The Girl From Cobb Street (2015)
The Nurse's War (2015)
Daisy's Long Road Home (2015)
The Buttonmaker's Daughter (2017)
The Secret of Summerhayes (2017)
House of Lies (2018)
House of Glass (2018)
A Tale of Two Sisters (2019)
The Dangerous Promise (2020)
Venetian Vendetta (2020)

About The Author

Merryn Allingham was born into an army family and spent her childhood moving around the UK and abroad. Unsurprisingly it gave her itchy feet, and in her twenties she escaped an unloved secretarial career to work as cabin crew and see the world. The arrival of marriage, children and cats meant a more settled life in the south of England, where she's lived ever since. It also gave her the opportunity to go back to 'school' and eventually teach at university.

Merryn has always loved books that bring the past to life, so when she began writing herself the novels had to be historical. She finds the nineteenth and early twentieth centuries fascinating to research and has written extensively on these periods in the Daisy's War trilogy and the Summerhayes novels, as well as in the Allingham

Regency Classics Series.

She has also written two timeslip/parallel narratives which move between the modern day and the mid-Victorian era, House of Lies and its companion volume, House of Glass.

The Tremayne Mysteries series is a new departure into crime but still historical (the 1950s) and still very much focussed on people and their relationships.

For more information on Merryn and her books visit
http://www.merrynallingham.com
You'll find regular news and updates on Merryn's Facebook page:
https://www.facebook.com/MerrynWrites
and you can keep in touch with her on Twitter
@MerrynWrites

Printed in Great Britain
by Amazon